NOCTE

NOCTE

A Novel

by Courtney Cole

***

Nocte:

Latin;
Noun; ablative singular of *nox* (night)
Adverb; by night
Pronunciation: Knock-tay

Lakehouse Press, Inc.

This book is an original publication of Lakehouse Press, Inc.
All rights reserved.

Copyright © 2014, Courtney Cole
Cover Design by The Cover Lure (Matthew Phillips)

Library of Congress Cataloging-in-publication data

Cole, Courtney
NOCTE/Courtney Cole/Lakehouse Press Inc/Trade pbk ed

ISBN 13: 978-0692305690
ISNB 10: 0692305696

Printed in the United States of America

Dedication

Insomniacs know that there is something about the night.
A darkness, an energy, a mystery that shrouds things.
It hides things at the same time as it illuminates them.
It is this thing
that allows us to examine our thoughts in a way that we
can't during the day,
It is this thing that brings truth and clarity.

This book is for Tristan.
My son whom I've passed insomnia to.
Always trust your own mind.
You know it best.

Foreword

I once considered not writing this story. It was too dark, too twisted, too much, *too, too, too.*

Obviously, I changed my mind. But I re-wrote in four different ways first, trying to make it different, more easily palatable, softer.

It didn't work.

So I went back to my original idea, the idea that I loved. The idea that I dreamed about and lived and breathed until it was done the way I wanted it, the *way it has to be.*

I know you're capable of reading it. I know you're capable of putting yourselves back together again when it's all over. I have faith in you.

Is this story dark?

Yes.

It is twisted?

At times.

Will it slap you in the face?

Absolutely.

Will it have you flipping the pages, trying to figure it out, trying to get to the climax, trying to breathe?

God, I hope so.

I wrote this story the way it needed to be written. I couldn't sugarcoat it. I couldn't water it down. It is this way because the story demands it.

I'm not sorry.

"By night, I am free.
No one hears my monsters but me.
My freedom is fragile, though,
Because every morning,
Over and over,
The night is broken
by the sun.
It's a good way to die."

--An early entry from the journal of Finn Price

I CAN'T I CAN'T I CAN'T
HEAR.
I CAN'T SEE
LIGHT
ANYMORE.
CALLA CALLA CALLA CALLA
SAVE ME, SAVE YOU.
SAVE ME.
SERVA ME, SERVABO TE.
SAVE ME AND I WILL SAVE YOU.

-- A later entry from the journal of Finn Price

There is nothing quite so terrifying as the descension of the human mind into insanity.
-Calla Price

"Secrets. Everybody's got 'em."
-Dare DuBray

PROLOGUS

My name is Calla Price. I'm eighteen years old, and I'm one half of a whole.

My other half-- my twin brother, my Finn-- is crazy.

I love him. More than life, more than anything. And even though I'm terrified he'll suck me down with him, no one can save him but me.

I'm doing all I can to stay afloat in a sea of insanity, but I'm drowning more and more each day. So I reach out for a lifeline.

Dare DuBray.

He's my savior and my anti-Christ. His arms are where I feel safe, where I'm afraid, where I belong, where I'm lost. He will heal me, break me, love me and hate me.

He has the power to destroy me.

Maybe that's ok. Because I can't seem to save Finn *and* love Dare without everyone getting hurt.

Why? Because of a secret.

A secret I'm so busy trying to figure out, that I never see it coming.

You won't either.

1

UNUM

Calla

-BEFORE-

Outside, a starless night sky yawns far and wide against a full moon that creates shadows. Inside, those shadows seem to morph into each other, creating twisted hands that drag their broken fingers along the darkened walls of the salon.

My mother insists on calling the formal living room a salon. Since she learned the term when she was in France years ago, it makes her feel sophisticated. And since we live in a funeral home on the top of an isolated mountain in Oregon, my dad lets her feel sophisticated in any way she chooses.

She's not here tonight, though, sophisticated or otherwise. She's on her way to her book club, to drink wine and gossip, oblivious to the fact that my entire world just imploded. And since my father and brother are both gone too, I'm alone for now.

Alone and with a broken heart.

Yet not *exactly* alone. I'm here in a dark funeral home with two dead bodies down in my father's embalming room.

Normally, this wouldn't be a big deal. When your father is a mortician, you learn to sleep under the same roof as dead people.

But tonight, with the storm causing the trees to bend and hiss against the house, and the electricity knocked out from the wind, it's alarming and dark and a bit terrifying.

My foot thumps against the side of the chair, an obvious sign that I'm agitated. I'm annoyed by my agitation, but honestly. I deserve to be annoyed.

Everything in my life was just turned inside out.

I turn my gaze out the windows, and stare at the cliffs. Jagged rock juts into the sky, which creates a haunting picture and only serves to remind me that I'm very isolated here at the top of our mountain. Also, it's lighter outside than it is in here, which is ridiculous.

I don't know why I'm scared of being alone, but I am. A therapist might say that it's because Finn and I are twins, and I've never had to be alone in my whole life. I even shared womb space.

It's why my parents just told us at dinner that they think Finn and I should go to separate schools. And I must say, I don't agree. I *strongly* disagree, in fact. Finn needs me because he's not like me. The mere thought of being apart gives me heart palpitations and I know I have to try talking to my mother about it.

Now.

No matter what else is going on with me, or what else I found out tonight, Finn will always take precedence.

I grab my phone and punch in mom's number because she's in her car alone, with no distractions. She'll have nothing to focus on other than what I'm saying. Maybe that means she'll finally hear me.

The phone rings once, then she picks up.

"Hi Calla. Is everything okay, hon?"

After the bombshell she dropped on us tonight, she's surprisingly cheerful.

"It's fine. The storm knocked out the power, but I'm ok. Hey, mom... *Finn can't be alone.* He needs to come to with me. I mean it. You don't understand how important it is." *Because I can't tell you over the phone.*

I eye his journal, lying on a nearby table. If mom and dad knew some of the stuff in there, the weird Latin phrases, the scratched out words, the craziness, then they truly wouldn't be giving me so much pushback.

But they don't know because they respect his privacy, and because of that, they're resolute in their desire to force independence on us.

Mom sighs now because this is a tired argument, and she's tired of having it.

"You know our feelings on this," she says firmly. "I get that you want to protect Finn. And I love that you're so protective, but Calla, he has to learn to live without that and so do you. You've got to have a life of your own, without constantly watching over your brother. Please trust us to know what's best."

"But mom," I argue. "After everything that happened tonight with... Something happened tonight. And more than ever, I know I can't leave Finn. I know him better than anyone."

"What happened tonight?" mom asks, quickly and curiously. "Did something happen with..."

"It's nothing I want to talk about over the phone," I interrupt her tiredly. "I just... I want you to promise me that you'll think about letting Finn and me stay together.

13

Please. I'm part him, and he's part me and that's what being a twin is all about. He might be different than me in one way, but we're the same in a million others. No one gets him like I do. He needs me."

Mom sighs again. "That's the whole point, honey," she says gently. "The *one difference* between you. Think back to that day, the day that we first knew about it. Tell me again what happened."

I'm the one sighing now because my heart is aching and I don't want to talk about this now. Maybe calling her was a bad idea.

"You know what happened," I say limply.

"Humor me," she directs me. Firmly.

"We were playing Capture the Flag in Kindergarten." I tell her reluctantly, like I'm reciting from a book. If I close my eyes, I can still smell the hot, dirty gym floor. "Finn had the flag. He was running." His skinny arms and legs were flying, his hair was damp on his brow.

"And then?"

My chest hurts a little. "Then he started screaming. And running in the other direction. He wasn't playing anymore. He was screaming about demons chasing him."

"And what else?" My mom's voice is sympathetic, but still very firm.

"And my name. He was screaming my name."

I can still hear him shrieking my name, his voice boyish and shrill and desperate.

Caaaaaalllllllllaaaaaaa!

But before I could do anything that day, he climbed the hanging rope all the way to the ceiling to get away from the demons.

The demons.

It'd taken four teachers to get him down.

He wouldn't even come down for me.

He was hospitalized for two weeks after that and diagnosed with Schizoaffective Disorder, which is a nasty cross between Schizophrenia and Bi-Polarism and very appropriately referred to as SAD. He's been medicated ever since. He's been chased by those effing demons ever since, too.

That's why he needs me.

"Mom," I murmur desperately, because I know where she's headed with this. But she's unrelenting.

"Calla, he called for *you*. Because he *always* calls for you. I know it's a twin thing, but it's not fair to either of you. You've got to be able to go to college and figure out who you are outside of being Finn's sister. He's got to do the same. I promise you, we're not doing this as a punishment. We're doing it because it's best. Do you trust me?"

I'm silent, mostly because my throat feels hot and constricted and I can't speak from the mere frustration.

"Calla? Do you trust me?"

My mom is so freaking insistent.

"Yes," I tell her. "Yeah, I trust you. But mom, it's not a problem for me. Because when Finn's on his meds, he's almost normal. He's fine."

Almost. There's only been a few break-through episodes. And a few periods of depression. And a few delusions.

Other than that, he's been fine.

"Except for the times that he's not fine," my mom answers.

"But…"

15

"No buts, Calla," she shuts me down, quickly and efficiently. "Honey, we've talked this into the ground. Now, I've gotta go. I forgot my reading glasses so I'm on my way back to get them. But the rain is bad so I need to focus on the road—"

She interrupts her own sentence with a scream.

A shrill, loud, high-pitched shriek. It almost punctures my ear-drums with its intensity and before I can make heads or tails of it, it breaks off mid-way through. And I realize that I heard something else in the background.

The sound of metal and glass being crunched and broken.

Then nothing.

"Mom?"

There's no answer, only loaded pregnant silence.

My hands shake as I wait for what seems like an eternity, but is actually only a second.

"Mom?" I demand, scared now.

Still nothing.

Chills run up and down my back, and goose-bumps form on my arms because I somehow know that she won't be answering.

And I'm right.

Mom died as she was screaming, as the metal crunched and the glass broke. The EMTs say that when they found her at the bottom of the ravine, the phone was somehow still in her hand.

2

DUO

Calla

-AFTER-

Astoria smells like dying.

At least, it does to me.

Embalming chemicals. Carnations. Roses. Stargazers. These things mix with the sea breeze and pine trees blowing through the open windows, forming an olfactory cocktail that smells like a funeral to me. That's fitting, I suppose, since I live in a funeral home. And my mother recently died.

Everything reminds me of a funeral because I'm surrounded by death.

Or mortem, as Finn would say. He's obsessed with learning Latin, and has been for the past two years. I don't know why, considering it's a dead language. But then again, I guess that makes total sense around here.

My brother, on the other hand, only makes sense part of the time. We're supposed to be preparing for college, but all he's interested in is scribbling in his journal, learning Latin and looking up morbid facts about death.

His journal.

The mere thought of the battered leather book sends a shudder down my spine. It's tangible proof of how crazy his thoughts can be, and because of that (and the fact that I promised him I wouldn't), I don't look into it.

Not anymore.

It scares me too much.

With a sigh, I stare down at him from my bedroom windows, down at the lawns of the funeral home. From here, I can see Finn and my father working on the landscaping, bent over in the early morning Oregon sun as they pull weeds from the flowerbeds that surround the house.

Finn's arms are skinny, his skin pale as he tugs at the roots, then drops the dusty weeds into a pile of wilted greens. I watch him for a minute, not with the eyes of his sister, but with the objective eyes of someone who might be seeing him for the first time.

My brother is slender and clean-cut, with an array of sandy brown curls haphazardly arranged in a halo. His eyes are pale blue, his smile is wide and bright, and he's beautiful in an artist kind of way.

You know, the kind of artist who forgets to eat because they're so passionate about their work... and because they forget to eat, they're slender and sinewy, all angles and bone. He's handsome though, sweet and quirky.

And I'm not just saying that because we're twins.

We don't look anything alike. The only thing we share is skin the color of cream and the same shape of nose, straight, aquiline, with a slight tilt on the end. Otherwise, I have green eyes and dark red hair, just like our mother.

Our mother.

I ignore the lump that forms in my throat when I think about her and I desperately try to put her out of my mind. Immediately. Because whenever I think about her, all I can think about is the hand that I played in her car crash. If I hadn't called her... if she hadn't answered.... she'd still be here right now.

Alive and breathing.

But she's not.

That weight threatens to crush my chest, and so instead of focusing on the guilt that blinds me, I focus on getting dressed. Because focusing on something, concentrating on monotony, sometimes distracts me from the grief.

Sometimes.

I throw some clothes on, yank my hair into a ponytail, and clatter down the gleaming mahogany steps, which incidentally, are the same exact shade as my mother's casket.

God, Calla. Why does every freaking thing have to come back to that?

I grit my teeth and force my stubborn mind to think of other things, but that's hard in a funeral home. Especially as I make my way out of the private part of the house and into the public areas.

All I can do is keep my eyes pointed forward.

Because even though no one is here yet today, there are two Viewing Rooms straddling this hall. There's a body in each one, laid out in their finest for all of their acquaintances to stare at.

They're dead, of course, with spiked plastic disks inside their eyelids holding them closed and thick pancake makeup smeared on their faces to give them some semblance of living color. It's a major fail, by the way.

Dead people don't look like they're sleeping, as everyone likes to say. They look dead, because they are. Poor things. I refuse to gawk at them. Death strips a person of dignity, but I don't have to be the one holding the filet knife.

Twelve steps later, I'm out the door and taking a deep breath, replacing the potent funeral home smells with the fresh air of the outdoors. Two steps later and I'm strolling across the dewy grass. My father and Finn both look up, then stop what they're doing when they see that I'm awake.

"Good morning, men!" I call out with faux cheerfulness. Because something my mother taught me was fake it 'til you make it. If you don't feel good, pretend you do because eventually you will. It hasn't worked yet, but I'm still holding out hope.

Finn smiles, causing the one dimple in his left cheek to deepen. I know he's faking it too, because none of us really feel like smiling these days.

"Morning, slacker."

I grin (fake). "It's a rough life sleeping until ten, but someone's got to do it. Do you guys want me to run in to the café and get some coffee?"

My father shakes his head. "Those of us who got up at a normal hour are already caffeinated."

I roll my eyes. "Well, do you want me to take Finn to Group, to make up for my laziness?"

He shakes his head and smiles, but the smile doesn't reach his eyes. Because it's also fake. Just like mine. Just like Finn's. Because we're all fakers.

"Actually," he eyes me, sizing up me and my mood. "That'd be great. I've got someone coming in today, so I'll be tied up."

By *someone,* he means a body to embalm, and by *today,* he must mean soon because he's already standing up and wiping off his hands.

20

I nod quickly, willing to do anything to get out of here.

Years of watching bodies come and go wears on a person. I've seen it all... accident victims, elderly people, still-births, kids. The kids are the hardest, but eventually, it's all hard. Death isn't something that anyone wants to think about, and no one wants to be surrounded by it all of the time.

My father might've chosen his profession, but I certainly didn't.

Which is why I'd rather take Finn to his therapy any day.

It's something my mother used to do, because she always insisted that it was better for Finn if someone was there, in case he wanted to 'talk' on the way home. He never does, and so I think she just wanted to make sure that he went. Either way, we keep up her tradition.

Because traditions are soothing when everything else has gone to hell.

"Sure. I can go." I glance at Finn. "But I'm driving."

Finn smiles at me angelically. "I called it when you were still in bed. It's the price of being a slacker. Sorry."

His grin decidedly says *Not Sorry.* And this time, it isn't fake.

"Whatever. Do you want a shower?"

He shakes his head again. "I'll just run in and change. Give me a minute."

He trots off, and I watch him go, observing for the fiftieth time, how much he looks like our father. Same height, same build, some coloring. Our father looks more like his twin than I do.

Dad watches him walk away, then glances at me.

"Thanks, sweetie. How are you doing today?"

He's not asking how I'm doing, so much as how I'm feeling. I know that, and I shrug.

"Ok, I guess."

Except for the freaking lump that won't go away in my throat. Except for the fact that whenever I look in the mirror, I see my mom so I have to fight off the urge to rip them all from the walls and throw them over the cliffs. Except for those things, I'm fine.

I look at my dad. "Maybe we should become Jewish so that we can sit in Shiva and not have to worry about anything else."

My dad look stunned for a minute, then smiles slightly. "Well, Shiva only lasts a week. So that wouldn't do us much good at this point."

Nothing will do us much good at this point. But I don't say that.

"Well, I guess I won't cover up the mirrors then." *Unfortunately.*

My father smiles now, and I think it might actually be a little bit real. "Yeah. And you'll have to keep showering too." He pauses. "You know, there's a grief support group that meets at the hospital too. You could poke your head in while you wait for Finn."

I'm already shaking my head. Screw that. He's got to give up trying to make me go to one of those. The only thing worse than drowning in grief is sharing a lifeboat with other drowning people. Besides, if anyone needs a grief group, it's him.

"I think I'll pass," I tell him for the hundredth time. "But if I change my mind, I'll look it up."

"Ok," he gives in easily, like he always does. "I understand that, I guess. I don't want to talk about it, either. But maybe one of these days...."

His voice trails off and I know that he's filing this under the One Of These Days folder in his head, along with a million other things. Things like cleaning out my mother's closet, picking her dirty clothes up out of their bathroom, putting away her shoes and her jacket. Things like that.

It's been six weeks since my mother died, and my father has left her stuff un-touched, like he's expecting her to come home at any minute. He knows this isn't the case since he embalmed her body and we buried her in her gleaming mahogany casket, but obviously it would be insensitive to point that out.

Instead, I hug him.

"Love you, dad."

"Love you, too, Cal."

Over his shoulder, my gaze freezes on the small ivy covered brick building down the path from the main house, and I stare at it for a minute before I pull away.

"Have you decided about the Carriage House yet?"

He and my mother had converted it into an apartment last year as an investment property, but they'd been in the process of trying to find a renter when mom died. Finn and I have been trying to get dad to let one of us live in it.

He shakes his head now. "You know, it's not really fair to give it to one or the other of you. I'm going to rent it out, after all."

I stare at him like he just grew a second head. "Really? But..."

But what a waste of a beautifully renovated space.

My father is unfazed. "You and Finn are going to college in the Fall anyway. It'd be extra income. That was our original plan, anyway."

I'm still stunned. "Well, good luck finding someone who wants to live here."

Right next door to a funeral home and crematorium.

"If you know of anyone, please let them know," my dad continues, ignoring my pessimism. I scoff at that.

"You know I don't know anyone." I don't go into the depressing state of my social life, which is nonexistent and always has been. It's always been something that worried my mom and dad, although Finn and I never much cared. We've always had each other.

Finn bounds down the stairs, his hair wet, interrupting our conversation.

"Since I smelled like sweaty feet, I took the world's fastest shower," he announces as he breezes past us. "You're welcome."

"Drive safe!" my father calls out needlessly as he heads inside. Because of the way my mom died, among twisted metal and smoking rubber, my father doesn't even like to *see* us in a car, but he knows it's a necessity of life.

Even still, he doesn't want to watch it.

It's ok. We all have little tricks we play on our minds to make life bearable.

I drop into the passenger seat of our car, the one my brother and I share, and stare at Finn.

"How'd you sleep?"

Because he doesn't usually.

He's an insufferable insomniac. His mind is naturally more active at night than the average person's. He can't figure out how to shut it down. And when he does sleep, he has vivid nightmares so he gets up and crawls into my bed.

Because I'm the one he comes to when he's afraid.

It's a twin thing. Although, the kids that used to tease us for being weird would love to know that little tid-bit, I'm sure. *Calla and Finn sleep in the same bed sometimes, isn't that sick??* They'd never understand how we draw comfort just from being near each other. Not that it matters what they think, not anymore. We'll probably never see any of those assholes again.

"I slept like shit. You?"

"Same," I murmur. Because it's true. I'm not an insomniac, but I do have nightmares. Vivid ones, of my mother screaming, and broken glass, and of her cellphone in her hand. In every dream, I can hear my own voice, calling out her name, and in every dream, she never answers.

You could say I'm a bit tortured by that.

Finn and I fall into silence, so I press my forehead to the glass and stare out the window as he drives, staring at the scenery that I've been surrounded with since I was born.

Despite my internal torment, I have to admit that our mountain is beautiful.

We're surrounded by all things green and alive, by pine trees and bracken and lush forest greenery. The vibrant green stretches across the vast lawns, through the flowered gardens, and lasts right up until you get to the cliffs, where it finally and abruptly turns reddish and clay.

I guess that's pretty good symbolism, actually. Green means alive and red means dangerous. Red is jagged cliffs, warning lights, splattered blood. But green... green is trees and apples and clover.

"How do you say green in Latin?" I ask absentmindedly.

"Viridem," he answers. "Why?"

"No reason." I glance into the side-mirror at the house, which fades into the distance behind us.

Huge and Victorian, it stands proudly on the top of this mountain, perched on the edge of the cliffs with its spires poking through the clouds. It's beautiful and graceful, at the same time as it is gothic and dark. It's a funeral home, after all, at the end of a road on a mountain. It's a horror movie waiting to happen.

Last Funeral Home on the Left.

Dad will need a miracle to rent the tiny Carriage House out, and I feel a slight pang of guilt. Maybe he really does need the money, and I've been pressuring him to give it to Finn or me.

I turn my gaze away from the house, away from my guilt, and out to the ocean. Vast and gray, the water punishes the rocks on the shore, pounding into them over and over. Mist rises from the water, forming fog along the beach. It's beautiful and eerie, haunting and peaceful.

But it's also a prison, holding me here beneath the low-hanging cloud cover.

"Do you ever wish we could move away? Like *far* away?" I muse aloud.

Finn glances at me. "Berkeley isn't far enough for you?"

I shrug. "I don't know. I'm talking someplace *far* away. Like Italy. Or Scotland. It'd be nice, I think. To get away from here. From everything we know."

From the memories.

From the people who think we're weird.

From everything.

Finn's face stays expressionless. "Cal, you don't have to go around the world to re-invent yourself, if that's what you want. You can do that in California. But you don't need to change yourself at all. You're fine the way you are."

Yeah. Being known as Funeral Home Girl is fine. But he's right. No one will know that in California. I can get as good a new start there as I can anywhere. I won't be surrounded by dead people, and people won't always be asking *How are you feeling?*

We drift into silence and I continue staring out the window, thinking about college and what my new life there might be like. Since my father has agreed that Finn and I should stay together, there's nothing scary about it. It's just exciting. And it will include a lot of expensive shoes and pashminas. I'm not exactly where what pashminas are, but they sound sophisticated, and so I need them.

"Well?"

Finn's insistent tone brings me out of my thoughts. He's obviously waiting on an answer to something.

"Well, what?"

"Well, did dad decide? About the carriage house. We could just share it, you know. I'm sick of smelling like formaldehyde all the time."

For real. I can't even count how many times I'd hear snide girls at school whispering as I walked past, old tired jokes like, "I smell dead people." I always wanted to tell them to quit ripping off old movies and come up with something original, but of course I never did. To them, I was Funeral Home Girl. But I never gave them the satisfaction of knowing that their words hurt.

"We don't smell like formaldehyde," I assure Finn. We smell like flowers. Funeral flowers. It's not much better.

"Speak for yourself," he grumbles. "Can we, or not?"

I shrug.

"Apparently, dad's going to rent it out, after all."

Finn stares at me for a second before returning his gaze to the road. "Seriously? I didn't know we were that hard up. We have mom's life insurance money, and the money from the funeral home."

"College is expensive," I murmur. Because that's the only explanation I can think of, other than maybe dad just wants to follow through with something that he planned with mom. Finn nods, because it's an acceptable answer. Obviously, sending two kids is expensive.

We're quiet as we drive the rest of the way, and still quiet as we walk the sterile halls of the hospital, our Chucks squeaking on the waxed floors.

"I'll meet you back out here in an hour," Finn tells me casually, as though he's going shopping instead of going to talk about his mental illness with other mentally ill people. Like always, Finn carries his cross like a champion.

I nod. "I'll be here."

Because I always am.

He walks away without looking back, disappearing into a therapy room. As I watch him go, I can't help but think, for the millioneth time, that it could've just as easily been me born with SAD. It's a thought that makes me feel panicky and guilty at the same time. Panicky, because sometimes I still worry that I might get it, that it might show up out of the blue. And guilty, because it should've been me in the first place. Finn is a better person than I am.

I'm the one who was born first, the one born bigger, the one born stronger...regardless of the fact that Finn really is *better*. He's funny and witty and smart, and his soul is as gentle as they come. He's the one who deserved to be healthy.

Not me. I'm the snarky, sarcastic one.

Mother Nature is a bitch sometimes.

I find a nearby bench in the sky-lit atrium, and curl up beneath an abstract bird painting, pulling out a book to read. Having my nose buried in a book accomplishes two things.

1. It lets people know I'm not in the mood to be talked to. Honestly, I seldom am. And 2. It kills the boredom while I wait.

The sounds of the hospital fade into a buzzing backdrop, while I immerse myself in blissful fiction. Fiction is best served alone. It's how I survived my school years, reading through lunches and awkward classes when no one talked to me, and fiction is how I survive waiting for Finn during long hours in the hospital psych wing. It's how I can ignore the shrill, multi-pitched yells that drift down the hallways. Because honestly, I don't want to know what they're yelling about.

I stay suspended in my pretend world for God knows how long, until I feel someone staring at me.

When I say feel, I *literally feel it,* just like someone is reaching out and touching my face with their fingers.

Glancing up, I suck my breath in when I find dark eyes connected to mine, eyes so dark they're almost black, and the energy in them is enough to freeze me in place.

A boy is attached to the dark gaze.

A man.

He's probably no more than twenty or twenty-one, but everything about him screams *man*. There's no *boy* in him. That part of him is very clearly gone. I see it in his eyes, in the way he holds himself, in the perceptive way he takes in his surroundings, then stares at me with singular focus, like we're somehow connected by a tether. He's got a million contradictions in his eyes....aloofness, warmth, mystery, charm, and something else I can't define.

He's muscular, tall, and wearing a tattered black sweatshirt that says *Irony is lost on you* in orange letters. His dark jeans are belted with black leather, and a silver band encircles his middle finger.

Dark hair tumbles into his face and a hand with long fingers impatiently brushes it back, all the while his eyes are still connected with mine. His jaw is strong and masculine, with the barest hint of stubble.

His gaze is still connected to mine, like a livewire, or a lightning bolt. I can feel the charge of it racing along my skin, like a million tiny fingers, flushing my cheeks. My lungs flutter and I swallow hard.

And then, he smiles at me.

At me.

Because I don't know him and he doesn't know better.

"Cal? You ready?"

Finn's voice breaks my concentration, and with it, the moment. I glance up at my brother, almost in confusion, to find that he's waiting for me. The hour has already passed and I didn't even realize it. I scramble to get up, feeling for all the world like I'm rattled, but don't know why.

Although I do know.

As I walk away with Finn, I glance over my shoulder.

The sexy stranger with the dark, dark gaze is gone.

3

TRIBUS

Finn

FuckYouYouCan'tDoAnything.   HurtMeMotherfucker.
YouCan'tDoAnything. You'reSoFucked. HurtMe. HurtMe.
HurtHer. Can'tDoAnything. KillMeNow.

Like always, I ignore them...the voices in my head
that whisper and hiss. They're always there in the
background, inside my ear. There are several of them,
mostly women's voices, but there are a couple men's
voices, too. Those are the ones that are harder to ignore,
because sometimes they feel like my own.

It's really hard to ignore your own voice.

And even though I can push them to the back of my
consciousness most of the time, I can never make them
go away. The colorful pills I used to take every day
couldn't even silence them, not always.

Because of that, since they made me nauseous and
didn't work anyway, I added another chore to my to-do
list the other day. It was an easy one to cross off.

~~Stop taking pills~~

~~Don't tell Calla or dad.~~

I picture my mental list in my head, with perfect
clarity, because that level of focus tends to muffle the

voices for a second. My list is on white notebook paper, lined with blue, a pink line running vertically down the left side. After I complete a task, I draw a mental line through it, crossing it out. It makes me ~~feel accomplished.~~

Without my list, I can't get through the day. It's too hard to think without it, too hard to concentrate. Without it, I can't even *appear* normal. Its compulsory for me at this point, just one more thing that makes me bat-shit crazy.

No one except Calla and my dad know how crazy I am. And even *they* don't know the extent of it.

Not all of it.

They don't know how I wake up in the night, and have to force myself to stay in bed, because the voices tell me to throw myself from the cliffs. To stop myself, I always dive into bed with Calla, because for whatever reason, she quiets the voices. But she can't be with me every minute.

She can't be with me during the day when my fingers itch to scratch into my skin, to pull my fingernails out, to run down to the bottom of the mountain and scream as I hurl myself into traffic.

Why would I itch to do these things?

Because of the fucking voices.

They won't shut up.

It's getting to the point where I don't know what's real and not real anymore, and that scares the piss out of me. It particularly scares the piss out of me because Calla and I will be separated soon. She thinks we're going to the same school, that I've consenting to going to

Berkeley with her. But I can't. I can't suck her down with me. I'd be the worst person in the world if I did.

So soon, I'll be at MIT and she'll be at Berkeley, and then what will happen?

She'll be fine, because she's sane. But what will happen to *me?*

As I come out of the therapy room, I bend and gulp a drink from the water fountain. A few drops of icy water trail down my neck and instantly the voices react.

Scratch it off.

My hand is already on my throat before I realize what I'm doing. Frustrated, I force my hand to my side.

I'm not going to hurt myself.

Jesus.

I have to stay sane.

Quickly, I find Calla curled up on her normal bench, staring into the distance. I cover the ground between us in twelve long strides.

"Cal? You ready?"

She stares at me like I'm a stranger, before realization filters across her face and she smiles.

"You ok?"

Calla's voice wraps around me like a blanket.

She keeps me sane.

It's always been that way, maybe even in the womb, for all I know.

Don't let her know Don't let her know Don't let her know.

~~*Don't let her know.*~~

I smile, a perfectly normal grin.

"Perfectus." *Perfect.* "You ready?"

"Yep."

We walk out of the hospital, into the afternoon sunlight and pile into the car. I start the engine and steer the car from the parking lot with shaking hands.

~~Act normal~~

Calla turns to me, her green eyes joined to mine. "You wanna talk about anything?"

I shake my head. "Do I ever?"

She smiles. "No. But know that you can. If you want to."

"I know." And I do.

"Did you know that ancient Egyptians shaved off their eyebrows to mourn the death of their cats?"

I change the subject and Calla laughs, shoving her long red hair out of her eyes with slender fingers. It's our thing, these stupid death facts. It's *my* thing, really. I don't know why. I guess it's from all the years of living in the stupid funeral home. It's my way of giving death the finger. Plus, by focusing on death facts and learning Latin and making my stupid mental lists, it gives me something to focus on. Any time I focus hard on something, it staves off the voices.

Trust me, I'll do anything for that.

"I didn't. But thank God I know now," Calla answers. "What would you shave off for me if I died?"

I would plunge to the bottom of the ocean for you. I'd comb it for shells and make you a necklace and then hang myself with it. Because if you aren't here, I don't want to be either.

I can't show her how panicky the mere thought makes me, so I shrug. "Don't give me the chance."

34

She looks horrified, as she realizes what she said, so soon after mom died.

"I didn't mean to...." She starts to say, then trails off. "I'm sorry. That was stupid."

Calla and I are twins. Our level of connection can't be understood by those who don't have it. I know what she means even when she doesn't. Her comment had come out before she remembered mom. It sounds stupid, but sometimes, we can forget our loss for a second. A blissful second.

"Don't worry about it," I tell her, as I turn onto the highway.

Fuck her. She has no right.

The voices are loud.

Too loud.

I close my eyes and squeeze them hard, trying not to hear.

But the voices are still there, still persistent.

She doesn't deserve you. Kill her you fucking pussy kill her now. Push her off the cliffs. Lick her bones. Lick her bones. Lick her bones.

I grip the steering wheel until my knuckles turn white, trying to force the voices away.

Lick her bones, suck her marrow, show her show her show her.

Today, the voices sound real, even though I know they aren't. They're not my voice, they're just masquerades, a scary mask, imposters. They're not real.

My voice is real.

Those voices are not.

But it's getting harder and harder to tell them apart.

4

QUATUOR

Calla

One thing about this mountain in the summertime, is that time seems to slow to almost a stand-still, and days blend into each other. Before I know it, one day bleeds into two, then three, before somehow, I find myself on Group Therapy duty again.

This time, however, I'm quick enough to call driving rights. I ignore Finn's indignant look as we get into the car, and I smile smugly at him (real, not fake) as I drive away from the house.

As I steer the car down the mountain curves, the tires squeak on the rain-soaked gravel. Finn stares out the window, lost in his thoughts as we pass 'the spot'. The place where our mother crashed and died.

A near-by tree hosts brightly-colored ribbons and a small plain cross. It's lonely here, reverent and quiet. It's a place that I usually ignore, because otherwise, it makes my heart hurt too much.

Unexpectedly, though, Finn lifts his head.

"Can you stop?"

Startled, I brake, then pull over. "What's wrong?"

He shakes his head. "Nothing. I just need to be here for a minute."

He gets out, his car door creaking as he closes it. I'm uneasy as I follow, because we've never stopped here before, not since we hung the ribbons and staked the white cross into the ground. It's sacred ground here, but it's also emotional ground. And emotional ground is dangerous for Finn to tread on.

"Whatcha doin'?" I ask as casually as I can, following him to the side of the steep incline, to the place where mom plunged over the side as she was talking to me. Balancing here, with our toes poking over the side, we can still see where the trees are knocked down and damaged from mom's car hitting them. I feel a wave of nausea.

"Do you think she was dead before she hit the bottom?" Finn asks, his voice emotionless. My heart squeezes in my chest.

"I don't know."

I've thought about it, of course, but I don't know. Dad didn't tell us and I can't bring myself to ask.

"What do you think about the other car?" Finn asks, his gaze staring down into the ravine and definitely not looking at me. I inhale, then exhale, pushing the guilt away, far away from me, over the mountain, over the cliffs, into the water.

"I don't know," I answer honestly.

It's the truth, because afterward, Dad wouldn't tell us what happened to the occupants of the other car. Who they were, how many. He thought I was feeling enough unwarranted guilt, enough pain and torment. He wouldn't talk about any of it and we were banned from turning the television on for weeks, just in case the news carried coverage. You'd think it would be maddening, but at the time, I was so immersed in grieving that I almost didn't notice.

The problem is, it didn't stop the guilt.

Because I killed people.

Staring down the side of this mountain, looking at the gouges carved into the trees from the metal of the crashed cars, the destruction of the forest...it's all evidence. Whoever mom hit is dead. That's apparent.

And that's my fault. I killed them just like I killed her.

The only real question is, how many were in the car? Was it one person? A couple? *An entire family?*

"Do you think there were kids involved?" I ask quietly. Because the thought of that... *God.* It's unbearable. I picture scared little kids strapped into car seats, covered in blood and terror. I squeeze my eyes closed to block out the imagined sight.

"I don't know," Finn answers, his voice just as quiet. "We could find out, if you want. We could look up the newspaper articles. If you think knowing would be better than *not* knowing."

I think on that for a minute, because it's tempting, *so* tempting. Then I shake my head.

"If dad won't tell us, then it's bad," I decide. "That means that I'm better off not knowing."

Finn nods and stares wordlessly out over the trees.

Finally he speaks. "But what was a car doing on this mountain? We're the only ones who live here. No one else has any reason for being here that late at night. The Home was closed."

It's a question I've wondered about ever since it happened. Mom was rounding the curve in the middle of the lane because she wasn't expecting anyone to be there.

But someone was.

And they'd hit each other head on.

"I don't know," I reply and my chest feels like ice, like my sternum will freeze and shatter. "Maybe they were lost."

Finn nods because that's a possibility, and the only one that makes sense, before he grabs my hand and holds it tight.

"It's not your fault."

His words are simple, his tone is solemn.

A lump forms, sticking halfway in my throat, in a limbo area, where it can neither be swallowed or cleared.

"It *is*." My words are just as simple. "Why aren't you mad at me for it?"

When Finn finally looks at me, his eyes are tortured, and blue as the sky.

"Because it can't be undone. Because you're the most important person to me. That's why."

I nod because now I know the truth. He's not mad at me because he thinks I'm not at fault. It's clear that I am. He's not mad at me because I'm all he has, because I'm a part of him.

"We've got to go. I'm going to be late."

I nod in agreement and we back away from the edge. With a last glance at the sad ravine, we climb back into the car, damp with the drizzle and our tears, and drive silently to the hospital.

When we're inside, Finn turns to me before he slips into his room.

"There *is* a grief group. You should check it out."

"Now you sound like dad," I tell him impatiently. "I don't need to talk to them. I have you. No one understands like you."

He nods, *because no one understands like him.* And then he disappears into the place where he draws his strength, around people who suffer just like him.

I try not to feel inadequate that they can help him in ways that I can't.

Instead, I curl up on my bench beneath the abstract bird. I pop ear-buds in my ears and close my eyes. I forgot my book today, so disappearing into music will have to do.

I concentrate on feeling the music rather than hearing it. I feel the vibration, I feel the words. I feel the beat. I feel the voices. I feel the emotion.

Someone else's emotion other than my own is always a good thing.

The minutes pass, one after the other.

And then after twenty of them, *he* approaches.

Him.

The sexy stranger with eyes as black as night.

I feel him approach while my eyes are still closed. Don't ask me how I know it's him, because I just know. Don't ask me what he's doing here again, because I don't care about that.

All I care about is the fact that he *is* here.

My eyes pop open to find him watching me, his eyes still as intense now as they were the other day. Still as dark, still as bottomless.

His gaze finds mine, connects with it, and holds.

We're connected.

With each step, he doesn't look away.

He's dressed in the same sweatshirt as the other day. *The irony is lost on you.* He's wearing dark jeans, black boots and his middle finger is still encircled by a silver band. He's a rocker. Or an artist. Or a writer. He's something hopelessly in style, timelessly romantic.

He's twenty feet away.

Fifteen.

Ten.

Five.

The corner of his mouth tilts up as he passes, as he continues to watch me from the side. His shoulders sway, his hips are slim. Then he's gone, walking away from me.

Five feet.

Ten.

Twenty.

Gone.

I feel a sense of loss because he didn't stop. Because I wanted him to. Because there's something about him that I want to know.

I take a deep breath and close my eyes, listening once again to my music.

The dark haired stranger doesn't come back.

5

QUINQUE

The rain might make Oregon beautiful, but at times, it's gray and dismal. The sound of it hitting the windows makes me sleepy, and itch to wrap up in a sweater and curl up with a book by the window. At night, when it storms, I dream. I don't know why. It might be the electricity of the lightning in the air, or the boom of the thunder, but it never fails to trigger my mind to create.

Tonight, after finally falling asleep, I dream of *him.*

The dark-eyed stranger.

He sits by the ocean, the breeze ruffling his hair. He lifts his hand to brush his hair out of his eyes, his silver ring glinting in the sun.

His eyes meet mine, and electricity stronger than a million lightning bolts connects us, holding us together.

His eyes crinkle a bit at the corners as he smiles at me.

His grin is for me, familiar and sexy. He reaches for me, his fingers knowing and familiar, and he knows just where to touch me, just where to set my skin on fire.

I wake with a start, sitting straight up in bed, my sheets clutched to my chest.

The moonlight pouring onto my bed looks blue, and I glance at the clock.

Three a.m.

Just a dream.

I curl back up, thinking of the stranger, and then condemn myself for my ridiculousness. He's a stranger, for God's sake. It's stupid to be so fixated on him.

But that doesn't stop me from dreaming about him again. He does different things in my dreams. He sails, he swims, he drinks coffee. His silver ring glints in the sun each time, his dark eyes pierce into my soul like he knows me. *Like he knows all about me.* I wake up breathless each time.

It's a bit unnerving.

And a bit exciting.

After two such nights of fitful sleep, rain and strange dreams, Finn and I kneel in front of plastic storage boxes, sorting through stuff from my closet. Piles of folded clothes surround us, like mountains on the floor. Rain pelts the window, the morning sky dark and gray.

I hold up a white cardigan. "I don't think I'll need many sweaters in California, will I?"

Finn shakes his head. "Doubtful. But take a couple, just to be safe."

I toss it into the Keep pile. As I do, I notice that Finn's fingers are shaking.

"Why are your hands shaking?" I stare at him. He shrugs.

"Don't know."

I eye him doubtfully, so used to watching him for any sign of a problem. "Are you sure?"

He nods. "Quite positive."

I let it go, even though it makes me uneasy. If I don't shield Finn from distress, he could have an episode. Obviously I couldn't shield him from losing mom, but I do my best to protect him from everything else. It's a heavy thing to shoulder, but if Finn can carry his cross, I can certainly carry mine. I unfold another sweater, then toss it in the Goodwill pile.

"After mine, we'll have to do yours," I point out. He nods.

"Yeah. And then maybe we should do mom's."

I suck in a breath. While I would like nothing more, just in the name of moving forward, there's no way.

"Dad would kill us," I dismiss the idea.

"True," Finn acknowledges, handing me a long sleeve t-shirt for the Keep pile. "But maybe he needs a nudge. It's been two months. She doesn't need her shoes by the backdoor anymore."

He's right. She doesn't need them. Just like she doesn't need her make-up laid out by her sink the way she left it, or her last book sitting face down to mark its page beside her reading chair. She'll never finish that book. But to be fair to my dad, I don't think I could throw her things out yet, either.

"Still," I answer. "It's his place to decide when it's time. Not ours. We're going away. He's the one who will be here with the memories. Not us."

"That's why I'm worried," Finn tells me. "He's going to be here in this huge house alone. Well, not alone. Surrounded by dead bodies and mom's memory. That's even worse."

Knowing how I hate to be alone, and how I especially hate to be alone in our big house, I shudder.

"Maybe that's why he wants to rent out the Carriage House," I offer. "So he's not so alone up here."

"Maybe."

Finn reaches over and flips on some music, and I let the thumping bass fill the silence while we sort through my clothes. Usually, our silence is comfortable and we don't need to fill it. But today, I feel unsettled. Tense. Anxious.

"Have you been writing lately?" I ask to make small-talk. He's always scribbling in his journal. And even though I'm the one who'd gotten it for him for Christmas a couple years ago, he won't let me read it. Not since he showed it to me one time and I'd freaked out.

"Of course."

Of course. It's pretty much all he does. Poems, Latin, nonsense... you name it, he writes it.

"Can I read any of it yet?"

"No."

His answer is definite and firm.

"Ok." I don't argue with that tone of voice, because honestly, I'm a bit nervous to see what's in there now anyway. But he does pause and turn to me.

"I don't think I ever said thank you for not running to mom and dad. When you read it that one time, I mean. It's just my outlet, Cal. It doesn't mean anything."

His blue eyes pierce me, straight into my soul. Because I know I probably *should've* gone to them. And I probably would've, if mom hadn't died. But I didn't, and everything has been fine since then.

Fine. If I think hard enough on that word, then it will be true.

"You're welcome," I say softly, trying not to think of the gibberish I'd read, the scary words, the scary thoughts, scribbled and crossed out, and scrawled again. Over and over. Out of all of it, though, one thing stood out as most troubling. One phrase. It wasn't the odd sketches of people

45

with their eyes and faces and mouths scratched out, it wasn't the odd and dark poems, it was one phrase.

Put me out of my misery.

Scrawled over and over, filling up two complete pages. I've watched him like a hawk ever since. He smiles now, encouraging me to forget it, like it's just his outlet. He's fine now. *He's fine.* If I had a journal, I'd scrawl *that* on the pages, over and over, to make it true.

"Hey, I'm going to go to Group again today. Do you want to come with? If not, I can go myself."

This startles me. He normally only goes twice a week. Have I missed something? Is he worse? Is he slipping? I fight to keep my voice casual.

"Again? Why?"

He shrugs, like it's no big deal, but his hands are still shaking.

"I dunno. I think it's all the change. It makes me feel antsy."

And shaky? I don't ask that though. Instead, I just nod, like I'm not at all freaked out. "Of course I'll go."

Of course, because he needs me.

An hour later, we've walked down the hallways filled with our mother's pictures, past her bedroom filled with her clothes, and are driving to town in the car she bought us. We both pointedly avoid looking at the place where she plunged over the side of the mountain. We don't need to see it again.

Our mother is still all around us. Everywhere. Yet nowhere. Not really.

It's enough to drive the sanest person mad. No wonder Finn wants extra therapy.

I leave him in front of his Group room, and watch him disappear inside.

I take my book to the café today for a cup of coffee. I've grown accustomed to the rain making me sleepy since I've lived in Astoria all my life. But I've also learned that caffeine is an effective Band-Aid.

I grab my cup and head to the back, slumping into a booth, prepared to bury my nose in my book.

I'm just opening the cover when I feel him.

I *feel* him.

Again.

Before I even look up, I know it's *him*. I recognize the feel in the air, the very palpable energy. I felt the same thing in my dreams, this impossible pull. What the hell? Why do I keep bumping into him?

When I look up, I find that he's seen me, too.

His eyes are frozen on me as he waits in line, so dark, so fathomless. This energy between us… I don't know what it is. Attraction? Chemistry? All I know is, it steals my breath and speeds up my heart. The fact that he's invading my dreams makes me crave this feeling even more. It brings me out of my reality and into something new and exciting, into something that has hope and life.

I watch as he pays for his coffee and sweet roll, and as his every step leads him to my back booth. There are ten other tables, all vacant, but he chooses mine.

His black boots stop next to me, and I skim up his denim-clad legs, over his hips, up to his startlingly handsome face. He still hasn't shaved, so his stubble is more pronounced today. It makes him seem even more mature, even more of a man. As if he needs the help.

I can't help but notice the way his soft blue shirt hugs his solid chest, the way his waist narrows as it slips into his jeans, the way he seems lean and lithe and powerful. Gah. I yank my eyes up to meet his. I find amusement there.

"Is this seat taken?"

Sweet Lord. He's got a British accent. There's nothing sexier in the entire world, which makes that old tired pick-up line forgivable. I smile up at him, my heart racing.

"No."

He doesn't move. "Can I take it, then? I'll share my breakfast with you."

He slightly gestures with his gooey, pecan-crusted roll.

"Sure," I answer casually, expertly hiding the fact that my heart is racing fast enough to explode. "But I'll pass on the breakfast. I'm allergic to nuts."

"More for me, then," he grins, as he slides into the booth across from me, ever so casually, as though he sits with strange girls in hospitals all of the time. I can't help but notice that his eyes are so dark they're almost black.

"Come here often?" he quips, as he sprawls out in the booth. I have to chuckle, because now he's just going down the list of cliché lines, and they all sound amazing coming from his British lips.

"Fairly," I nod. "You?"

"They have the best coffee around," he answers, if that even *is* an answer. "But let's not tell anyone, or they'll start naming the coffee things we can't pronounce, and the lines will get unbearable."

I shake my head, and I can't help but smile. "Fine. It'll be our secret."

He stares at me, his dark eyes shining. "Good. I like secrets. Everyone's got 'em."

I almost suck in my breath, because something is so overtly fascinating about him. The way he pronounces everything, and the way his dark eyes gleam, the way he seems so familiar because he's been in the intimacy of my dreams.

"What are yours?" I ask, without thinking. "Your secrets, I mean."

He grins. "Wouldn't *you* like to know?"

Yes.

"My name's Calla," I offer quickly. He smiles at that.

"Calla like the funeral lily?"

The very same." I sigh. "And I live in a funeral home. So see? The irony isn't lost on me."

He looks confused for a second, then I see the realization dawn on him.

"You noticed my shirt yesterday," he points out softly, his arm stretched across the back of the cracked booth. He doesn't even dwell on the fact that I'd just told him I live in a house with dead people. Usually people instantly clam up when they find out, because they instantly assume that I must be weird, or morbid. But he doesn't.

I nod curtly. "I don't know why. It just stood out."

Because you *stood out.*

The corner of his mouth twitches, like he's going to smile, but then he doesn't.

"I'm Adair DuBray," he tells me, like he's bestowing a gift or an honor. "But everyone calls me Dare."

I've never seen a name so fitting. So French, so sophisticated, yet his accent is British. He's an enigma. An enigma whose eyes gleam like they're constantly saying *Dare me.* I swallow.

"It's nice to meet you," I tell him, and that's the truth. "Why are you here in the hospital? Surely it's not for the coffee."

"You know what game I like to play?" Dare asks, completely changing the subject. I feel my mouth drop open a bit, but I manage to answer.

"No, what?"

"Twenty Questions. That way, I know that at the end of the game, there won't be any more. Questions, that is."

I have to smile, even though his answer should've annoyed me. "So you don't like talking about yourself."

He grins. "It's my least favorite subject."

But it must be such an interesting one.

"So, you're telling me I can ask you twenty things, and twenty things only?"

Dare nods. "Now you're getting it."

"Fine. I'll use my first question to ask what you're doing here." I lift my chin and stare him in the eye.

His mouth twitches again. "Visiting. Isn't that what people usually do in hospitals?"

I flush. I can't help it. Obviously. And obviously, I'm out of my league here. This guy could have me for breakfast if he wanted, and from the gleam in his eye, I'm not so sure he doesn't.

I take a sip of my coffee, careful not to slosh it on my shirt. With the way my heart is racing, anything is possible.

"And you? Why are you here?" Dare asks.

"Is that your first question? Because turn-about is fair play."

Dare smiles broadly, genuinely amused.

"Sure. I'll use a question."

"I brought my brother. He's here for... group therapy."

I suddenly feel weird saying that aloud, because it makes my brother sound *less than* somehow. And he's not. He's *more than*. Better than most people, more gentle, more pure of heart. But a stranger wouldn't know that. A stranger would just slap him with a *crazy* label and let it be. I fight the urge to explain, and somehow manage not to. It's not a stranger's business.

Dare doesn't question me, though. He just nods like it's the most normal thing in the world.

He takes a drink of his coffee. "I think it's probably kismet, anyway. That you and I are here at the same time, I mean."

"Kismet?" I raise an eyebrow.

"That's fate, Calla," he tells me. I roll my eyes.

"I know that. I may be going to a state school, but I'm not stupid."

He grins, a grin so white and charming that my panties almost fall off.

"Good to know. So you're a college girl, Calla?"

I don't want to talk about that. I want to talk about why you think this is kismet. But I nod.

"Yeah. I'm leaving for Berkeley in the fall."

"Good choice," he takes another sip. "But maybe kismet got it wrong, after all. If you're leaving and all. Because apparently, I'll be staying for a while. That is, after I find an apartment. A good one is hard to find around here."

He's so confident, so open. It doesn't even feel odd that a total stranger is telling me these things, out of the blue, so randomly. I feel like I know him already, actually.

I stare at him. "An apartment?"

He stares back. "Yeah. The thing you rent, it has a shower and a bedroom, usually?"

I flush. "I know that. It's just that this might be kismet after all. I might know of something. I mean, my father is going to rent out our carriage house. I think."

And if *I* can't have it, it should definitely go to someone like Dare. The mere thought gives me a heart spasm.

"Hmm. Now that *is* interesting," Dare tells me. "Kismet prevails, it seems. And a carriage house next to a funeral home, at that. It must take balls of steel to live there."

I quickly pull out a little piece of paper and scribble my dad's cell phone on it. "Yeah. If you're interested, I mean, if you've got the balls, you can call and talk to him about it."

I push the paper across the table, staring him in the eye, framing it up as a challenge. Dare can't possibly know how I'm trying to will my heart to slow down before it explodes, but maybe he does, because a smile stretches slowly and knowingly across his lips.

"Oh, I've got balls," he confirms, his eyes gleaming again.

Dare me.

I swallow hard.

"I'm ready to ask my second question," I tell him. He raises an eyebrow.

"Already? Is it about my balls?"

I flush and shake my head.

"What did you mean before?" I ask him slowly, not lowering my gaze. "Why exactly do you think this is kismet?"

His eyes crinkle up a little bit as he smiles yet again. And yet again, his grin is thoroughly amused. A real smile, not a fake one like I'm accustomed to around my house.

"It's kismet because you seem like someone I might like to know. Is that odd?"

No, because I want to know you, too.

"Maybe," I say instead. "Is it odd that I feel like I already know you somehow?"

Because I do. There's something so familiar about his eyes, so dark, so bottomless. But then again, I *have* been dreaming about them for days.

Dare raises an eyebrow. "Maybe I have that kind of face."

I choke back a snort. *Not hardly.*

He stares at me. "Regardless, kismet always prevails."

I shake my head and smile. A *real* smile. "The jury is still out on that one."

Dare takes a last drink of coffee, his gaze still frozen to mine, before he thunks his cup down on the table and stands up.

"Well, let me know what the jury decides."

And then he walks away.

I'm so dazed by his abrupt departure that it takes me a second to realize something because *kismet always prevails* and I'm *someone he might like to know.*

He took my dad's phone number with him.

6

SEX

Finn

NOCTE LIBER SUM NOCTE LIBER SUM
BY NIGHT I AM FREE.
ALEA IACTA EST THE DIE HAS BEEN CAST. THE DIE
HAS BEEN CAST.
THE DIE HAS BEEN FUCKING CAST.
SERVA ME, SERVABO TE. SAVE ME AND I WILL SAVE
YOU.
SAVE ME.
SAVE ME.
SAVE ME.

"Hey, bro." Calla walks into my room, abruptly, unannounced, and I instantly close my journal, hiding my thoughts behind its brown leather cover. "What's up?"

I smile, swallowing my panic, hiding everything carefully and completely behind my teeth.

"Not much. You?"

"Not much. Just restless."

She hops onto my bed, sitting next to me, her fingers immediately tracing the letters on the front of my journal. She knows enough not to open it.

I shrug. "We should do something."

~~Act normal.~~

She nods. "K. Like what? Wanna drive to Warrenton beach?"

To see the old Iredale wreck? We've seen it a million times, but whatever.

"Sure," I answer simply. Because sometimes saying fewer words makes it easier to conceal the crazy.

We climb off the bed and Calla turns to me, grabbing my elbow.

"Hey, Finn?"

I pause, staring down at her. "Yeah?"

"You've seemed....off this whole week. I thought when you went to group a second time it'd help, but you still seem strange. If something's wrong, you'd tell me, right?"

You can't You can't You can't You can't. You're crazy crazy crazy crazy.
Don't Tell Her Your Secret Secret Secret.

I swallow back the voices.

~~Act normal.~~

"I'm fine," I lie. A blissful lie to spare her worry, to spare my pride, to spare me the humiliation of being dragged away to a padded room, to a place where keys are thrown away and the crazy people are forgotten, replaced by medicated shells.

"Promise?" Calla is hesitant, her red hair standing out like fire against my white curtains. She almost always accepts my word, but this time, she knows me. She knows I'm lying.

"Repromissionem," I assure her. She rolls her eyes.

"You know, sometimes, Latin just complicates things. That took you five syllables to say what you could've said in two."

I smile and shrug. "It's a dignified language. It has character."

"If by dignified, you mean *dead*, ok."

She laughs and I pretend to, because honestly we're shells anyway, medicated or not. We're not the people we used to be. We just look like it on the outside.

We clatter down the creaky steps of our house, bickering back and forth, doing our best to seem normal because mom always said fake it 'til you make it. We're definitely doing our part.

As we round the corner into the large, elaborate foyer, the distinct roar of a motorcycle splits apart the serene atmosphere of the funeral home. We stare at each other.

We don't typically get mourners on motorcycles this far up the mountain.

Dad steps past us, eyeing Calla curiously.

"Thanks for referring someone to me for the carriage house. I wasn't expecting your help with that, considering how much you wanted it for yourself."

Calla stops still, frozen in place, while she stares at dad.

"He called?"

He?

Her voice is filled with anxiety and happiness and hope. I stare at her. What the hell is this?

Dad nods. "Yeah. This morning. That'll be him now, to look at it."

Calla spins around and stares out the window, and I look over her shoulder.

A black, aggressive motorcycle, a Triumph, is parked on the circular drive, as a tall dark-haired guy stands in front of it, removing his black helmet.

Calla is so absorbed in watching him that she doesn't realize how closely I'm watching *her*.

She smiles a beatific smile. "It's been days since I told him about it. I thought he didn't want it."

My dad raises his eyebrow. "He still might not. He's just here to look at it. Really quick—how did you meet him?"

She pauses. "I met him in the café at the hospital the other day. I've bumped into him a couple of other times. He's been there visiting someone. He seems nice."

Nice.

Dad doesn't push her because the guy is already walking up the porch steps. "Excuse me while I go show him around."

I don't bother to ask her who the hell this guy is, or why she chose to invite him into our life by renting out the apartment that both she and I wanted for ourselves. I don't have to ask. I can see it written all over her face.

She's glowing as she looks at him, an expression I've never seen on her face. She's interested in him. *Very* interested.

Apprehension builds in my belly as I watch my father shake his hand, as they walk side by side down to the carriage house.

The guy looks decent enough, but there's something about him. Something unsettling, separate from the way my sister is staring at him in rapt fascination.

GetRidOfHimGetRidOfHimGetRidOfHim.

I ignore the voices, and watch the carriage house door close behind them.

A heaviness settles around me, something dark and oppressing, because even though I want to save my sister from me, I don't know if I'm ready.

I smile at her. "Ready to go?"

She pauses, glancing back outside, hesitant now as she stares at the closed door of the Carriage House.

"Um... let's have a raincheck, ok?"

I suck in a breath, startled that she would ditch me for this guy. I should've known from the new look on her face. The look of intoxication. But having it actually slap me in the face for the first time is still shocking.

She has an interest outside of me. Something that came between us, even though the moment is small... even though it's just a stupid drive to the beach.

Even though I want to be unselfish, I don't know if I can handle it.

We were outsiders our whole childhoods and all the way through high school. And while it sucked, it was also a hidden blessing, because since I was all Calla had, she focused solely on me. We've always been everything to each other.

Bile rises up in my throat as I watch her descend the porch steps and walk across the lawns, her chin stuck out, and her hands buried in her hair as she arranges it over her shoulder.

I need her. I need things to stay the same. But I can't risk her. I can't suck her down. I can't let my craziness swallow her then spit her out. But I need her.

My thoughts are contradicting and confusing and swirl around in my brain until I can barely focus. I stagger to the window seat and stare down, my forehead pressed against the glass as I try to catch my breath.

Serva me, servabo te.

Save me, and I'll save you.

As I remember the dark-haired guy's confident stride, I have a feeling that he's someone I won't be able to save her from.

But the die has been cast.

I see that now.

7

SEPTUM

Calla

He came.

I think I'm in shock as I linger near the house, trying to seem like I'm casually sitting at the little table on the side porch, like I'm *not* waiting with bated breath for them to re-emerge.

I can't believe he's here.

It's been days since he took dad's phone number, and I waited every day, but he didn't call. I thought he wasn't going to, that I'd imagined the chemistry, the connection. Maybe even that I'd imagined *him.*

But he re-appeared in my dreams, again and again. Smiling at me, staring at me, *being with me.* My subconscious is definitely trying to urge me toward him, maybe even toward living again. I don't know.

All I know is that he's here, out of the blue today, with his dark eyes and British accent and on a motorcycle, no less.

Kismet prevails.

My lungs feel fluttery, along with my heart, my stomach and my ovaries. All of it feels quivery, like a shaking ridiculous mess. It feels like it's meant to happen, that I keep bumping into him, and dreaming about him, and now he's here in my life.

It almost takes my breath away.

This feeling only grows more pronounced when the Carriage House door finally opens and my father and Dare step back out. They shake hands and my father immediately heads back toward the house, a small smile on his lips. Halfway across the lawns, he diverts his course and heads for me.

Stopping in front of me, he stares down.

"The last few weeks have been hard. Too hard. I'm not going to pretend to know what you're going through, because our paths are different and we feel our loss in different ways. All I'm going to say is this. Be careful. You're naïve and innocent and your mother would know what to say right now, but I don't. This the first time you've seemed interested in something in weeks. So all I'm going to say is be careful. Ok?"

I'm utterly speechless because my father's expression is so *knowing*. It's like he looked inside my head and saw the connection I feel toward Dare, the interest, the intrigue. He's nervous for me, but yet he's still willing to rent the Carriage House to Dare because he needs the money. And because he thinks Dare will distract me from my grief.

I nod. "Ok."

He nods back, then walks into the house without another word. From behind me, I swear I can feel Finn staring at me, his gaze beating between my shoulder blades from the windows, but I shake it off. I'm not doing anything wrong.

Or am I?

Because as Dare looks up and meets my gaze, he smiles a mischievous smile that makes me think I am.

Dare me.

To do what? That question makes me tingly.

Dare slowly walks across the yard, and motions to the chair across from me. "Is that seat taken?"

I roll my eyes. This game again?

"No."

He doesn't ask, he just sits in it, stretching his long legs out and crossing them at the ankles and stares at me, like he belongs in that chair. I raise an eyebrow, but he's still silent.

"So, you have a British accent, but your last name is DuBray. How does *that* work?" I finally ask, desperate to make him stop staring at me. His mouth twitches.

"Is that your third question?"

Frustration bubbles up in me, regardless of how cute things sound coming out of his mouth.

"Do I have to count every single question I ask? I'm only making polite conversation."

He shakes his head, and smiles just a bit. "Fine. I'll give you this one in the name of polite conversation. My father died when I was a baby and he was French. My mother was British, so we moved there. I've lived there my whole life, hence the accent."

His beautiful, beautiful accent. I nod. "I'm sorry about your father."

He shrugs. "He was a good man, but it was a long time ago."

I itch to ask him how old he is, but I resist the urge. I can't use another question already. Besides, I'd bet money that he's twenty-one. Or so.

"Can you speak French?" I ask hopefully, because Lord have mercy that would be hot.

"Oui, mademoiselle," he answers smoothly. "Un peu. A little bit."

Be still my freaking heart. I stare at him, enthralled.

"So," he finally says, changing the subject so very casually, as though he's not the coolest, sexiest man alive. "How do you survive living in a funeral home? Have you ever seen a ghost?"

I ignore my pounding heart and raise an eyebrow. "I'll take this question to mean that you did, in fact, have the balls to rent the carriage house?"

He chuckles, a raspy, husky sound that vibrates right into my belly.

"The fact that I have balls of steel is now unarguable," he announces with a grin. "And I'm never nervous. Not even about ghosts. Also, since I gave you one answer, turnabout is fair play, right? So... have you ever seen a ghost?"

I've not seen one, but the ghost of my mother is here... present in every picture, pile of clothing and memory of this house. But of course I don't say that.

I shrug instead. "I've never seen one. As far as I'm concerned, there is no such thing."

"Really?" he answers, sounding doubtful. "That's disappointing."

"You're going to be in the Carriage House anyway," I tell him. "There aren't any dead people out there. I mean, I assume you're renting it, right?

Please be right.

63

He nods. "Yeah. Thanks for letting me know about it. It's just what I've been looking for. A nice little space with gorgeous scenery."

As he says the words *gorgeous scenery,* he stares straight at me, with purpose.

I'm his gorgeous scenery. I suddenly can't breathe enough to even try to ask him why he wants to be in Astoria in the first place.

"Kismet," I manage to eke out.

He nods. "Kismet."

Dare stares at me, long and hard and dark, and I manage to take one deep breath, then another.

"So I'll be seeing you," he says, abruptly ending our conversation by standing up.

"When are you moving in?" I ask, suddenly panicky at the thought of him leaving. He brings with him an air of comfort, of excitement, of something charged and dangerous and new. I don't want to let that go just yet.

He grins.

"Now. I brought my bag."

His bag? I follow his gesture to see a duffel bag strapped to the back of his bike. One bag.

"That's it?"

"I travel light," he answers, heading back to the Carriage House. To his *home,* which is now only a hundred feet from my own.

"I guess you do," I murmur. I watch the way his wide shoulders sway, and the way the breeze flutters his dark hair. He grabs his bag and ducks into his new home and I realize that I forgot to ask him something.

How long he's staying.

***

Dinner feels different tonight, mainly because I know Dare is a hundred yards away.

I serve up spaghetti, which is the easiest meal on the planet to prepare, and garlic bread and corn. My father eats with gusto, while Finn, as usual, pushes things around on his plate. His meds make him lose his appetite.

We're eating late, because my father worked late.

At the thought of his 'work', I can't help but glance at his hands. I know he washed them several times when he came upstairs, but just the thought of what he'd been doing with them, what he'd been handling, grosses me out. I know that a scant hour or so ago, he was jamming a needle into a dead person's neck and replacing all of their blood with chemical fluid.

And now he's eating with those same hands.

It's gross and it's hard to swallow my blood-colored spaghetti sauce.

"So, how was your day?" I ask Finn, trying desperately to think of something else. I hadn't seen him all afternoon. He shrugs.

"Good, I guess. I finished going through my closet. I've got a few boxes for Goodwill, dad."

My dad nods, but I see something on Finn's face, something flicker, and I widen my eyes. *Don't do it*, I try and tell him telepathically. *Don't mention mom's stuff. Don't.*

And he doesn't. Instead, he looks at me.

"Actually, I have something I want to tell you guys."

We both look at him, waiting. My breath catches because he looks so serious.

What the hell?

I see him swallow hard. Not a good sign.

"I've decided to go to MIT after all."

My stomach plunges into my shoes and the silence in the room is heavy. I look at my dad and he looks at me, then we both stare at Finn while I try and remember how to speak so that I can argue.

"No," I manage to say. "You can't go alone. *Finn.*"

He feels the pleading in my eyes and looks away, at the walls, out the windows.

"Please don't try and talk me out of it," he tells us, but he's mostly telling me. "Cal, I want to go with you. I do. But this is for the best. It's something I have to do. I have to be alone, and figure out how to be alone. How to stay sane alone. Do you understand?"

No. A thousand times No. A millions times NO.

I'm shaking my head, but my father leans over and puts a hand on my shoulder. A warning to be silent. I stare at him helplessly.

"I think that's good," my father says. "Your mother and I..." his voice trails off like he's in pain and he pauses for a second. "Your mother and I both thought that was for the best. Some separation so that you can grow independently. This is good."

My dad sounds so proud. Like Finn is doing something heroic, like he's saving a kid from a fire or moving a tortoise off a free-way. But it's not heroic because he's being self-destructive. I can see it in his eyes, and the way he holds his shoulders and won't look at me.

Put me out of my misery.

The words in his journal are all I can see when I look at him.

But when he looks back into my eyes, his are filled with something else. Pleading.

Let me do this. Let me go.

Let him do what?

Learn to live alone? Shoulder things alone? I take a shaky breath and Finn still stares at me. And stares. And stares. And finally I break under the pale blue weight of it.

"Ok."

The word comes out like an exhale.

Finn raises an eyebrow. "Ok? No kicking or screaming?"

I shake my head. "No. Not if you're sure. I fought mom and dad over it, but I'm not going to fight *you.*"

I feel resigned and sad and panicky, and I already feel alone. But what can I do? It's Finn's choice. His gaze softens now.

"You're not fighting me," he points out. "You're doing what I know needs to be done. And you know it too, Calla."

No, I don't. I know just the opposite, actually.

But again, what can I do? His mind is made up.

I don't say anything, because I can't. So I nod wordlessly instead.

I push my food around on my plate because when I try to swallow it now, it sticks in my throat like some sort of gelatinous sludge. Dad and Finn keep watching me, waiting for me to protest or argue or throw a fit. But I don't. In spite of myself, I somehow remain calm, cool and very collected until the minute that I can excuse myself and make a break for it.

I rush outdoors, ignoring the fact that Finn calls out from behind me. I flee the yard, sucking in air as I run down the path leading to the beach. The trail looks like a silvery ribbon in the dusky moonlight, twisting and turning through the green wet underbrush and gleaming dark rocks.

The trees form a canopy over the path, and it's unsettling here alone in the dark. The shadows give me goose-bumps, because I don't know what they're hiding. But even still, even with the moon slivering in through the tree tops and with the wind calling incoherent words through the pine needles, I'm still grateful to be here, rather than in my dining room.

I push myself forward, away from the destructive path that Finn seems to be insistent on, and towards the path to the ocean.

When I reach the beach, my heels sink into the damp sand, and I'm thankful that it's low tide. My legs won't get wet. I make it to the rocks within minutes, and just as I approach them, a shadow steps away from the boulders.

It's tall and unexpected, because no one ever comes here.

It pauses, and I suck in a breath.

Then it steps into the moonlight and I realize who it is.

Dare.

Because he lives here now.

"Hey," he greets me, his voice husky and soft and British. There is welcome in his eyes, and a sincere appreciation for how I look, a hungry expression, as his gaze flits over me. It makes the blood flush through my cheeks and my chest. He likes what he sees.

I swallow hard.

"Are you all right?" he asks, his head cocked and his eyes glinting in the moonlight. "I couldn't help but notice that you ran down the mountain."

God. I want to sink into the sand. I must look like a crazy person.

"I'm fine," I tell him. "I just... my brother upset me and I needed a minute to breathe."

"And when you're upset you run down to the beach in the dark? Alone?" Dare cocks his head again and I'm not sure if he's judging me. I look away.

"No. I just... my favorite place is down here. I come here a lot. Not just when I'm upset."

"Show me." Dare's voice is husky and soft, and it isn't a request. "Your favorite place, I mean."

I don't hesitate. I don't know why. Maybe because he's been in my dreams so often, it's like I know him already.

"Ok."

I lead him along the beach another hundred feet or so, through the rocks and into a secluded inlet. Hidden by the night, a horse-shoe shaped cove waits for us in the dark.

"Watch where you step," I tell him, although I know it's hard to see. "This cove is covered in tidal pools. Actually, wait here for a minute."

I reluctantly let go of his arm and venture away to find a few pieces of smallish driftwood. I lug it back to the cove and hunt for a canvas bag that I keep here for just these occasions. It's not under the rock I usually keep it under, so I nose around for a while longer, until Dare calls out.

"Looking for this?" he holds it up. I nod, taking it from him.

"Yeah. Thanks." Pulling the lighter from the bag, I set the wood ablaze.

It instantly fills the inlet with an ethereal violet light.

Dare stares at it, mesmerized. "It's purple."

69

"It's the salt from the ocean," I explain. "It makes the flames purple and blue. But don't breathe in the smoke. It's gorgeous, but toxic."

"So look, don't breathe?" Dare looks amused.

I nod. "Exactly. Instead of breathing the smoke, why don't you turn around and look at the cove?"

He does as I ask and I can see on his face that he's impressed. Small pools are scattered around us, with sea life in each one, plants and shells, crabs and seaweed. Everything seems magical, as the night glows violet.

"During high tide, these are covered up. In fact, you can't get to the back of the cove. But during low tide, the water is sucked out and you can walk right in and look at everything the water covers up."

"This is incredible," Dare decides, walking around and examining everything. "No wonder it's your favorite place." He moves lithely, casually. Easily.

In fact, being with him is easy. As each moment passes, I feel less panicked and terrified about Finn, and more comfortable with Dare.

Even though he's clearly sophisticated, he's still as comfortable as my favorite pair of jeans. It's like...he doesn't judge me. He doesn't ridicule me. He simply accepts things as I offer them and doesn't push me for more.

While he kneels to examine a pool, I examine him. He's wearing dark clothes tonight, dark jeans and a black hoodie. The graceful way he moves makes even a hoodie seem elegant. He's graceful and refined, nothing like the boys were in school.

It's refreshing. And knee-weakening.

He turns to me, his gaze dark and curious.

"How did your brother upset you?"

70

The panic comes back to me in a rush, and for a minute, I stare past Dare, out to sea.

"We're twins. He wants to go to a different college, but I don't agree. He needs me."

Dare stares at me, trying to figure me out. I see the wheels turning. He opens his mouth, but I interrupt before he can say anything.

"You don't understand," I tell him preemptively. "My brother has an issue. A mental issue. He's medicated, but he needs me."

If I meant to scare him, and I don't know if I did or didn't, it doesn't work. Because Dare just nods, unfazed. "That's commendable," he tells me. "That you care so much."

My head snaps back. "Of course I do," I snap. "Why wouldn't I? He's my brother."

Dare smiles and holds up his hands. "Calm down," he says soothingly. "I was just making an observation. Not everyone cares that much, family or not."

I stare at him. "That's a sad thought. Why are you out here anyway? In the dark? Alone?" I throw his words from earlier back at him in an effort to change the subject. He smiles in appreciation of my effort.

"Because I was bored. And I thought I could see the stars better from here."

He's right. We definitely can. Up on the mountain, the trees block them.

And he likes the stars? Is it possible for him to get more perfect?

He points upward.

"That's Orion's belt. And that over there.... That's Andromeda. I don't think we can see Perseus tonight." He pauses and stares down at me. "Do you know their myth?"

His voice is calm and soothing and as I listen to him, I let myself drift away from my current problems and toward him, toward his dark eyes and full lips and long hands.

I nod, remembering what I'd learned about Andromeda last year in Astrology. "Yes. Andromeda's mother insulted Poseidon, and she was condemned to die by a sea monster, but Perseus saved her and then married her."

He nods, pleased by my answer. "Yes. And now they linger in the skies to remind young lovers everywhere of the merits of undying love."

I snort. "Yeah. And then they had a corny movie made for them that managed to butcher several different Greek myths at once."

Dare's lip twitches. "Perhaps. But maybe we can overlook that due to the underlying message of eternal love." His expression is droll and I can't decide if he's being serious or just trying to be ironic or something, because *the irony is lost on you.*

"That's bullshit, you know," I tell him, rolling the metaphorical dice. "Undying love, I mean. Nothing is undying. People fall out of love or their chemistry dies or maybe they even die themselves. Any way you look at it, love always dies eventually."

I should know. I'm Funeral Home Girl. I see it all the time.

Dare looks down at me incredulously. "If you truly believe that, then you believe that death controls us, or maybe even circumstance. That's depressing, Calla. We control ourselves."

He seems truly bothered and I stare at him, at once nervous that I've disappointed him and certain that I'm right.

I *am* the one surrounded by it all the time, after all…by death and bad circumstances. I *am* the one whose mother just died and I know that the world continues to turn like nothing ever happened.

"I don't necessarily believe that death controls us," I amend carefully. "But you can't argue that it wins in the long run. Every time. Because we all die, Dare. So death wins, not love."

He snorts. "Tell that to Perseus and Andromeda. They're immortal in the sky."

I snort right back. "They're also not real."

Dare stares at me, willing me to see his point of view and I'm suddenly confused about how we started out talking about love and are now talking about death. Leave it to me to work that into conversation.

"I'm sorry," I offer. "I guess it's a hazard of living where I do. Death is always present."

"Death is big," Dare acknowledges. "But there are things bigger than that. If there's not, then this is all for nothing. Life is worth nothing. Putting yourself out there, and taking chances and all that. All of that stuff is bollocks if it can just disappear in the end."

I shrug and look away. "I'm sorry. I just believe in the right here and right now. That's what we know and that's what we can count on. And I don't like to think about the end."

Dare looks back at the sky, but he's still pensive. "You seem rather pessimistic today, Calla-Lily."

I swallow hard, because I do sound like a shrew. A jaded, ugly, bitter person.

"My mom died a few weeks ago," I tell him and the words scrape my heart. "It's still hard to talk about."

He pauses and nods, as though everything makes sense now, as though he's *sorry* because everyone always is. "Ah. I see. I'm sorry. I didn't mean to open a wound."

I shake my head and look away because my eyes are watering and it's embarrassing. Because God. Am I ever going to be able to think about it without crying?

"It's ok. You didn't know," I answer. "And you're right. I'm probably jaded. Being surrounded by death all the time… well, I guess it's made me ugly."

Dare studies me, hard, his eyes glittering in the light of the driftwood fire which reflects purple flames into his black bottomless depths.

"You're not ugly," he tells me, his voice oh-so-beautiful. "Not by a long, long shot."

His words make me lose my train of thought. Because of the way he's looking at me right now… *like I'm beautiful*, like he knows me, when I'm really just Calla and he doesn't.

"I'm sorry I'm so emotional tonight," I tell him. "I'm not usually like this. It's just… there's a lot going on."

"I see that," he answers quietly. "Is there anything I can do?"

You can call me Calla-Lily again. Because it seems intimate and familiar, and it makes me feel good. But I shake my head. "I wish. But no."

He smiles. "Ok. Can I walk you back up to the house at least?"

My heart leaps for a second, but the idea of facing Finn right now isn't one I enjoy. So I shake my head.

"I'm not really ready to go back yet," I tell him regretfully. Because it's the truth.

He shrugs. "Okay. I'll wait."

My heart thunders in my ears as I pretend that I'm not thrilled with that. We sit in the sand, so close that I can feel the warmth emanating from his body, so close that whenever he moves, his shoulder brushes mine. I shouldn't get so much pleasure from that, from the accidental touches, from his warmth.

But I do.

We sit in such a way for an hour.

In silence.

Staring at the ocean and the sky and the stars.

No one has ever felt comfortable like this to me before, with silence that isn't awkward. No one but Finn. Until now.

"Did you know that the Italian serial killer Leonarda Cianciulli was famous for turning her victims into tea cakes and serving them to guests?" I ask absently, still staring out at the water.

Dare doesn't miss a beat. "No. Because that's an odd thing to know."

I feel the laughter bubbling up in me, threatening to erupt.

"I agree. It is." It's something my brother shared with me yesterday.

Dare smiles. "I'll be sure to work that in at the next party I attend."

I can't help but smile now. "I'm sure it'll go over well."

He chuckles. "Well, it's a conversation starter, for sure."

I don't move because I sort of want to stay here forever, even though the dampness of the sand has leached into my jeans and now my butt is wet.

But even though I don't want this to end, the darkness is so black now that it swallows us up. It's getting late.

I sigh.

"I've got to go back."

"Okay," Dare answers, his voice low in the night, and if I didn't know better, I'd think I detected regret in it. *Maybe he wants to stay here longer, too.*

He helps me to my feet, and then keeps his hand on my elbow as we walk over the driftwood and through the tidal pools and up the trail. It's that thing that real men do, the guiding a woman across the room thing. It's gentlemanly and chivalrous and my ovaries might explode from it because it's intimate and familiar and sexy.

When we get to the house, he removes his hand and I immediately feel the absence of his warmth.

He looks down at me, a thousand things in his eyes that I can't define but want to.

"Good night, Calla. I hope you feel better now."

"I do," I murmur.

And as I pad up the stairs, I realize that I actually do.

For the first time in six weeks.

8

OCTO

Finn

JumpJumpJumpJumpJumpJumpJumpJumpYouFuckingCow ardJump.

"Hey," Calla's voice is soft from my doorway.

I yank away from my open bedroom windows as though the sills are on fire. I'd seen Calla walk up the path with *him,* but I hadn't realized she was already back in the house.

"Hey," I stammer, as I move far away from the windows and try to tune out the fucking voices that taunt me. "About earlier. Are you mad?"

Calla sinks onto my bed, sitting on her hands. She stares at me hesitantly.

"No. I'm just worried. You know why."

I do. My journal. I also know that she still hadn't ratted me out to my dad. Because she knows my deepest fear... of being locked away.

YouDeserveChainsChainChainsChains.

I grit my teeth.

"Don't be worried, Cal. I've got this."

She takes a breath so shaky that I can hear it from here. "This is the thing. I haven't told dad about the things I read because I'm taking it on myself to make sure you're fine. That you stay safe. That you get better.

If I'm not with you to do my job and everything blows up, then that's on me. And I don't want to live with the guilt of something like that. I carry enough guilt already."

My heart feels like a concrete block as I stare at her vulnerability.

"Calla, mom's accident wasn't your fault. You know that."

Her eyes are so bleak as she stares back at me. "Do I?"

"We've told you a hundred times, Cal. You called. She didn't have to pick up the phone. It was raining so hard. She should've let it go to voicemail. That was her choice. Not yours. She crossed the center-line. Not you."

Calla closes her eyes. "Either way. I wouldn't be able to stand it if something happened to you. Do you understand?"

I swallow hard. "Yes. But I promise. I'll be ok."

She raises an eyebrow. "Promise?"

"Repromissionem," I assure her, my entire being forcing out the lie. It comes out sounding like truth which is fine because honestly, I don't know the true answer to this question.

~~Sound normal.~~

She rolls her eyes. "Again. Two syllables are easier."

I smile. "What did you need, anyway?"

Her eyes widen, then narrow. "I just wanted to check on you. I hate it when you seem off. It makes me nervous."

"Don't be. Nervous, I mean," I tell her. "It's ok."

She nods. "Ok."

But she isn't convinced and there's nothing I can do to make her that way. I know her better than the back of my hand, so I know that.

"I just wanted to say goodnight," she tells me finally. "And that I love you. And that if you change your mind, even if it's the last minute, it's fine. I hate the idea of being apart, Finn. But more than that, I just want you to be ok. So if this is what you need, I'll try to be ok with it."

Her eyes fill up with tears and she looks away, but I reach out a hand and lay it on hers. She looks at me, her chin quivering.

"It'll be ok." My voice is assured. Confident. "*I'll* be ok."

She nods.

"Reprommissionem?" Her voice is still shaky.

"Promise."

~~Lie.~~

9

NOVEM

Calla

The ocean breeze blows back his hair, and Dare smiles in the sun. His teeth gleam and I giggle at something he said.

I reach for him and he grabs me, holding me close.

"You're going to be the death of me," he says against my neck, his lips brushing my skin.

"Why?" I manage to breathe, my hands splayed against his chest. He smells like the woods.

"Because you're so much better than I deserve."

I wake up in wonderment, because *hello*. I'm so not better than he deserves. My subconscious mind must be on drugs, but regardless of that, my dreams are heaven.

I shower and make my way downstairs for a late breakfast/ early lunch. The pickings are slim in the pantry.

"We're out of lemons for lemonade," I tell my dad as we munch on cereal. "We're also out of sandwich meat, spaghetti sauce, bread, milk... basically anything we can use to make dinner." He nods, unconcerned and I sigh.

I feel like he's been slipping. Like he cares less and less about real life issues every day, and more on his grief about mom. He cares about his job, of course. But that's nothing new. He's always been a workaholic. In fact, that's where he was the night mom died. In town, picking up a body.

I force my attention from that, onto anything but that.

"I'll go to the store today," I tell him, getting up and stretching. "Do you know where Finn is?"

My father keeps his face buried in his newspaper, but still pulls out his wallet and hands it to me. "No."

I sigh again. "Ok. Well, if you see him, tell him I'll be back later."

I take his wallet and slip out the door, grateful for a chance to be away from his blank expression. I know we all cope in different ways, but Jesus.

The mid-day sun gleams on the wet road as I steer my car down the mountain. The birds are chirping in the trees, and I roll my windows down to let the brisk air in. I take a deep breath, then dance in my seat as a happy song comes on the radio.

Thank you, God, I whisper in my head. Happiness, in any form, is hard to come by these days and I'll take it where I can get it. Reaching down, I roll the volume dial up, pumping up the music, filling my car so that happiness is all I hear and all I feel.

I only look away from the road for a second.

For one brief moment.

When I look back up, a tiny animal is sitting in the middle of the road. It happens so fast that I only see two green eyes looking at me, and gray fur, and I yank the wheel hard to avoid hitting it.

My car rumbles off the road and I slam on the brakes, my wheels skidding in the dirty gravel on the shoulder.

I skid to a stop, at least a foot from the edge, but still, I'm horrified and frozen. I can't breathe as I sit still, as I eye the edge and suddenly, it seems very close to me. Like I could've plunged over the side, just like my mom.

My breath comes in heavy gasps, my heart flutters in my chest as I hear her screaming, as I see the rain from that night, the steam rising from the road, the sound of her shrieking tires in my ear. It all swirls around me like stuttered pictures from a movie, re-living itself in ways I can't stop. I put my hands over my ears to block out the screaming, and my chest contracts and contracts.

I'm having a heart attack.

But I'm not.

It has to be a panic attack.

I'm panicking.

I can't breathe.

I throw open the car door and the roar of it is loud. I scramble out, and bend over, trying like hell to breathe, and failing miserably, my hands on my knees, my mouth open, gasping impotently.

"Stand up," a calm voice says quickly. "If you can't breathe, stand up."

I do, arching my back with my hands on my hips, my face turned up to the sun.

One.

Two.

Three.

Four.

By five, I can breathe a small breath.

By six, I take a large one.

By seven, I'm able to move my head, to look and see who is with me.

Dare stands in front of me, concern swimming in his dark eyes, his lithe form hovering by my car. It's like he's afraid to approach me, afraid that I'm a wild animal poised to attack.

"I'm sorry," I tell him, my lungs still feeling fluttery. "I don't know what happened."

He takes a step, his eyes wary and concerned. "Are you okay?"

Am I?

I look around, at my car, at my open car door, at the way I just melted down in the street. But I nod, because I can't do anything else.

"Yeah. I just... there was something in the road. I almost hit it. I think it might've been a kitten. I might've even hit it. It happened so fast, I don't know."

I bend over again, and Dare pulls me up.

"Stand up," he reminds me. "It opens your diaphragm up."

Right. Because I'm melting down and can't breathe. For a minute, I decide this must be how Finn feels all the time. So crazy, so helpless.

"I'm sorry," I mumble, my hand reaching back for my car fender to lean on. Dare cocks his head, so calm in the face of my panic.

"For what?"

"For falling apart," I whisper. "I don't know what's wrong with me."

He's unfazed. "Tell me what happened," he suggests softly, and his hand is on my back now, rubbing lightly between my shoulder blades, reminding me to breathe.

"I told you... I was driving down the mountain and swerved because of a cat. I... don't know why I panicked."

"Maybe because your mom just died in a car crash?" Dare prompts gently, more gently than I would've ever guessed he could. "Maybe it scared you?"

"I don't know," I admit. "I just kept hearing her scream. She... I was on the phone with her when she died."

I whisper that like a confession, because I know I'm the reason she's dead. Dare doesn't lower his gaze and once again, he doesn't judge.

"That's terrible."

I nod. "Yeah."

I realize suddenly that the roar I'd heard a minute ago wasn't my car door, of course. It was Dare's motorcycle. "Were you going to town?" I ask him half politely, half truly curious, but mostly just to change the subject.

He shakes his head. "No. I was coming back. I returned a library book."

I'm not sure what I'm more focused on, the fact that he reads, or the fact that he was coming up the hill and I was going down, just like the night mom died.

She was coming up, someone else was going down.

"We could've hit," I realize, a chill running down my spine.

Dare looks confused, his full lips parted. "Pardon?"

I shake my head. "I'm sorry. I was just...I'm happy I steered over to the side, rather than to the middle. Or you might've hit me."

It's a morbid thought and what the hell is wrong with me?

Dare stares at me, probably worried that he's with some sort of psychopath, but he hides it nicely. "But I didn't," he points out. "We're both fine."

Are we?

"You're shaking," he says simply now. And with that, he rubs my arms, and somehow, I don't know how, I fold into him. It feels right, it feels normal, it feels so freaking good, it feels like I've stepped into one of my dreams.

He startles for a second, and then lets me stand there, my forehead pressed to his shirt as he rubs my back. His scent is so soothing... so woodsy and masculine and perfect. He smells just like I dreamed he would. I breathe it in, then sniffle and that's when I realize that I'm crying.

I'm an utter mess today.

He must think I'm a lunatic.

"I'm so sorry," I apologize finally, stepping away from him. "I don't know what's wrong with me."

"You've had a lot to deal with," he says understandingly. "Anyone would be edgy."

Would anyone be having a panic attack in the middle of the road, crying on a beautiful guy that she's only just met?

I look at him. "You must think I'm crazy."

He shakes his head solemnly. "Nope."

"Because I'm not," I insist.

His mouth twitches. "Never."

I have to giggle now, at the ridiculousness of this situation.

I look at him and somehow, he seems so out of place out here among nature, with his slender, refined body and black eyes.

"Did you see the kitten?" I change the subject.

He shakes his head. "I just saw the dust from your tires on the shoulder."

I'm worried now because I don't want to be a cat killer on top of everything else. Dare takes one look at my expression and rushes to assure me, probably because he doesn't want me to cry on him again.

"I'll go look for it," he tells me quickly. "Why don't you go back up to the house so you're not standing on the side of the road?"

I hesitate. "I should wait for you. I mean, you're doing it for me, after all."

He smiles, a wide bright smile. "You can repay me on a different day. For now, you should get out of the road."

"But the groceries," I murmur, already heading back to the car.

"We'll get them later."

We.

Dazed a bit, I start up my car, do a three-point turn and head back up to my home. I'm still dazed as I cross the yard and sink into a chair on the porch to wait.

Twenty minutes later, Dare's bike idles back up the drive.

He's empty-handed.

"I couldn't find anything," he calls out as he climbs off the bike and idles towards me. "I think maybe you saw a raccoon or something."

I hesitate, trying to picture the animal I'd seen.

"It seemed too small to be a raccoon," I offer.

"Maybe it was a baby," he suggests.

Or maybe I've gone nuts and it wasn't anything at all. But of course, I don't say that.

"Thank you for looking," I finally say, my gaze dropping to his feet. His boots are covered in dew and tiny bits of leaves. He really did trek out into the mountain to look.

"Want to go get your groceries now?"

I nod reluctantly, for some reason dreading the idea of driving down the mountain again.

Dare looks at me. "Want me to drive you?"

My head snaps up. "You want to come?"

He grins. "I need some shampoo. I'll be happy to drive if you want."

"Weren't you wanting to read or something?"

He rolls his eyes. "I read at night when I'm trying to go to sleep. I'm perfectly free at the moment. In fact, I'll be free tonight, too."

The mere thought of Dare in his bed, sprawled out, naked, his muscles gleaming in the moonlight, it spreads heat to my cheeks and I yank my eyes back up to his, focusing on reality, not on Dare in his bed.

He grins. *Dare me.*

"Perhaps we should focus on the *now*," he suggests lightly, as if he knows that he was just undressed in my mind. I internally combust, then nod.

"Yeah. I'd better get some groceries."

I toss him my keys and we drive down the mountain.

We.

Dare and me.

It's an exhilarating thought, and one that for the moment, distracts me from sadness.

That's a miracle in itself.

10

DECEM

Finn

You'reAMiserableMiseraleMiserableExcuse, the voices hiss and I clench my teeth and draw around them, drawing faces and then scratching them out every time a voice says something. Before long, the page is covered in scribble.

Calla's gone and I don't know where she is, and for the first time in weeks, I'm alone.

I don't like it.

I don't like it.

A motor roars through the yard and I go to the window, looking down. The new guy stands on the edge of the grass. Calla stares up at him, her hand so close to the guy's chest.

GetAwayFromHer.

GetAway.

I watch, enthralled, horrified as my sister smiles.

It's like she knows him. Like she belongs there, smiling with him.

I'm alone and she's there.

It's wrong.

It's wrong.

I grit my teeth again, because it's not wrong. My sister is an adult and she can do what she wishes and obviously it's normal for her to smile at a guy.

But not him, the voices protest, so many of them that I can't tell them apart. There's something about him, something wrong, something he's hiding.

He's hiding.

YouCan'tTellHerSheWon'tBelieveYou. For the first time, I agree with them. Calla would never believe me if I voiced this reservation, because I don't have any proof.

All I have is a feeling.

And we all know I'm crazy.

11

UNDECIM

Calla

I sort through the million different kinds of pasta sauce, picking one, before I find Dare in the shampoo aisle.

I'm halfway to him when my eye falls on Dove, the kind of shampoo my mother used. I can almost smell her hair as she hugged me, and my throat clams up and I pointedly look away, because that's what I have to do when something reminds me. I have to ignore it and put it away for later. Because I simply can't deal with it now.

"Are you ready?" I ask Dare. He nods, then eyes my heaping cart.

"Good thing we brought your car and not my bike," he observes. I have to laugh, but I don't want to explain how my father is sliding, how we're out of every imaginable thing in my house. So I don't.

Instead, we check out and load our stuff into the trunk and get on our way.

But once we're on the road, Dare turns to me.

"I could use a drink. Could you?"

I'm giddy that he thinks I'm old enough, but I shake my head. "I'm not twenty-one," I tell him sheepishly, but honestly, why am I embarrassed? My age is not my fault.

Dare grins, unaffected. "I meant a soda, young one."

"Oh. Well, I know a coffee house. And they have sodas."

"Let it be so, then," he announces theatrically, like he's at the helm of the Starship Enterprise.

"You're not a Trekkie, are you?" I ask, scared that I might finally be finding a fault in this seemingly perfect guy as I turn the car down a narrow city street. He glances sidelong at me.

"What's that?"

"You're from England, not Mars, right?" I demand. "A trekkie. Someone who watches marathons of star trek and goes to star trek conventions dressed as an Ewok. You're not that. Hopefully."

"I take offense to that," he says seriously. "First, an Ewok is from Star Wars, not Star Trek. Any good trekkie would know that."

He pauses and I'm appalled because oh-my-gosh there's no way.

"And also that you'd think so little of me. I'm not a trekkie. I'm a die-hard Whovian. I don't think I can be both."

Dr. Who, England, of course. I smile limply and pull into a parking spot.

"I just admitted a guilty pleasure," he tells me, with his hand on the handle. "It's your turn. What's one of yours?"

Honestly, I haven't thought about *any* pleasures in six weeks.

"Um." *Daydreaming about you.* "I like the Arctic Monkeys."

He barks out a laugh as I name the British band, and gets out of the car, coming around to open my door while

I'm still fiddling with my seat belt. I look up at him, mesmerized by his manners.

"I'll try and look past that," he says solemnly as I brush past him, inhaling his cologne on my way.

He opens the coffee house door for me, too, and we wait in the trendy line for our turn. He looks at me.

"And this is what I'm afraid the hospital café will turn into," he says quietly, like he's sharing a secret. I nod, completely serious.

"Yeah. I can see that there's a need to worry."

I picture the sterile hospital environment, shrouded with the screams from the Psych Ward and giggle. "Tons of need to worry."

Dare raises his eyebrows. "I'm glad we agree."

We get our sodas, but instead of heading to the car, Dare heads for a table. "Do you mind if we sit for a minute? I'm sure our food will be fine for a few minutes in the car."

"Ok."

I sit across from him and play with my straw, and we stare at each other. After a minute, he smiles and I decide that his smile might be my new favorite thing.

And then I promptly feel guilty for having a favorite anything.

My mother is dead and I killed her. I'm not allowed to enjoy things anymore.

I stare at him as flatly as I can, ignoring the way little fingers lap at my stomach, urging it to flip over and over as Dare looks at me, as his silver ring glints in the sunlight.

What is it about that one motion, that one tiny thing, that always sticks in my head? It's so stupid. Such a silly thing to focus on.

"As me a question," Dare finally says, breaking the silence. "I know you want to."

"I don't," I answer evenly.

"You lie."

I sigh. "Maybe."

He grins wickedly enough to send a nervous thrill through me. "So ask me."

"Um, let's see. How long are you staying here?" I ask conversationally, like I'm not dying to know the answer.

He shrugs. "I'm not sure yet."

I stare at him. "That's not an answer."

"It has to be, because that's the truth."

"But sometimes the truth is deceptive," I fling back at him, and this sobers him right up.

"What do you mean by that?" he asks, somewhat defensively. *Hmm. Interesting reaction.*

"I just meant that sometimes, the truth is so crazy that it doesn't seem true. Like you saying you don't know how long you'll be here. You have to know how long you'll be here."

He stares at me, amused now. "But I don't."

"You're frustrating," I tell him. He grins. "Guesstimate, then."

"Fine," he says, sounding satisfied. "If you're worried about me leaving, I'll guesstimate. I guess... I'll be here as long as it takes."

"As long as what takes?" I ask.

He shrugs.

I want to throat punch him.

"You're *seriously* frustrating," I answer. He laughs.

"I've heard that before," he admits.

"I bet," I grumble.

93

He's laughing and the sound of it vibrates my ribs, filling my belly with warmth. It's a warmth that I don't deserve to feel. I try to shove it down, try to shove it away, but the guilt keeps coming back, present in everything I do.

No matter what.

I shouldn't be sitting here enjoying myself, that's for sure.

I shouldn't be fantasizing about this sexy man, dreaming about him, wishing I could be with him. I don't deserve it. I squeeze my eyes tightly shut, and when I open them, I notice something on Dare's boot, mixed with the grass from the mountainside.

Blood.

"Um. What's that?" I ask stiltedly, because I already know.

He follows my pointing finger, then meets my gaze.

"It's blood. I didn't realize it was there."

"What's it from?" My words are calm, much calmer than my racing heart.

"From a raccoon," Dare sighs.

My eyes meet his. "I hit it, didn't I?"

He nods slowly.

"I killed it?"

He nods again. "It's dead."

"Why didn't you tell me before?" My voice is shaky now, and I fight to control it.

His dark gaze doesn't waver. "Because there's nothing we can do about it. It's dead, and I'm sure it was instantaneous. It didn't suffer and I didn't want you to feel bad about it. I'm sorry. I should've just told you."

Oh my God. I'm a menace to society. I know it was just a raccoon, but it had a life, and then it came into contact with me, and now it's dead.

"We should go," I say quietly, pushing away from the table and heading for the door without waiting for him to respond. He does follow me, though, and when we reach the car, he turns to look at me in confusion.

"Did I do something?"

"Of course not," I tell him tiredly. "Nothing at all. I should just be getting back. I'm sure my brother is wondering where I am."

I haven't left him alone this long in forever.

I drive this time, because I've got to be normal. I've got to put what happened this morning out of my head. You fall off a horse, you get back on. Your mom dies in a crash, you have to drive again.

When we're sitting in front of the funeral home, I kill the ignition, and Dare hops out, grabbing eight bags of groceries while I carry four.

"You don't have to cart these in," I tell him as we tumble in through the back door. He doesn't reply, he just heads straight to the kitchen, as though it's his house, as though he's been there before.

Curiously, I follow him, watching him begin to unload the items, putting the milk in the fridge and going straight to where the sugar belongs, sliding it into place.

"How do you know where everything goes?" I ask stupidly, watching him put the bread away. "You don't seem the type to know your way around any kitchen, much less mine." He pauses, lifting his eyebrow.

"It says Bread Box," he points.

I flush.

"And the rest is common sense," he adds, opening the cabinet above the stove and putting away the salt.

Still. He moves around with such familiarity.

I'm... imagining things, I decide. *Of course I am.*

When everything is done, Dare leans back against the counter. "Today was fun," he tells me, his eyes gleaming, his body stretched out.

I nod. "Thank you for taking me to town."

He smiles.

"Anytime."

He starts for the door, then pauses and turns. "I mean that," he adds. "I'd like to do that again. Go have a soda with you, I mean."

He's so beautiful as he stands bathed in the sunlight in my doorway. I gulp hard, trying to swallow the guilty lump in my throat. With everything that I am, or ever will be, I want to say yes.

But I can't.

"I...uh...." *I don't deserve to.* "I don't know if I'll be able to. My brother needs me."

I turn around, because my eyes are watery and hot, and I'm ridiculous and I don't want Dare to see me cry again.

Dare's voice comes from right behind me, six inches away.

"Calla, look at me."

I stare pointedly at the walnut cabinets, trying not to let the hot tears spill, because as much as I'm trying to hold them in, the tears keep welling up.

One escapes, slipping down my cheek.

Dare pulls me around, then drops his hand, staring me in the eye. He's so intent, so serious. He wipes my tear away with a thumb.

"You deserve to have a life, too," he tells me, his voice even. "You can take care of Finn and still take care of you."

I don't deserve it.

"You don't understand," I start to say, then decide I'd sound crazy if I tried to explain.

"You can't say that, because you don't know me," I say instead, my voice harsh and stilted.

Dare runs a hand through his hair and his eyes glint like obsidian. "I guess not."

And then he abruptly turns and walks out, his shoulders wide as he strides across my lawn, away from me.

Something bothers me as I wipe off the counters, and it isn't until I flip off the lights and walk into the Great Room that I realize what it is.

He acts like I disappointed him.

I don't know why.

12

DUODECIM

Calla

I haven't seen Dare in days, which is strange since he lives here now. But not so strange, considering that I've somehow disappointed him.

I've heard his motorcycle roar to life in the mornings, then I hear him come back home late at night, but I haven't personally seen him for seventy-two long hours.

"I wonder where he goes every day?" Finn muses at breakfast, as we hear his bike roar down the mountain. My father shrugs.

"Don't know. It doesn't matter to me. He paid for three months of rent in advance, so as far as I'm concerned, he's not my business until September."

Three months in advance? That's interesting. I chew my biscuit as I consider that. Is that how long he's staying?

I feel Finn watching me, waiting for a reaction, but I don't give him one. For some reason, I don't want to let him know how much time I spend musing about Dare DuBray, how I've laid in bed for three nights, obsessing about his voice and what it might be like if it was whispering into my ear in the dark.

"Want to do something today?" Finn asks, after taking a swig of orange juice. I shrug.

"Sure. Like what?"

He eyes me over his glass. "Maybe we could go to the cemetery?"

And just like that, it feels like he stomped on my solar plexus, squeezing out every last vestige of oxygen from it.

"Why would we do that today?" I manage to ask around the constricted muscle. Our father is unusually silent as he watches our interaction.

Finn levels his gaze at me. "Because we haven't been there yet. I don't want mom to think we've forgotten."

Dad makes a choking sound and picks up his plate (which incidentally is one of a set of 16 perfectly matched china plates from their wedding) before rushing away to the kitchen, and I glare at my brother.

"Mom's dead. She's doesn't *think* anything."

Finn's gaze doesn't falter. "You don't know that. You have no idea what she sees or doesn't see. Now, do you want to go visit her today?"

There's a stern tone to his voice, something firm and judgmental. I swallow hard because I'm so not ready for that.

"I can't...yet," I finally tell him quietly. His blue eyes soften although he doesn't look away.

"I don't think it'll get easier with time," he answers. I shake my head.

"That's not what I'm hoping for. It's just that... *I'm* not ready. Not yet."

"Ok," Finn gives in. "What else would you like to do today?"

I look out the window, my gaze instantly drawn to the water.

"I'm hungry for crab legs."

Finn smiles, the slow one that I love. "Crab fishing, it is."

So I dump my dishes in the kitchen and jog upstairs to change into old scrubby clothes and a floppy hat to protect my white skin from the sun. I meet Finn in the foyer.

"Do you have sunscreen in that thing?" Finn eyes my giant beach bag. I nod.

"Of course."

We head out to the trail that leads to the beach, then climb over the rocks and strewn seaweed to get to the rickety pier. Our little boat bobs gently in the slip, it's graying sides faded by the sun.

As we step aboard, I lick the briny air from my lips, while the breeze rustles the hair away from my face. There's already crab traps loaded in the cargo hold, and Finn releases the anchor so we drift out in the bay.

The sun beats down through the thin material of my sleeves, and I imagine that even now more freckles are forming, but I don't care. All I care about is moving through the water, over the swells and further into the ocean.

Finn leans down and grabs a crab pot, dropping it over the side. The orange buoy bobs in the waves to mark the spot as we move to a different location, and then we drop another. We drop five total before we drift further out to sea and lay limply in the sun on the hull of the boat.

I stare up at the sky, at the blueness of it, and watch the way the white clouds frolic with each other, bouncing and stretching and existing in the air. It makes me wonder if it's where Heaven is. Or if there's even a Heaven at all. I ponder this, of course, because of mom. Because she's always in the back of my mind. And because Finn ripped the Band-Aid off that wound this morning.

"Maybe Heaven is another dimension," I muse out loud. "Maybe the people there exist right now, moving and talking alongside us, we just can't see them. And maybe they can't see us, either."

Finn lays back, his arms behind his head, his eyes closed.

"I think they can see us."

"So you definitely think there's a Heaven?" I ask doubtfully. "How can you be sure?"

"I can't," he answers. "But it's what I believe. Mom did too."

That catches my attention and I stare at him. "How do you know that?"

He's unconcerned with my anxious tone. "Because she told me once. She used to love those Chicken Soup for the Soul books, remember?"

Of course I remember. "She got me Chicken Soup for the Teenage Soul last year. She put in my Christmas stocking." I'd wanted an iTunes card.

Finn grins without opening his eyes. "Well, she put Chicken Soup for the Grieving Soul in the foyer waiting room. I read it one day when I was bored, and she caught me."

I giggle because I can only imagine how happy she probably was... to think that she was finally influencing Finn's literary taste. She loved those freaking books.

"One of the stories was about the afterlife. Sort of. It was her favorite."

Finn falls silent and I wait.

And wait.

"And?" I prompt him. He opens an eye.

"And? Oh, you want to hear the story?"

I roll my eyes. "Obviously."

"Fine." Finn is clearly bored with this, but he humors me. "Once upon a time, there was a colony of water bugs. They were a close colony, a family. Where one went, the others went. But every so often, one would straggle away on their own, crawl onto a lily pad, and never return. This was a great mystery to the family of water bugs. They couldn't figure out what was happening to their family members, or why they disappeared. They talked about it often, and worried about it, but they could never figure it out."

Finn opens his eyes now, and stares out at the water, past me, past the waves, and out to the horizon. He fixes his gaze on the red lighthouse in the distance, on the pelicans that dive for their dinner around it, and the waves that break apart against the rocks.

"Well, one day, another water bug climbed onto the lily pad, drawn there by invisible forces from within itself, forces it didn't understand and couldn't control. As it sat there in the sun, it transformed into a beautiful dragonfly. It shed its water bug skin, and sprouted iridescent wings that gleamed in the sunlight. Wings so large and strong, it was able to fly into the air, doing loops in the sky.

"The new dragonfly was ecstatic with it's new body and thought to itself, 'I need to go back and tell the others. They need to know that this is what happens so they won't be scared.' So he dipped and dove through the air, directly at the water. But unfortunately, he couldn't dive below the surface to where the water-bugs were swimming. In his new form, the dragonfly was no longer able to communicate with his family. He felt at peace, though, because he knew that someday, his family would all transform too, and they'd all be together again."

Finn pauses and looks at me. "And such it is with Heaven. People die, they go on to another place, a better place, but they can't communicate with us anymore because they're in a different form. But it doesn't mean that it's not just as real. Or that we won't find out for ourselves one day."

My throat feels gunky and tight, so I clear it. "Mom believed this?"

Finn nods. "Yeah. She told me."

The story is beautiful and it makes me want to cry, and it also makes me resent Finn just a little bit because he shared that moment with mom and I didn't. But I push that irrational thought away. It's enough that I know now.

We float for a while in silence, and I drag my fingers through the water.

At least an hour passes before Finn finally speaks again. "We need to go to the cemetery, you know."

I nod. "Okay."

He raises an eyebrow. "Okay?"

I nod again. "Yeah. Soon."

He smiles, a real smile, and we float randomly for another hour before he finally points the rudder toward the first crab pot. As we approach, I reach over the side and drag it in, pulling the wet chain into the boat. The crab pot is empty. But the next one isn't, nor the next. We end up with five crabs, a good haul for the day.

My stomach rumbles at the mere thought of drowning their legs in butter and putting them into my belly.

We float inland, and Finn steers the boat into the slip, while I stuff my hat into a bench and then transfer the crabs into a bucket. Their legs make scratching sounds as they slide around against the plastic, and for just one brief moment, I allow myself to feel guilty because I'm going to drop them into boiling water later.

"What the hell?" Finn mutters, staring ahead of us, past the trail, past the treescape, and into the clearing behind the Carriage House. I follow his gaze and almost audibly gasp when I see Dare.

He's back from town now, and dressed in workout clothes, shorts and a cut off ratty t-shirt. He's repeatedly punching the side of the woodshed.

Over and over and over.

Thud. Thud. Thud. Thud.

Like a machete or a thresher or a piston.

Sweat drips down his face, and blood drops from his hand, as he pummels the wood, punching at it like a machine.

"What the hell," I echo Finn's sentiment, before I shove the crab bucket into his hands and take off up the trail to get to Dare. Finn protests from behind me, but I don't stop and I don't slow down.

I skid to a stop next to Dare, pulling at his elbow. He smells like sweat, so I can't imagine how long he's been out here, hurting himself.

"Dare, stop," I tell him. "You're bleeding."

He shakes my hand off, not looking at me, and punches again.

Blood splatters the ground and onto my bare foot.

104

"Dare."

Thud.

"Dare." My voice is stiffer now, like ice, and finally he stops, his arm dangling at his side. He doesn't look at me, but his breaths are coming in pants. I wait, and eventually the pants slow down to shallow, even breaths.

"What's wrong?" I ask him. "Why are you.... what's wrong?"

I wait.

He's silent. Finally, he rocks back on his heels, and sinks to the ground, to his knees.

"Nothing's wrong," he finally tells me, his voice like wood.

"Nothing?" I find that hard to believe. "Then why are you breaking your hands?"

I kneel down in front of him, lifting his hands to examine them. The knuckles are beyond scraped, beyond cut. They're mashed. A bloody pulp, actually. "I think you might've actually broken them."

He yanks them away. "I didn't."

"Ok."

I eye him warily. If there's one thing I've gotten good at, it's sorting through crazy situations. "Can I help you clean them up?"

I hold my breath until he climbs to his feet.

"I've got it." His voice is curt and dismissive, and he turns to walk away. What the hell? Where is the guy who has been so engaging? So charming? He's apparently been replaced by this cold stranger who has an affinity for hurting himself.

I grab his elbow. Out of my periphery, I notice Finn standing in the distance, watching. Waiting.

"It's ok," I call to my brother. "You don't have to wait."

Finn shakes his head, but so do I. "Go on," I call out. "I'll be up shortly."

Reluctantly, he walks away with the crabs and Dare looks at me.

"You don't need to stay. I don't need help."

"Yes, you do," I argue. "You just don't realize it."

"And you do?"

"Yes."

Dare stares down at me, his eyes chilly. "No, you don't. Because as you so clearly pointed out, you don't know me. You can let go of my elbow now."

My fingers slip away, confused by his iciness, by his words, but he still follows me into the Carriage House and into his little kitchen.

As we go, I can't help but notice how neat he keeps the little home. The bed is made, the counters are wiped off, there are no dirty clothes piled on the floor. Impressive for a young single guy.

I turn the water on and let it run, waiting until it gets warm before I hold his hands beneath it. He sucks in his breath but doesn't say anything. I grab a clean dish-towel and wrap his hands in it, and he leans against the counter. As he does, the shirt at his waistband lifts a bit, exposing a flat ribbon of his belly.

The skin looks soft as velvet, although the muscle looks hard as steel. I itch to run my finger along it, to touch it and find out.

But of course, I don't because it's not exactly socially acceptable.

"Why are you upset?" I ask instead, as I open his freezer. I pull out some ice, and dump it into two baggies, one for each hand.

Dare doesn't open his eyes.

"I'm not."

"You lie."

It's a statement, not a question.

He sighs.

"Maybe."

I push him into a kitchen chair, and hold the ice onto his hands.

"Definitely."

He opens his eyes finally. "Do you know what it's like to not be able to change something?"

I ogle him. Seriously?

"My brother is crazy and my mom died in a car crash," I tell him. "Of course I know what it's like."

He sighs and looks away like I'm trivial and just don't understand.

"Your brother doesn't seem crazy," he answers. "I mean, from the way you've talked about him."

"That's true," I answer carefully. "But just because we can't see something doesn't mean it's not there."

Dare looks at me, his eyes dark as night. "True."

He gets up and pulls his shirt off, wincing slightly as he moves his hands. He tosses the blood-splattered tee in the sink, and I can hardly breathe on account of his abs. Rippled like a washboard, they hover in my face, and I want to trace those ripples with my fingers, to follow the thin, dark, 'happy trail' into the edge of his shorts to see where it leads.

But I know where it leads.

And that bursts my cheeks into flame.

"How do you live here?" he asks quietly, and I lift my gaze to follow his. He's staring out the window now, at the black smoke that billows from the crematorium stacks. I'm the one who almost cringes now, at the mere fact that he recognized the smoke for what it is. *Burning bodies.*

I shrug. "I'm used to it. There are creepier places."

He looks at me, unconvinced. "Oh, yeah?"

I nod. "Yeah. I know of one off-hand."

"I'd like to see that place sometime," he tells me. "Or I won't believe it."

I smile. "Deal. *If* you tell me what's wrong with you. Why are you punishing your hands? What did they ever do to you?"

"I don't really want to talk about it right now," Dare tells me, leaning once again against the counter, so casual that it's painful. "Unless you're using one of your questions and I'm obligated to answer."

I don't miss a beat. "I am."

He sighs because he saw that one coming, and I almost fall into the blackness of his eyes because they're bottomless wells. "I'm mad at myself," he finally says, as though that's an answer.

"Obviously," I say wryly. "But the question is...why?"

He stares at me now, with a painful gaze, something so wretched and awful that it makes my stomach flip. "Because I can't change something. And because I'm letting it get to me," he finally replies. "Something that I can't control. It's stupid. So it pisses me off."

"Emotions piss you off?" I ask, my eyebrow raised.

He smirks now, and the heaviness lifts.

"They are when they're stupid."

He turns to walk out of the kitchen, and I suck in my breath hard.

A tattoo is inscribed across the top of his back, spanning his shoulder blades.

LIVE FREE.

I've never seen such a fitting tattoo, for a guy with such a fitting name. If anyone *lives free*, it's Dare.

"I love your tattoo," I call out to him, as he walks from the kitchen to the bedroom, out of my sight.

"Freedom is an illusion," he calls back.

I want to ask him why, but I don't want to use a question, so I let it go. For now.

He emerges a minute later in a clean shirt.

"We've got some gauze and tape up at the house," I tell him. "Will you come with me so that I can bandage you up? Finn and I caught some crabs today. Stay for dinner."

I'm not asking. It's an instruction. And surprisingly, Dare nods.

"Ok."

I lift an eyebrow. "Ok?"

He smiles and the Dare I know is back, the charming and friendly one. "Yeah. I want to see if they really scream when you drop them into the pot."

I must recoil a bit, because he chuckles. "I'm kidding. That's a myth, right?"

I nod. "They don't have vocal cords. But it sounds like a scream sometimes, when the air bubbles out of their stomachs."

"That's a pleasant thought," Dare says wryly.

"I just don't think about it," I shrug. "Because they're delicious."

"Sadistic yet practical," Dare observes as he holds the door open for me.

I grin. "That's my hamartia."

Dare shakes his head. "I don't believe in fatal flaws."

I pause, staring up at him. "Really? Then what, pray tell, will be your downfall?"

Dare pauses too, purveying me with his arms dangling limply at his sides.

"There's a very good chance it'll be you."

13

TREDECIM

"How can you possibly say that?" I stutter. "You only just met me."

Dare's lip twitches and he starts walking toward my house. "I'm a very intuitive guy, Calla-Lily. I guess you can just call it a feeling."

I feel like I'm walking on a cloud of confusion as we make our way to my house. I barely greet Finn when we walk in, and he immediately knows that something is up, although he doesn't ask for details. Instead, he just calmly assesses me.

"Everything ok?" His voice is slow and even, and I nod.

"Yeah."

He nods. "Good. I'm not feeling well, so I'm going to eat in my room."

He turns and disappears into the back hallway before I can say anything. I suspect that his absence has more to do with Dare's presence and less to do with not feeling well. I sigh as my father comes through the kitchen door.

He glances at Dare. "Would you like anything to drink?"

"Sure. I'll have whatever you're having," Dare answers.

My father is gone for a minute, and comes back out with a beer. "You looked like you could use something stronger than lemonade."

Dare almost looks relieved, and takes a big gulp. "Thanks."

As Dare wipes his mouth with one of smashed up hands, my dad eyes the damage, but doesn't say anything.

It's strange how everything is socially acceptable and comfortable, despite the fact that Dare's hands are mangled and everyone is ignoring that fact.

"Let's go find the first aid kit," I tell Dare. He nods and sets his beer down, and dad heads into the kitchen.

"The crabs will be ready in five," he calls over his shoulder.

"We'd better hurry," I murmur to Dare as I lead him through the halls. We pass the Viewing Rooms and the Great Room and never once does Dare say anything about the Funeral Home smell.

After we quietly walk the length of the halls leading to the basement, I gently push him into a seat outside of my father's Embalming Room. "Be right back," I tell him.

I push open the door, and ignore the instant change in temperature that sends goose-bumps forming down my arms and legs. I also ignore the reason it has to be so cold in here. Cold = Death. It's an equation that was long ago impressed in my head. It's one reason I'd love to move someplace tropical. Because Warmth = Life.

I dig in a cabinet for gauze and medical tape, rustling around loudly enough that I don't hear Dare walk into the room. It's only when he speaks from behind me that I jump.

"So, this doesn't look that scary," he observes, his quiet voice loud in the silence.

I whirl around, my heart pounding. "Sorry," he says quickly, holding up a hand. "I didn't mean to startle you."

"It's all right," I tell him. "I just wasn't expecting to hear a voice."

He nods, his lip twitching. "Yeah, I guess that would be a bad thing in here usually."

I nod, still willing my heart to slow down as I grab the supplies I need.

Dare turns in a slow circle, eyeing the wall of coolers, the metal tables in the middle with the run-off trays, the sterile walls, the medicinal smell.

"This room is creepy," he announces, focusing in on the run-off trays. "I don't see how your dad can do what he does."

"I don't either," I agree, as I pull him from the room. "I hate being in here. The last time I was down here was when they wheeled my mom in."

She'd been in a bag, completely covered by black canvas. I thought she needed me with her, to hold her hand, so she wouldn't be alone. But I'd only lasted until the zipper reached her chest, and I saw her yellow shirt turned red with blood. Then I was out of here like a shot.

I poke a long swab of iodine at his knuckles, and Dare doesn't even flinch. "Surely your dad didn't... your mom..." his voice trails off as he realizes how sensitive that subject is.

I swallow hard. "He did, actually. I have no idea how. But he said he couldn't trust anyone else to take care of her. I don't know why he bothered. The casket was closed, anyway."

My chest clenches up, and I dab, dab, dab at Dare's cuts and then wrap his hands with gauze and tape.

He looks into my eyes, a long, slow look. "I'm sorry. It was thoughtless of me to ask. I'm not usually so clumsy with words."

I shake my head. "It's ok."

He examines my hands, moving deftly to bandage his. "I'm not going to ask how you learned to do this so well."

I can't help but smile. "Smart. Although I have to say, it's nice to work on someone living."

I snort when Dare does a double take. "Kidding. I don't work on the bodies. Ever."

He exhales and I laugh, and then put the supplies away. When I turn back around, Dare is trailing a finger down one stainless steel cooler door.

"Are there any... I mean, is anyone in here?" He doesn't even sound nervous.

I nod. "Yeah. I think there's one."

Dare raises an eyebrow. "And it seriously doesn't bother you to sleep in the same house?"

I shrug. "I've never known anything different. My father has been a mortician my whole life. I used to get made fun of in school. *Funeral Home Girl.* That's what they called me."

I don't know why I said that, and apparently Dare doesn't either because he studies me now.

"Why would they do that? It's not like you chose your father's profession."

"I know. Who knows why kids do what they do? They can be cruel. But I lived. And Finn did too. They used to tease him for being crazy."

Dare's eyes are dark as he looks into mine. "So you were basically all each other had growing up," he says slowly. "No wonder you're close."

I nod. "Yeah. That about sums it up."

"So that's why you were upset the other night on the beach. Because you don't want to be separated from Finn." Dare's voice is so calm, so slow and so steady. I nod, sucked into the vortex of that comfort.

"Yeah."

He nods. "I can understand that. What's wrong with your brother? You said he's..."

"Crazy," I interject. "I shouldn't call him that. He's not. He's just got a mental issue. He's medicated though."

I hear the condensation in my voice and cringe. My brother is *more than*, not *less than.*

"He's harmless," I add. "Trust me."

"I do," Dare answers, his eyes gleaming. "Trust you, I mean."

That answer causes my heart to thud. I don't know why. It's not like others don't trust me. My dad, Finn. My mom used to. But to hear that Dare trusts me, it's like an intimacy, words that roll off his tongue and meant only for me. I like it.

"Ready to eat?" I manage to ask casually. Dare nods and we make our way up the stairs and into the dining room. When he holds my chair out for me, I manage not to swoon.

***

The sound of cracking crab legs fills the air, along with the fishy smell of the meat. It makes my stomach growl in sort of a Pavlov's reaction to melted butter. Across from me, Dare eats his like a pro.

He's clearly done this before. I watch as he expertly cracks the leg, then picks the meat out in one deft movement. Most people utterly muck it up.

"So, where do you live, Dare?" My father asks this casually as he takes a bite of biscuit, but his tone is anything but casual. I know it, and Finn knows it, but thankfully, Dare doesn't know him well enough to see that my father is pumping him for information.

"My family lives outside of Kent, in the English countryside by Sussex," Dare answers just as easily. I might be imagining things, but his eyes seem guarded.

"Oh?" My father raises an eyebrow. "You don't say. You're a long way from home then, fella. What brings you to the Pacific Northwest?"

I'm of course at attention now, blissful that my father is asking him these questions so I don't have to. My questions are numbered and valuable.

Dare smiles politely.

"I'm just here visiting. America is beautiful, particularly this area." He skillfully skirts the actual question, something that we all clearly see. However, there's no way we can politely ask for a better answer.

Crack. My father splits open another crab leg. "I guess you're used to the rain, coming from Sussex. My wife grew up in England. That's why she never minded the rain here."

Dare nods. "I'm very used to it."

We all fall silent and continue eating, and I can practically see my father wanting to ask more questions.

"You *are* twenty-one, right?" he asks as Dare takes a swig of his beer. "I don't want to contribute to the delinquency of a minor." He says it jokingly, but he means it. Dare smiles.

"I'm twenty-one exactly."

I knew it. He's definitely more of a man than a boy. Even more so than the calendar says. His eyes are even older than twenty-one. He's seen a lot. I can tell. Just how much though, is the question.

As we eat, I watch him easily maneuver the crab legs and eat without making a mess. He eats four in the time it takes me to eat two.

"Do you like lobster, too?" I ask him after a few minutes. "You seem to like crab."

Dare smiles a blindingly white smile. "I love lobster. Pretty much any shellfish, really."

"Me too," I tell him.

We continue eating with the sounds of cracking and dipping and chewing.

Finally, I glance at my father. "Is Finn all right?"

My father nods slowly. "Yeah. I'm sure."

Suddenly, the quietness of this house, which is actually a mausoleum, my father's tension, Finn's strange absence…all of it smothers me and I suck in a deep breath.

Dare glances at me, his eyes so freaking dark. "You ok?"

I nod. "Yeah. I just…I'm restless. You know how you didn't believe that I know someplace creepier than here?"

He nods slowly, interested, his eyes gleaming. "Yeah."

I smile. "Want to see it tonight?"

117

My dad coughs a little. "Calla, I'm not sure that tonight is the best night for that. It's dark, you could get hurt."

I roll my eyes. "Dad, Finn and I have been there a hundred times over the years. It's fine."

I look at Dare. "You up for it?"

He grins. "I never say no to an adventure."

14

QUATUORDECIM

Finn

From my window, I watch them go and the darkness from outside seems to bleed into my room, into my heart, into my blood.

LetHerGoLetHerGoLetHerGo.

I swallow back the hateful words as I watch my sister get into our car with him. Bile rises in my throat because my sister is mine and distancing myself is the last thing I want to do, but at the same time, it's the only thing I can do.

DoWhatIsRight.

That's my voice. Finally. Breaking through the crazy, through the voices, through the words.

I've got to do what is right.

What is right.

What is right.

ProtectYourSecret.

The other voices come back, hissing, reminding.

My secret.

That's what it comes back to now.

Always.

No matter what.

15

QUINDECIM

Calla

Dare sprawls on the passenger side seat, taking up every inch of space as I drive us carefully down the mountain. I don't even glance at my mother's cross as we pass, and although I'm sure Dare has seen it and wondered about it, he doesn't mention it.

"So where exactly are we going?" he asks in his sexy as hell accent as we turn onto the highway at the bottom of the mountain.

I glance at him and smile.

"Are you scared?"

He shakes his head, rolling his dark eyes.

"Hardly. I've got you to protect me."

I laugh at that because the idea of little me protecting huge him is laughable. But then I shake my head. "You're going to have to wait."

So he waits while I drive. Into the night, along the quiet highway, until we turn off and head into a quiet part of town, then out onto the edge, where it's darkened and only a few city lights twinkle in the night.

We drive beneath the old burned out sign, the words that form a rickety neon arch, faded purple and created back when neon signs were cutting edge. The bulbs have long ago been broken, a glaring reminder that this place is sad and abandoned.

JOYLAND, the letters spell out.

Even the letters look spooky, all darkened and jagged. There's nothing joyful about this place anymore, other than the memories that it contains, memories of riding the old train with Finn, laughing with him on the bumper cars, running through the haunted house. But that was all before they closed this place, of course. Afterward, Finn and I came here to be alone, to huddle together and talk amongst the creepy buildings because we found it amusing to scare ourselves. But we haven't been here since mom died. I guess real life is scary enough.

I pull into an abandoned parking spot, between faded orange lines, among a sea of other empty slots.

"My parents used to bring Finn and I here when we were little," I explain. "But the owner apparently got into tax trouble and overnight, this place was locked up and abandoned."

Dare looks around, at the black parking lot, the darkened gates, and at the rickety Ferris wheel looming above the gated horizon, it's spindly bars a haunting white against the blackness of night.

"So you just come here and sit in the parking lot or what?" he speculates, his face blank. I chuckle.

"No. We figured out a way in a long time ago."

Dare grins now, as realization spreads across his face. "Ohhhh. Breaking and Entering. Always a crowd favorite."

I chuckle again. "Somehow I'm guessing this will be a first for you."

I open my door and the creak echoes through the night because there are no other noises here to mask it. It feels like we're on the edge of the world, all alone, and if we take one wrong step, we'll vault over the side.

"It's all right," I call over my shoulder as I head for the park. "The owner is long gone. We heard he's overseas now so I'm sure he doesn't care who pokes around. We're not the first, and we won't be the last."

I feel Dare behind me, so close that I can smell his cologne, as I lead him along the fence. Finally, I see what I'm looking for... the jagged hole that someone cut away years ago. It's just the size for a person to crawl through.

I duck through it, and Dare doesn't hesitate to follow. The idea that he trusts me enough to follow without question makes my belly warm. He barely knows me.

But as I turn and pause, staring up at his handsome face, the look in his eyes melts my insides. Because he *wants* to know me. That much is clear.

I swallow hard, then turn back around, surveying the scene in front of me.

The Midway is empty, completely abandoned and dark, like something out of a horror movie. The carnival games line each side, with grotesque clown faces and peeling race cars, and the gleaming paint of Whack-a-Mole as it watches me from afar with gleaming eyes.

Trash blows in the breeze like paper tumbleweeds, and there is graffiti on a few of the buildings, evidence that we certainly aren't the first here. TURN BACK, is written in artful red and black. DROP DEAD is painted directly beneath it in glowing orange. And then, at the very bottom, painted in eerie, morbid white, is DEATH COMES TO US

ALL. I don't bother mentioning that my brother painted that one.

"Interesting," Dare says slowly, as he pivots in a circle. "But I wouldn't say it's creepier than a funeral home."

"That's because this isn't what I want to show you," I tell him mischievously. He glances down at me.

"Well, I'm ever ready," he announces. "Lead on."

I giggle at his formal tone, which even still is sexy with his accent, and without thinking, I reach behind and grab his hand in the dark. I almost startle at the contact, at the feel of his warm fingers and strong hands. He's surprised by it, but he doesn't shirk away. Instead, he grips my hand firmly, yet softly, and I pull him along, enjoying the very idea that I'm touching him right now.

I'm holding hands with Dare DuBray.

We walk through the dead center of the Midway, past the Old Mill boat ride, with it's rotting boats bobbing in the murky moat, past the hanging swings, their chains creaking as they move in the wind, and past the bumper cars, with the defunct cars all shoved together in the middle.

I stop in front of Nocte, Joyland's version of a house of horrors.

Dare reads the dark sign, the black letters that seem to drip with blood. "Nocte, huh?"

I nod. "It means *by night* in Latin. Finn used to love this place. And I think it's what started his love of Latin."

I don't mention my theory that Finn loved this place because the grotesque horror of it made even him feel sane. That's why we still come, because it still has the same effect, maybe even more so. The atmosphere of abandonment adds to the horror, making it seem real, somehow. So when he walks through it, he's the sanest thing in the room, aside from me.

Dare and I stand staring up the winding drive, toward the deserted mansion that seems to leer at us from above, some of its windows broken out and winking. Plants line the drive, and weeping trees form a canopy, creating a shadowy walkway.

Dare glances at me. "Ok. It's creepy."

I smile, even as chills already form along my spine. "You haven't seen anything yet."

I tug on his hand, and we start up the drive. "When this was running, they used to have ghosts and zombies jumping out along the way, scaring you, telling you to turn back." I pause, staring up at him. "Do you want to turn back, Dare?"

My voice contains a flirty challenge, and he hears it. He turns to me, grinning.

"Not on your life." The moonlight shines down on him, illuminating the dark stubble that lines his jawline, and glinting off the ends of his hair. He seems to shine, for a moment, and I itch to reach up and touch his face.

But I don't.

Instead, I smile. "Let's do it, then."

We climb the creaky stairs of the porch, cross the creaking boards, then turn the brass handle of the door. Dare steps fearlessly over the threshold.

"Which way?" he turns to me. I pull out my flashlight and shine it around the familiar foyer. Red velvet lines the walls, hanging in an ominous way reminiscent of blood. It smells musty and old in here, oxygen deprived and dusty.

"That way," I point to the right, toward the hall that I know leads to the bedrooms.

Because suddenly, I just have to be close to him. It's a need, not a want. An unconscious pull, a call that I desperately want to answer.

We inch along the hall, with every other step creaking, and I catch Dare glancing behind us several times.

"Scared?" I ask cheekily.

"Not at all," he answers calmly, stepping around a mannequin lying in a pool of fake blood. The mannequin seems to stare up at me with lifeless eyes, eyes that seem too knowing to be glass, too real to be fake. It's part of the draw of this place. It's creepily real. And now, since it's abandoned and dark, it's scarier than they ever meant for it to be.

As we walk, I know without looking where Dare is. It's like I'm a planet and he's my axis... or my sun. I feel his heat, I feel his presence, and I ache to lean into it, to fold into him, to absorb his strength.

It's a sudden urge, and I'm startled with the intensity of it.

I'm startled because I've never felt it before, not like this. It's enough to make me feel guilty, because it distracts me from other feelings that have overwhelmed me lately...the blinding grief.

I swallow hard as I lead him to the first bedroom.

Stepping inside, I shine the light around, at the mannequin lying on the bed, with the rope around its neck and the knife in its chest. She stares at me accusingly with matted blond hair, like she wants to know what the hell we're doing with this intrusion.

I don't know what I'm doing.

That's the truth of it. What I know is that I like the way Dare makes me feel. I like being distracted from pain. I like the way my heart flutters and my stomach flips whenever he's around. That's what I know.

I turn my attention from the mannequin to her surroundings. The bed-sheets are splattered with 'blood' and on the wall, THE GOOD DIE HERE, drips in ominous red, supposedly written by the murderer's finger dipped in the victim's own blood.

"Are you?" I ask Dare with a smirk. "Good, I mean?"

He looks at me sharply, then his mouth tilts into a smile. "I've had no complaints."

I shake my head because obviously that isn't what I meant, but it's funny so I laugh anyway.

"Hmmm. Then we might be in danger. If you're good, I mean."

I scoot closer to him and suddenly, I'm in his personal space. I'm pressed against his chest, and the rock hard solidity of it surprises me. He's lithe and slender, so I didn't expect him to be so…immovable, so muscular and hard.

I take a deep breath, inhaling his masculine smell, and stare up at him.

He's staring down at me, his gaze connected to mine, just like the first day I saw him. But this time, there's something in his eyes that wasn't there before, there's an expression there that I've only seen in my dreams. Want. *For me.* It shakes me to my core, causing my breath to linger on my lips.

I reach up to touch his face, my fingers grazing his jaw, his stubble teasing my fingertips.

"I'm ready to ask my fourth question," I tell him, my voice wobbling slightly. His nearness makes me dizzy.

"Go on then," he answers, his voice ever calm.

"Do you have a girlfriend back home?"

My words sound childish, almost. Because *girlfriend* seems so juvenile. Because my feelings seem huge and adult.

Dare sucks in his breath, and reaches up to enclose my fingers within his own, holding them in place as he stops me from exploring the rest of his face. He stares into my eyes and I can't read him now.

"No."

He's holding my hand against his chest and I feel his heart beat against my palm.

Thump. Thump. Thump.

It's loud in the silence.

The chemistry between us is palpable enough to touch, weaving around us, pulling us together, the air snapping with its electricity.

But he doesn't move.

And I don't either.

I want him to kiss me. I imagine the way his full lips would feel, firm, yet soft. I imagine the way his hands would feel on my back, pulling me closer, closer, closer.

But he doesn't move and neither do I.

And then suddenly, he releases my hand and steps back.

"So is this all you've got, then?" he asks, his voice teasing me now. The sexual tension is sadly broken.

I can't help but smile though. For the simple reason that it was there in the first place.

"Yeah. I guess your balls of steel saved you today," I tell him. He grins again, and then we make our way toward the foyer. As we cross the parlor though, I see something interesting, and pause next to the door-jam.

127

DD and CP are inscribed inside a heart. Corny and sweet. I trace the letters with my finger.

"What a coincidence," I murmur, for some reason aching on the inside, aching to be *that* CP and for Dare to be *that* DD. Because Corny or not, it's so intimate, so heartbreakingly personal. It smacks of first love, of high-school sweethearts, of things that are normal.

My hand falls away and I keep walking... because we're not those initials, and my life is not *normal.*

When we step outside, I take a deep breath of fresh air, breathing in the moon and stars and pine trees.

"There was more to see in there," I tell him softly, on the edge of the darkened driveway. The corner of his mouth tilts.

"Let's leave that for another day," he suggests as we walk.

I nod because our moment back in Nocte wasn't imagined. Maybe it scared him, like it sort of scared me, and that's why we're running from it now.

Because it was sudden and hot and blinding... like a shooting star.

After we're back in my car and driving toward home, I glance at him.

"Maybe you could give me a ride on your motorcycle sometime? I've never been on one."

He nods. "Maybe."

He stares out the window, careful to stay on his side of the car. I muse about that for a second, but refuse to dwell on it. But I'm so busy dwelling on it five minutes later that what Dare says next seems to come from left field.

"I'm ready to ask you a question," he tells me softly, his voice husky and seeped with the night.

I raise an eyebrow. "Okay. Shoot."

I'm expecting him to ask about a boyfriend, or my dating history, or even how old I am. He doesn't. His question actually slams into me with the force of a freight train, returning me to my reality.

"Can you tell me about your mom?"

There's a solid beat before I can make myself speak.

"Why?" I manage to croak, still stunned.

Dare shrugs, but his expression is soft, his dark eyes liquid.

"I don't know. It just feels like a way to know you better."

That answer, of course, melts my ovaries and I relax, the small of my back slumping against the seat.

I take a deep breath and grip the steering wheel hard enough to turn my knuckles white.

"What do you want to know?"

He stares at me for a second, before reaching over and loosening my grip on the wheel. His fingers are dry and warm, where mine are cool and clammy.

"Whatever you'd like to tell me. For instance...are you like her? Do you look like her?"

I smile. "I wish I was like her. She was artistic and amazing. I'm...not. But I do look like her. I look exactly like her, actually, which is probably hard on my dad right now. Finn looks like him."

"So she was born in England? Why did she move to America?"

It's my turn to shrug. "She was. But I don't know why she left. She said she didn't get along with her parents very well. She hasn't spoken to them in years, and I've never personally met them."

"Huh. Interesting," Dare murmurs. "I think it's good you can talk about her. When my mom died, I couldn't talk about her for almost a year."

I do a double-take. "Your mom's gone, too? You only mentioned your dad before. I'm so sorry! What happened?"

Dare stares out the windshield, into the night. I can tell he's not really seeing it.

"She died in an accident."

My stomach tightens into a knot for him, because God, I know that grief, that sudden, shocking, annihilating grief. I wouldn't wish it on anyone.

"I'm so sorry," I tell him limply. He nods.

"Yeah, it sucks. But I know how you're feeling right now, at least. I realized after my mom died that it always helps when someone knows what it's like."

He's right. It's hugely comforting.

"It's hard," I admit to him. "It's especially hard because it was my fault. I called her at night when it was raining. If I hadn't done that, she would still be here."

Dare looks at me sharply. "You can't believe that. That it's your fault, I mean."

I look away. "Of course I can. It's true."

"It's not," he argues. "I personally believe that when your number is up, it's up. Surely, living in a funeral home your whole life, you believe that, too. Sometimes, there isn't an explanation for something."

"And sometimes, there is. In this case, the explanation is a telephone call."

Dare shakes his head. "It's going to take some doing to convince you that you're wrong. I can tell."

130

"You can try," I tell him resolutely. "But if Finn and my father can't do it, I doubt you can."

"Challenge accepted," he says seriously, and the look in his eyes takes my breath away.

"Why do you care?" I ask him suddenly. "You barely know me."

He's silent for a second, fiddling with the silver band on his middle finger. When he looks back up, his eyes are filled with a hundred things I can't name.

"Because I feel like I do. Because we're the same in so many ways. Because I know how horrible it was to lose my mother. I can only imagine how hard it is when you think it's your fault."

Yeah, I think to myself. *It's almost too much to bear.*

"It *is* hard," I admit. "But sometimes, when you least expect it, someone tosses you a lifeline."

His eyes meet mine and I see that he knows exactly what I'm saying. *That he might be my lifeline.* There's no reaction, though, only a silent acceptance and maybe a spark of satisfaction.

We fall quiet now, comrades in this special club of having lost our mothers. It's not a club that anyone enjoys belonging to, but I know that I, for one, feel even closer to him now.

After a few minutes, I can't stand the silence anymore.

"You'd better be careful with those questions," I tell him, feigning a smile. "You've only got eighteen left."

16

SEDECIM

Finn

My secret is eating me alive, clawing at my skin, trying to get out. But I can't, I can't, I can't.

You'reCrazyCrazyCrazyAndEveryoneKnowsIt.

I stare at my journal, at the brown leather cover, and I grab it, hurling it across the room. It slams into the wall, then flutters unharmed to the floor. I rush to grab it, to clutch it to my chest as I rock with it on the floor.

After a minute, something occurs to me.

Of course.

I can't tell Calla, but I can tell my journal, the way I've spilled every other thing in my life onto its pages.

I grab a pen and then I press hard enough that it almost pushes through the page, as if my secret is bursting to get out as the words rush out through the ink.

Once it's there, I feel better, calmer, as though I've confided in an old friend. I close the cover and leave it on the windowsill. As I flip off the light and walk through the door, I almost miss the hissing whisper in my mind....the sharp female voice that I just can't get away from.

Coward.

17

SEPTEMDECIM

Calla

I take a cleansing breath and reach for the sky as I do my morning yoga on the edge of the cliffs. From here, I can see to the edge of the horizon, all the way out to where the water meets the sky.

"Why do you do this here?" Finn's voice comes from the trail, soft in the morning air. "You know it's dangerous."

I hold back a smile. "You know I'm not close enough to the edge to worry." I palm the ground, then hoist myself up into a Forward Fold. I stretch to my feet, feeling every tendon, muscle and ligament elongate as I roll to my toes.

"Why are you up so early?" I ask without opening my eyes. I count as I stretch.

Five.

Six.

Seven.

Finn sighs. "I don't know. I can't sleep."

Eight.

Nine.

Ten.

I finally turn around, and notice that my brother's face is weary and pale. This alarms me. "You're not feeling better yet?"

He shakes his head. "No."

A surge of panic shoots through me and I fight to tamp it down. It's just insomnia, for God's sake. Not an instant red flag.

"You're taking your meds, right?"

He seems to hesitate before he answers. "Yeah."

I raise an eyebrow. "Yeah?"

He nods.

"Do I need to take you to Group today?"

He hesitates again. "Maybe. I'm going to lie down for a while though. I might go to the afternoon session."

"Ok." I desperately try to hide my concern, because I know he doesn't want me to hover. He wants to find his autonomy, not become even more tethered to me. It hurts. *A lot.* But he doesn't need to know that. "Just yell at me when you're ready."

He nods and heads toward the house, pausing when he hits the edge of the trail. I worry because he's starting to stay secluded in his room. A *lot.*

His shoulders are so skinny as he calls back to me.

"Calla?"

"Yeah?"

He smiles a watery smile. "Did you know that Queen Victoria loved Albert so much that she insisted on being buried in his dressing robe, holding a plaster cast of his hand?"

I shake my head, rolling my eyes. "You're so weird and random, bro."

He grins like everything is fine, like he's back to normal. "I know."

Then he disappears down the trail.

135

I sit back down in the reddish dirt, trailing my finger through it. Before I know it, I've written Dare's name, with a flourish at the end of the *e*. A flourish shaped like a heart.

"A penny for your thoughts?"

Dare's wry voice comes from behind me and I cringe because apparently the trail leading to these cliffs is Grand Central Station today. And I'm humiliated because *obviously* I'm thinking of him. I flush, the heat spreading from my chest to my face, and I don't want to turn around.

But I do.

Dare's handsome face is amused and a teench arrogant. He's dressed in jogging clothes, although he's not sweaty, so he hasn't run far yet.

"My thoughts are more expensive than that," I announce. He grins even wider.

"I'm sure. We still have that little matter of secrets to discuss, by the way."

This confuses me. "Secrets?"

His eyes meet mine, gleaming ebony. "Yeah. Everyone's got 'em, remember?"

Oh, yeah. That's exactly what he said when we first met. "Maybe. But not me."

Dare rolls his eyes. "Somehow I doubt that. You had Nocte hidden up your sleeve, remember?"

I smile at that. "Yeah. And we didn't stay long enough to see it all."

"Another time," Dare answers quickly. I nod.

"Definitely." He doesn't seem excited though, and that bothers me. He seemed excited last night. He's an enigma, a contradiction. His emotions change by the day. Today, he's cool and detached. He's almost reserved or hesitant. It's so strange.

"I'll catch you later, Calla," he says quietly, before bolting off in a long-strided jog.

That's when my heart almost stops, because his strides are so long, he's in perilous territory within two steps.

"Stop!" I scream out, my voice splitting the sky like a knife. Dare freezes, turning to look at me in confusion, his eyes wide.

I'm on my feet now, my heart pounding in my throat.

"Carefully step back this way," I tell him. "Now."

Realization washes over his face as tiny balls of gravel and dirt begin to give way around his feet. He quickly lunges toward me, diving at the ground right before a huge hunk of earth breaks free, falling over a hundred feet to land in the ocean below.

Dare is in a heap at my feet, and my heart pounds as I stare down at him.

"You can't stand that close to the edge," I utter needlessly, my throat still hot and tight.

He looks over his shoulder at the ledge, then takes in the small yellow warning sign to our right. It's a sign that should be larger and red, bright red, bright enough for someone to notice.

He looks at me, then shakes his head. "I should've known better."

I nod. "There's no way you could've known. The ledge is really thin. It won't hold weight. I should've told you when you first came, but I didn't think about it."

Because I'm not used to having anyone but my family staying up here.

Because he flustered me with his *Live Free* tattoo and his contradictions.

He smiles, a slow smile, but not a genuine one. This one is forced, fake. It's his go-to smile, which means that we all have fake go-to smiles. All the world is a stage and we all smile falsely upon it.

"Well, I'd say you made up for it by saving my life."

Honestly, though, he doesn't sound happy about that. His eyes are so sad, so closed now, so glittery.

Aren't you happy to be alive?

I want to ask it. I'm so tempted, too tempted. He's got everything that most people want. Good looks, wit, charm. And he doesn't seem happy with it. Is it because he's an orphan now?

"Why do you seem so sad?" I blurt out, unable to stop myself.

Dare stares at me, studying me, considering my words. He raises an eyebrow.

"Official question?"

I nod, silently. *Yes. Official question.*

He sighs, and it sounds lost up here as it floats away over the edge, and he looks out over the ocean.

"Because I lost everything."

I'm the silent one now, because it's hard to stomach the rawness in his voice, the emotion that he can't quite hide. Dare surprises me by adding something, something so startlingly personal that it takes my breath away.

"I'm not sure if I can be found."

He looks at me with eyes so black, blacker than black, blacker than night.

"That would insinuate that *you're* lost. Not just that you've lost everything," I point out, careful not to ask it as a question. He nods curtly.

"Maybe I am." His voice has a scalpel's edge.

138

He's lost.

"And if I'm lost," he continues. "How can I possibly find someone else?"

He confuses me with his vague words. "Are you looking for someone else?"

"Aren't we all?" His gaze impales me and my heart twinges because the look on his face is vulnerable and broken.

But then it's gone, as fast as it appeared. He looks at me again, his eyes clear now, closed, bright. He once again appears cocky and arrogant and he flashes his go-to smile.

"Sorry. That seemed dramatic. Chalk it up to my near-death experience."

I smile back, grim and quiet. "I had a near death experience too, once. Actually, I had a *death* experience when I ate some nuts in the fourth grade. I died for a minute and a half."

Dare stares at me. "How was it?"

What a strange question.

"Uneventful," I admit.

"Well, how very anti-climactic of it," he acknowledges. And the fact that he's so blasé about mortality makes me laugh, and then we're both standing on the edge of a cliff laughing in the face of death.

It seems right.

When we're silent again, he eyes me.

"Why are you sitting out here on the edge of nowhere?" he asks.

I raise an eyebrow. "Official question?"

He laughs and rolls his eyes. "God no. I just thought you might offer it as a bonus."

I roll my eyes too. "Don't hold your breath. Talking about myself is my least favorite thing."

He smiles for a minute because I'm throwing his own words back in his face, but then sobers, staring deep into my eyes, examining my soul.

"I'd think you'd enjoy it," he tells me quietly. "It's such an interesting subject."

Just like that, my heart thunders and pounds, my stomach rolling over and over and over. There's something so stimulating in his voice, something so attractive and real.

Live, Calla, the Universe whispers.

"I'm glad you think so," I finally answer, sounding perfectly casual, as I try to live.

He nods slowly. "I do. Not that it means anything."

It means everything.

But I don't say that, of course. Instead, I begin to walk and Dare walks with me, instead of continuing his run. At one point, he grasps my elbow and helps me step over a rotting log. When he removes his hand, I feel its absence immediately. His touch had been branding-iron hot.

Or so I imagined.

Our walk back is silent, but the air is charged.

We pause outside of the carriage house.

"Thanks again," he says, his voice husky and quiet.

I nod. "Anytime."

He smiles, a real one this time, and I collect it, putting it in my jacket so I can hold it for later.

Then he walks inside, his shoulders swaying and the sunshine fading into the backdrop because something about him shines so bright.

I fall into a chair on the side porch, thinking about Dare, about his complexity, his mystery, his endless contradictions. I pull his smile out of my pocket and examine it, because it's beautiful and real and I want to hold it forever.

I don't see Dare again all day, but when I retire to my room for the night, there is a bouquet of calla lilies on my bed.

The note is written in dark scrawling handwriting, that simply says, *Thanks again.*

The mere idea that Dare had somehow managed to get inside of my room and stand this close to my bed, sets the butterflies free in my belly. They whirl and twirl and fly against my ribcage as I collapse into bed.

I fall asleep with the flowers in my hand, and thoughts of Dare in my head.

His smile is the last thing I think of before I drift away into oblivion, and it reappears, over and over, in my dreams.

18

DECEM ET OCTO

Finn

I wake with a start, from the nightmares of broken glass and burning metal.

It'sRealRealRealReal. She's deadddddddddd. The whispers hiss and laugh.

I gasp for air, gripping the bedclothes tight, as I fight the clouds of confusion and panic and fear.

Without a second thought, I pad down the hall to Calla's room and climb into the empty side of her bed. Something stabs me in the back, and I pull out a bouquet of flowers. I stare at them for a second, puzzled. Then I realize... Dare must've given them to her. Suddenly and overwhelmingly annoyed, I get out of bed and crush them under my heel.

I want her to be happy, I do.

I do.

But... Not yet. I just can't be without her yet.

Calla quiets the voices.

She's the only thing that does.

I crawl back in beside her, curling up next to her and then I fight for sleep, ache for it, pray for it. And finally, finally, finally, the blackness comes, covering me up like a blanket, and hiding my crazy. For now.

19

NOVEM

Calla

I wake with a start.

My dreams were strange tonight.

Dare was in them, of course, but instead of the sweet images I usually dream, this one was more of a nightmare. He was telling me something terrible, something that I couldn't quite hear, but my heart could feel. It was something dark. I could see his lips move, but no sound came out. Until he told me that he'd go away, if I wanted him to.

And that was it.

I'm awake now in a cold sweat because dream or not, I don't want him to go away.

I apparently have a very real fear of loss now.

I toss and turn, trying to get back to sleep, but since Finn is in my bed and my thoughts are troubled, I'm not successful.

So I pad downstairs, and out the door to the side porch. I curl up in a chair and stare down the mountainside, at the rustling trees and the black skyline.

The air is fresh and clean, and borderline chilly. I shiver in the breeze, and as I do, I glance at the Carriage House.

A light shines in there, through the window, warm and soft.

Dare's up. It's the middle of the night, and he's up.

Without even thinking about it, I get up and walk in that direction. I find myself standing next to his front windows, staring in, oblivious to the fact that I'm only dressed in a nightgown.

He's sitting at the desk in the living room, staring in apt concentration at a paper in front of him. He bends over it, working diligently, and I'm left to wonder what he's working so hard at.

The light inside is warm and beckoning, but of course, I can't knock. It's three a.m. So I watch from the shadows for a bit longer, and just when I'm ready to turn around and head home, Dare stands up and walks into the kitchen.

Curiosity is killing me, so I dart around the edge of the house to the windows on the other side of his living room. From this angle, I'll have a good view of his desk. Peering in, I gasp.

When I first saw Dare, I'd been right. He *is* something artistic. He's an artist.

And he's working on an amazingly beautiful drawing of me.

My breath is suspended as I peer closer, and leaning my forehead against the glass, I study the picture.

His skill is amazing. And the way he's drawing me is exhilarating.

In the picture, I'm walking away from him, and I'm completely naked except for a pair of high heels.

Breathless, I study the drawing... enchanted with the way he imagines me to be. I'm slender and pale, but pale in a beautiful way, an ethereal way. My hair is long and lush, my muscles curvy and perfect. Through his eyes, I'm feminine and delicate and perfect.

I scan the entire drawing as my cheeks grow hot with the sheer thought that he imagines me like this... that he imagines me naked.

And then my heart stutters and pauses in my chest as I see something.

A birthmark on my side.

The size of a quarter, it's the color of coffee with cream.

Startled, my fingers subconsciously flutter to my side, to feel the place where the very real, very intimate birthmark lingers on my skin.

How did Dare know?

There's no possible way he could've ever seen that birthmark, unless he's somehow seen me shower or changing clothes.

He must be watching me.

What the hell?

I'm churning this through my mind with such intensity, that I forget to step away from the window, and Dare scares the shit out of me when he appears directly in front of me, his surprised face in front of my own.

I yank backward and so does he, then he narrows his eyes as he stares out into the dark.

At me.

I back away and then take off down the path toward my house, because of a hundred things. Because I'm embarrassed that he caught me spying on him, because I'm nervous and confused about his picture, and because in spite of everything, I'm flattered and excited that he was drawing me at all.

I haven't gotten twenty yards, though, before Dare is tugging on my elbow.

"Calla, what are you doing out so late?"

His dark brow is furrowed as he stares into my face.

I stop and stare upward, into his dark eyes and without bidding, the image of the beautiful portrait he'd drawn with his own hands pops into my head. It was so lovingly rendered, so perfectly drawn.

"You were drawing me," I say simply, my hands dropping to my sides. I don't know how I feel, other than confused.

He actually seems flustered.

"Yeah. I...it's a hobby."

"You're really good," I tell him. "So good that you were able to draw a birthmark you've never seen before."

Long pause.

Finally, Dare sighs. "What do you mean by that?"

I sigh back. "The birthmark on my side. You've never seen it, so how did you draw it? Have you been watching me? If so, why?"

Another long pause.

"Uh, I'm not stalking around spying on you, if that's what you're implying," Dare finally answers. "I sit outside sometimes, and you go outside a lot. When you came back from sailing the other day, you weren't wearing a cover up. I noticed it then."

Oh. *Obviously.*

"I'm an idiot," I breathe. "I'm sorry."

He shakes his head. "No worries. I can see where you might jump to that conclusion."

Yeah, because I'm wacko.

He glances at me again. "I should be apologizing to you. For drawing you in such an... intimate way. I'm sorry. I hope I haven't made you feel uncomfortable."

If by uncomfortable, he means incredibly flattered, then yes. He has.

"It's okay," I tell him quickly. "You made me look beautiful. Who could be mad about that?"

"You *are* beautiful," he says evenly, his eyes flickering with a million different things. The air is charged, thick with something exciting, and I long to reach up on my tiptoes and kiss him.

"You never said what you're doing out so late," Dare reminds me, interrupting my tempting thoughts.

I look around, hunting for a feasible answer, but the quiet forest doesn't give me a thing. "I just couldn't sleep. I saw your light...."

"I couldn't sleep either," Dare confides. "I draw when that happens."

"You draw *me*," I say slowly. "Why me?"

Of all people in the world, why me?

He grins, a slow, sultry grin that seriously curls my toes.

"I don't only draw you, Calla-Lily. I draw everything that I find interesting."

He finds me interesting. My heart hammers, and I forget that a few minutes ago, I thought he might be a stalker.

"You do?"

He nods. "I do."

I'm shivering now from the night breeze and Dare notices.

"You should run up to bed, Calla," he suggests. "It's cold out here."

I nod wordlessly. "Ok. Good night, Dare."

"Good night."

I scamper up the walk, and the entire way, Dare watches me go. I feel it. But when I turn around at the top of my porch steps, he's gone.

I feel buoyed and amazing and wonderful, until I get back to my bed and remember that Finn's in it. Next to the bed, my flowers have been smashed, by Finn, presumably.

All of my amazing feelings plummet as I realize that I can't feel wonderful about Dare. I can't feel wonderful about anything, as long as there is something so seriously wrong with my brother.

I fall asleep with dark clouds hanging around me, consuming my joy.

20

VIGINTI

The ocean crashes against the shore, the mist spraying against me as I lounge against one of the rocks in the inlet. It's low tide, so I can linger here for hours before high tides comes back in to cover all of the exposed pools.

All I want to do is daydream about Dare. To fixate on the fact that he fantasizes about me naked.

But I can't. Not right now. Because in my jacket pocket, my fingers rest on the tattered leather cover of Finn's journal. After realizing last night that Finn is even more troubled than I realized, I know I've got to figure it out.

So when he and my dad went out to work on the fence, I took his journal. It's something I had to do because he's obviously not going to tell me himself. He'll think it's lost... and I'll have to go along with that. It makes me feel dirty, and awful for lying to him, because I know how much his writing means to him.

But he's just going to have to write in something else.

I've got to do whatever it takes to protect him from himself.

My breath hitches in my chest as I pull the book out. Because the last time I read it, it scared me for weeks.

His hidden thoughts terrified me then, and they'll terrify me now.

Regardless, I open the cover with shaking fingers.

And then I'm still.

Absolutely, completely still.

A folded paper is inside the front cover, but I can already see what it is.

Dare's drawing of me.

When did Finn get it? In the middle of the night?

Unable to breathe, unable to feel, I unfold the paper carefully and then my heart spasms.

MINE is scrawled across the beautiful sketch. Everywhere. Big letters, small letters, in-between letters. Scrawling bold writing.

MINE MINE MINE MINE MINE MINE.

I can't breathe.

I can't think.

All I know is that my fingers are trembling and my heart is spasming and what the hell is going on?

Finn crept out of my bed, down to Dare's house, and stole this picture in the middle of the night. Hell, he might've even been watching me the whole time and that's how he knew it even existed.

Chills run down my back, causing me to shiver and shiver and shiver.

Why?

What is wrong with my brother?

Forcing myself to focus, I flip through the pages of his journal because this is where I'll find answers. There's a tarot card, which is odd, but I take it back in and fly through the pages until I get to where I'd left off the last time I'd read it. The writing is bold and heavy, which is odd since Finn's fingers and arms are light as a feather, scrawny and thin.

My chest constricts as I read his words. They're written in all different sizes, in scratches and scrawls, the scribbles of the insane.

NOCTE LIBER SUM   NOCTE LIBER SUM
BY NIGHT I AM FREE.
ALEA IACTA EST   THE DIE HAS BEEN CAST.   THE DIE HAS BEEN CAST.
THE DIE HAS BEEN FUCKING CAST.
SERVA ME, SERVABO TE.   SAVE ME AND I WILL SAVE YOU.
SAVE ME.
SAVE ME.
SAVE ME.

The entire page is more of the same, desperate Latin phrases and random words. And of course the weird symbol. I don't even bother trying to interpret that. My brother loves weird symbols and scribbles them all over the place. I don't even blink until I reach the bottom of the page, where there are stick figures with their faces scratched out. Two of them, a man and a woman. The woman has flaming red hair.

Me.

I swallow hard and slam the book shut, staring out to sea, willing my mind to forget what I just read.

What does he need saved from?

Insanity?

Save me and I will save you. From what?

Do I need saved, too? Is that why he scratched my eyes out?

A lump forms in my throat, heavy and hot and acrid.

I can't do this. I knew it would be insane in his journal, I just didn't know how much. And I just…can't do it today. I need a break from the crazy.

Because my brother is crawling into my bed and scribbling MINE across an intimate, nude sketch of me. If anyone else were to see it, they'd think he was truly sick, maybe even sexually depraved. That's not the case. I know that because we're two halves of a whole. We're connected and because of that, he feels like he owns me. Like I'm his. Like he's mine.

My thoughts are swirling together and nothing makes sense and I don't know what to do.

I can't think about it right now.

It's too much.

It's too much.

I pull out the little bag with the lighter, and then I light the drawing on fire, because no one can ever see it. If they do, they'll lock Finn away because they won't understand.

I can't let that happen.

I watch it burn, I watch the corners curl and turn black, then I let it go up in flames, the ashes blowing away into the ocean.

And then I tuck the journal in my pocket and walk through the rain (*when did it start raining?*) to the house.

The stones on the trail are wet and I slip a few times, scraping my hands, but I still don't hurry.

The rain is cleansing.

Maybe it'll wash away the crazy.

Because I don't know what to do about it anymore.

Maybe Finn has gotten to a place where I can't fix him anymore.

The thought terrifies me, paralyzes me, and I find that I'm rooted to the ground outside of the Carriage House, my feet enmeshed in the ground, unable to move, unable to carry me one step further.

The rain soaks me and my hair is dripping. My teeth start to chatter, but still I can't move. The panic, the desire to run far from my home, cements my feet to the ground. It's insane, but I still can't move. My feet are stones, too heavy to lift.

The front door of the Carriage House is suddenly thrown open, and Dare darts out, jogging down the cobblestone path.

Without a word, he covers my head with a jacket as he pulls me into his home. His t-shirt is black, his shorts are black, his eyes are black as he rubs my arm with a towel, pushing me into a living room chair.

"What are you doing out in the rain, Calla?" he asks, his hands massaging my arms through the terry cloth. I lean into him, my forehead pressing against his muscle, against his solidity.

I love his solidity.

He's strong and real, unmovable.

"I don't know," I murmur. "I just... I didn't want to go home, I guess."

Dare pauses, gazing down at me, a hundred things wavering in his eyes. "Any reason why not?"

I shrug. "I don't know. Just a feeling."

A sudden overwhelming feeling. The funeral home felt ominous and huge and I couldn't go there, not with Finn's issues hanging over my head, not with my mother gone forever.

"We've been looking for you," he continues, eyeing me, rubbing the cold off my skin.

"You have?" I ask, confused. "But I haven't been gone very long."

He pauses, and I think I see concern in his eyes, but he quickly conceals it.

"You've been gone since this morning," he says calmly.

Isn't it still morning?

I look at the clock on his wall.

Six p.m.

My heart pounds, loud and heavy, as I look again.

It's still six p.m.

How can that be possible? I was so immersed in worrying about Finn that I lost hours of time?

"I think I might be going crazy like my brother," I blurt out, my cold hands grabbing at Dare's warm ones. His eyes soften and he stops, his hands so warm and dry and strong.

"You're not," he assures me. "You've just had a lot to deal with. Anyone would struggle. Trust me."

Anyone would lose several hours out of their day and not even realize it?

"Did you?" I demand. "When your parents died, did *you* struggle?"

"Of course," Dare assures me, cupping my hands now, enveloping them in his own. "Everyone does. And you have more to deal with than the average person. Calla, you're surrounded by death here. The funeral home, your mom... it's hard. Let's just put it that way."

He sits next to me, and I inhale him, breathing in the scent of man and rain and security and want.

I want him.

That's what I know.

The more I'm around him, the more I want him. I want his assuredness, his sexiness, his shoulders, his hips. I want his comfort, I want his voice, I want all of him.

More than anything I've ever wanted.

I reach a cold hand up, tracing his jawline once again, the way I did the other night. This time, though, he doesn't stop my hand. He doesn't stop my fingers from running across his lips, feeling the softness that lingers there.

The electricity feels like it's going to snap in the air, and electrocute me with the intensity, but it doesn't. It just creates a current that runs from me to Dare and back again, lighting me up, making me tingle in places I've never felt before.

I swallow hard.

"Kiss me," I whisper, looking hungrily into his eyes. He blinks, then stares, his mouth tightening.

"I shouldn't," he answers, low and husky.

"Do it anyway," I reply, hoping, praying, holding my breath.

Then he does.

He lowers his beautiful face and his lips come down on mine, soft, firm, real. I sigh into his mouth, into the spearmint breath that absorbs my own, into the thing I've been wanting for weeks.

He feels so comfortable, so exciting, so natural to me. Kissing him is like taking a breath. It gives me life.

He pulls away abruptly, though, leaving my heart pounding and my breath broken, and then he stands up.

"I shouldn't have done that," he mutters, taking the towel into the kitchen. I leap to my feet and chase him.

"Why not?" I demand. "I'm eighteen and I know exactly what I want."

I want you.

But he's already shaking his head. "You don't know what you want," he tells me regretfully. "Because you're upset, and you've got more to deal with than most people ever will. It's not a good time for this. It's not fair of me to take advantage of you right now."

"You're not—" I start to say, but he puts a long finger against my lips.

"I am," he says firmly. "I can't do that. Not today."

But he doesn't say *never.*

I stand still, my breathing harsh and ragged. Then I turn and walk away, humiliated with the rejection, but buoyed by it, too.

Because he didn't say never.

He didn't say never because he draws me at night and so I know he thinks about me too.

I walk out the door into the rain, ignoring the way he calls after me. I walk straight to my house, straight to my room, and after dropping my clothes and Finn's journal onto the floor, I step into the shower.

The hot water floods my senses, blocking out the memory of his smell.

I envision his hands holding my own, and I squeeze my eyes shut.

He thinks that's he's not what I need, but he's *exactly* what I need.

He distracts me from my pain. From my worry. From my fear.

But even as I have the thought, the truth of what he said slams into me.

It's not a good time right now.

It's not a good time because he doesn't want to be a d*istraction.*

He deserves to be a *focus.*

And in my current state, I can't focus on anything, except for maybe saving my brother from insanity. Dare deserves more than that.

But my selfish side wants him anyway.

I slide to the floor and close my eyes, letting the water wash my tears away.

***

I don't know how long I stayed in the shower, or how long I've been curled up in the window seat of my room since. All I know is that my father and Finn came home, and Finn disappeared into his room. I heard him rustling around in there.

I heard him clamoring down the stairs, yelling for me, yelling for Dad.

And now he's coming back up, stomping angrily, bursting through my door.

"Where's my journal?" he demands, his pale blue eyes like icicles, his thin hands clenched into fists at his sides.

For the first time in my life, I lie to my brother.

To his face.

"I don't know," I say simply, staring at him, not blinking. I don't look away, because I don't want to accidentally glance at the bottom drawer of my desk, where I have stashed his little book.

"You do, too," he says angrily. "It was in my room, and now it's not."

"I don't have it, Finn," I tell him again. "Why are you so upset? It'll turn up."

After I have a chance to read it.

Finn's face is taut and anxious and I do feel guilty for inflicting distress on him. I know what happens when he gets upset, but it's a chance I have to take. I can't help him unless I know what is truly bothering him. And this is the only way to find out.

"If you find it," he says limply, turning to leave. "Don't read it, Calla."

I don't answer, so he stops in his tracks, glancing back at me, his desperate gaze meeting mine. "You can't read it, Cal."

I can't help but stare into his eyes, fascinated by the utter desolation I find there. The level of his despair over a simple book is staggering.

"Why do you feel so strongly about this, Finn?"

My question is simple.

But his answer is not. He turns back to me, and his face crumples and he cries.

"Because things have to happen in order, Calla. They have to. In. Order. Can't you see? Can't you?" His skinny shoulders shake and I pull him into my arms and my hands stroke his back as he breathes harshly against me, his chest rising and falling against my own.

"I see," I tell him, which is another lie because I don't.

It's minutes and minutes before he steps away, before he's gathered control of himself enough to step out of my bedroom. But the look on his face is haunting when he does, as he closes the door and the last thing I see is the despair.

God, this hurts.

But I'm his protector. If I don't do it, no one will.

And sometimes, we have to do things we aren't proud of to protect those we love.

So I lock my door and pull out his book, curling up once again in my window seat so I can invade his privacy.

Below me, I see Finn go outside, and pull out an ax. He takes his aggression out on the wood, chopping piece after piece, even though this is summer and we won't need it for months. In fact, we won't even be here when it turns cold. But my father will.

So Finn chops wood for our father, while I turn my attention to his journal.

The craziness it contains spirals and leaps on the page, and I find myself holding my breath as I read.

I'M DROWNING. DROWNING. DROWNING.
IMMERSUM IMMERSUM IMMERSUM
CALLA WILL SAVE ME. OR I WILL DIE. OR I WILL
DIE. OR I WILL DIE.
SERVA ME, SERVABO TE. SAVE ME AND I WILL SAVE
YOU.

SAVE ME.
SAVE ME.
SAVE ME.
CALLA CALLA CALLA CALLA CALLA CALLA CALLA
CALLA
I WILL SAVE YOU CALLA. CALLA CALLA CALLA.

I tear my eyes away from the painful words, wrenching them away, because once again, just like always, Finn calls out for me when he's afraid.

Even in written words on the pages of his journal.

He thinks I'm the only one who can save him and I have to agree.

But he also thinks he needs to save *me,* which is slightly ridiculous.

I'm the only one who understands. I'm the only one who knows. And I can't tell anyone, because if I do, my father will have no choice but to send Finn to a mental institution, and I know enough to know that he'd never get out. They'd keep him.

So I have to save him without telling anyone.

And the only way to do that, is to read his innermost thoughts. All of them.

I shift my gaze out the window, into the rain, and I'm startled to find Finn gone, but Dare is in his place. Jogging along the trail, up from the beach, he strides confidently and unaffected by the downpour.

In fact, when he's on the edge of the lawns, out in front of my window, he stops abruptly.

Then his gorgeous face tilts upward and his eyes meet mine.

I stop breathing.

I stop thinking.

I just lift my hand to the glass, pressing it there, as though Dare's hand is resting against my own. The rain runs in rivulets down the pane, around my fingers like tears, and Dare's eyes soften. Without a word, he lifts his hand.

He holds it there, as though he's touching me. As though he's comforting me from things he has no knowledge of.

But what *I* know, is that he *is* comforting me.

His *presence* comforts me.

He knows it. That's why he stands in the rain for several minutes more, for *so long,* until he's absolutely drenched, until finally, finally, he drops his hand and continues on his way, through the rain and onto the trails.

He disappears into the canopy of trees, and then he's gone.

Gone from me.

I realize something as I linger with Finn's crazy thoughts in my lap.

I've never felt quite so alone before.

21

VIGINTI ET VNUM

I somehow pull myself together by morning, after losing hours of sleep, tossing and turning and panicking. By morning, I'm calm.

I have to be.

I can't fall to pieces because I have to put Finn back together.

At breakfast though, he seems utterly normal and grins at me over his cereal.

"I'm sorry I fell apart last night," he tells me casually, putting his spoon down and taking a bite of his bagel. He has an appetite. This is good.

I smile hesitantly. "It's ok. I'll keep an eye out for your journal, Finn. It'll turn up, I promise."

He smiles angelically. "I know."

His calm demeanor almost alarms me, as though he knows I have his journal. But that can't be true. If he knew, he'd freak out, and tear my room apart hunting for it.

"Do you want to do something today?" I ask him as I pour my orange juice.

"Can't," he mumbles around his bagel. "I'm going to sort through my stuff, and lean it down."

"Do you want help?" I feel my eyebrows knit together. He's acting so aloof.

He shakes his head. "Nah. I'm still not feeling that great. You should go do something with Dare."

This snaps my head up. He wants me to do something with Dare? What the hell?

He shrugs, then chuckles because my astonishment is apparent. "What? You're leaving at the end of the summer. You should have a summer fling. It's on every girl's bucket list, right?"

I roll my eyes at that, although my insides are leaping. He isn't going to make me feel guilty for spending time with Dare? It's like the Heavens are opening up and God is smiling upon me.

"I don't know," I answer. "I'm too young to worry about a bucket list."

"Just go," he tells me, pushing away from the table. "Dare was asking Dad how to get to Warrenton last night. You should take him yourself."

The fact that I've been there a million times before doesn't matter, because I've never been there with Dare.

"I'll be back in time to eat dinner with you!" I call to him. He waves over his shoulder without looking.

I've been dismissed.

Suddenly I feel like I've broken out of jail, like I'm free and I have to hurry and make my getaway. I all but run for the Carriage House, and I'm still breathless as I knock on the door.

I'm even more breathless when Dare answers it.

Because he's shirtless.

In fact, he looks like he just stepped from the shower because his hair is wet. And his chest is bare. I can't help but stare at the bare skin, the muscled abdomen, the lithe torso, and the perfect, chiseled V that disappears into the top of his jeans. A silver belt buckle shaped like a skull is positioned perfectly-centered a few inches beneath his belly button.

I swallow hard, then swallow again.

The corner of Dare's mouth twitches.

"Yes?" he asks, his lip curling at the corner. He has to know the effect he has on me. He probably has it on everyone.

I swear to God my intention is to ask him to go to Warrenton Beach. But my tongue has a mind of its own.

"Draw me," I breathe, surprising me and surprising him. His eyes widen, and he stares at me.

"Draw you," he repeats slowly, hesitantly, his eyes never leaving mine.

I nod. "You've drawn me from your imagination, but wouldn't a real model be better?"

Without waiting for a reply and before I can think the better of it, I nudge past him and enter his little house. He stares at me, his eyes like black molten lava, and I can tell he's trying to figure out how to handle me. So before he can say anything, I turn, forcing a confident grin.

"Where do you want me?"

Don't reject me. That's all I can think as I stare at his gorgeous face, and I must be crazy because there's no way he's going to do this.

"Calla," he says huskily, his tongue darting out to lick his full bottom lip.

"Don't," I interrupt him before he can turn me away. "Draw me, Dare. I want you to."

He stands as still as a statue, studying me, his body so long and lean.

"Please," I add finally, my whisper husky. "Where do you want me?"

I count the beats as he stares at me, as he ponders me.

One.

Two.

Three.

Four.

Fi--

"Just a minute," he finally answers, interrupting my internal counting, his eyes black as night.

He crosses the room and pulls a chaise lounge to the middle of the living room.

"You can sit there."

He sounds so professional. I do as he asks, and I perch on the edge of the seat, my nerves dancing along my skin, disbelief pulsing through me.

He's going to do it. He's going to do it.

"Close the blinds," I tell him softly, as I unbutton my shirt.

I can't believe I'm doing this.

I can't believe he's letting me.

I watch him swallow hard, his Adam's apple moving in his throat, while he does as I instruct. When the room has been darkened, he pulls a seat up in front of me, his sketchbook in his hand.

"Are you ready?" he asks, his voice level. He keeps his eyes on my face.

I shake my head.

"Not yet."

And then I take off my bra.

Dare clears his throat and opens his sketchbook, the picture of a professional, and I swear I feel ten thousand flames lapping at my body as every inch of me flushes.

I stand up and shove my shorts to the floor.

Dare doesn't move. It doesn't even look like he's breathing.

His eyes are frozen on me, appreciation flaring to life in them, and then he stares into my eyes, his gaze deep and dark.

"Calla," he begins again, and he starts to move, to get up.

"Don't," I tell him sharply. "Please. I need this. I want to be...distracted."

His eyes seem guarded now as he studies me, but he still stands up. He walks to his closet and comes back with one of his dress shirts. A white button-up. He hands it to me.

"Put this on," he tells me. "Leave it unbuttoned."

My heart pounds as I do what he asks.

He waits, then adjusts the opening of the shirt to fall just right against my skin, so that only the top curves of my breasts show. He buttons one button there, and then pulls the shirt open so that my belly button and hip are exposed.

He settles back into his chair.

"So I'm a distraction, then?" he asks simply, bringing his pencil to the page and drawing a flowing line. The beginning of my hip.

I flush. "You're far more than a distraction. But today... I need distracted." I swallow and his eyes meet mine, then he looks away.

"Lay back," he tells me brusquely. He gets up and comes to me, bending and moving my hair over my

166

shoulder. His hand brushes my skin and a fire erupts, a heat, a raging lava-like liquid, churning in my belly, and I ache for him to lay down with me, to feel him next to me.

But he doesn't. He stares down at me, studying me.

"Arch your back a bit," he tells me. So I do. He slides a small pillow behind it.

"Bite your lip," he tells me. "Not hard. Just enough to look like you're thinking about something. Fantasizing, maybe."

Oh God. I can totally do that.

He smiles, just a little, and returns to his seat.

His hands move across the page, quickly, then slowly. He looks up at me, his eyes so so dark, then he returns his attention to the page.

The electricity in this room is charged. It's real. It's smothering. It's exhilarating. I can't breathe.

Dare meets my gaze.

"Are you okay?"

I nod. "I am now."

Now that I'm here. Now that you aren't rejecting me. *Now that you see me.*

The edge of his lip curves up, and he swoops his hand, then bends his head in concentration.

"So what brought on this scene from Titanic?" Dare asks me tritely, eyeing me above the top of his paper. I feel a blush spread from my forehead to my chest and I look away.

"I'm not...it's not," I practically stammer. The cool air drifts over my body, forming goose-bumps everywhere.

Dare pauses. "No?"

I shake my head. "No. I just wanted... to feel something else."

"Something other than?" Dare waits.

"What I've been feeling," I clarify. "Craziness. Sadness. I just want to be someone else just for a minute."

Dare examines his picture, then sits back in his seat a minute.

"Why would you want to be anyone else?" he asks softly. "Calla Price is amazing."

He stands up and comes to me, staring down. His expression is guarded and intense and he lingers above me. His dark eyes trace the outline of my naked hip, the curve of my thigh, and then suddenly, he follows his gaze with his finger. He runs it lightly from my knee to my hip, his fingertip scaldingly hot.

"You want me, don't you?" I whisper, the words hesitant and afraid, hopeful and anxious.

His eyes are ablaze as he answers. "I've always wanted you."

Any answer I can possibly give him his frozen in my throat, jammed against my tongue and so all I can do is move. I turn to give him better access, so that he can touch me, so that he can move his fingers and grip me tight and shove his tongue down my throat and...then he takes his finger away and offers me his hand.

I stare at his extended hand in confusion, but then let him pull me to my feet.

I stand toe to toe with him, my bare breasts almost pressed against his body. If I just rocked forward a little bit, his hips would be pressed to mine and....

He raises an eyebrow. "Do you want to see it?"

It. The picture. I forgot.

I nod, swallowing hard.

He hands me the picture and it's beautiful.

168

I look like a model, draped casually over a settee. Dare made the curtains flutter in the wind behind me, and he created an ocean view through the windows. The light shines in on me and I seem like an ethereal creature, something otherworldly.

"It's beautiful," I breathe.

"You are," he agrees. He hands me my shirt and I hesitate.

I don't want to put it on. I want.. I want... I want... *Dare.*

But his expression is no-nonsense and professional and he's not touching me anymore.

Now isn't the time.

I put my clothes on and hug the picture to my chest.

"Can I keep it?"

"Of course."

He turns to move the chaise back to where it belongs and I pause.

"I was just thinking..." I begin. "That I'd like to go to Warrenton Beach today. Would you like to go, too?"

Dare narrows his eyes, but there's laughter in them. "Is this you, trying to get a bike ride in addition to a portrait?"

I narrow my own. "Is this you, offering to give me one?"

Dare hesitates, and something in his eyes is troubling, something unsure, but finally he shrugs. "I don't see why not. It doesn't look like rain."

He heads toward his bedroom.

"I'll grab a shirt."

If you must.

He calls out at me.

"If you look in that chest by the door, you'll find an extra helmet."

I do as he says, and sure enough, there's one there.

"Why do you have an extra?" I ask, pulling it out and closing the lid.

"Because you mentioned that you might want a ride," he answers, re-emerging from his room, a shirt in his hand. "Safety first, and all that."

He pulls the shirt over his head, and I'm not sure what I'm more enthralled with. His rippling abs, or the fact that he bought me a helmet.

Specifically for me.

It's enough to make my stomach flip.

"Thanks," I murmur.

He throws a look in my direction that can only be classified as sizzling. His near-black eyes spark with heat, and it's enough to set my nerve-endings on fire.

I gulp.

"Are you ready right now?" Dare asks me. "You can leave your picture here."

I shrug, trying to be casual. "It's as good a time as any."

He grins. "That it is, Calla-Lily."

22

VIGINTI DUORUM

When we're standing in front of Dare's bike, a shiny black Triumph, it looks aggressive and intimidating, and I'm suddenly nervous.

Dare glances at me. "Don't have the balls?"

I toss my hair back and laugh.

"I think we just established that I don't have balls. Right?"

I could swear he flushes as he shakes his head.

"That's true. I just saw that for myself."

And now I'm the one flushing as I see my reflection in his dark eyes, as I remember how I'd just laid in front of him, half naked.

Dare motions for me to climb on behind him, which I do.

"Hold on tight, Calla-Lily."

Don't worry.

Within moments, we're gliding down the mountain road and my arms are wrapped around Dare, and the nervousness fades away.

Because I belong here with him.

I belong perched behind him with my chest is pressed into his back. It sends sparks shooting through all of my nerve endings. His heat bleeds into me, his strength, and I want to soak it all in.

I rest my cheek against his shoulders and lazily watch the scenery blur past as we sail through town, and then over the Youngs-Bay bridge. The heavy bike vibrates between my legs, and I can suddenly appreciate the appeal of the bike and the open road. No wonder Dare has LIVE FREE tattooed on his back.

There's nothing more freeing than this.

We hug the road with the wind in our faces and too quickly, the ride is over.

Dare guides the bike into a parking spot and we dismount. It takes a second to get my land-legs again, and Dare grins as he supports my elbow. His touch is electric and I want it. And I can't think because lying half-naked in front of him has addled all of my thoughts.

"Well?"

It takes me a minute to realize that he's talking about the motorcycle ride.

"I loved it," I announce. "Let's do it again."

He winks at me. "Well, we'll have to get home somehow. But first, let's take a look at this wreck, shall we?"

I grin and pull him toward the beach, to where the remains of the old wreck rise out of the mist. It's weathered bones look at once ghostly and impressive, skeletal and freaky.

Minute by minute, I'm brought out of the charged sexual atmosphere from his cottage and into the brisk sea air of the moment.

"The Iredale ran aground in 1906," I explain to him as we walk. "No one died, thank goodness. They waited for weeks for the weather to clear enough to tow her back out to sea, but she got so entrenched in the sand, that they couldn't. She's been in this spot ever since."

We're standing in front of her now, her masts and ribs poking out from the sand and arching toward the sky. Dare reaches out and runs a hand along one of her ribs, the same hand that he slid along my naked hip, the same exact movement, calm and reverent.

I swallow hard.

"It's a rite of passage around here," I tell him. "To skip school and come out here with your friends."

Except I never had any friends, other than Finn.

"So you and Finn came here a lot?" Dare asks, as though he read my mind, and his question isn't condescending, he's just curious.

I nod. "Yeah. We like to stop and get coffee and come sit. It's a good way to kill the time."

"So show me," Dare says quietly, taking my hand and pulling me inside the sparse shell. We sit on the damp sand, and stare through the corpse of the ship toward the ocean, where the waves rise and fall and the sea gulls fly in loops.

"This must've been a good place to grow up," Dare muses as he takes in the horizon.

I nod. "Yeah. I can't complain. Fresh air, open water... I guess it could only have been better if I didn't live in a funeral home."

I laugh at that, but Dare looks at me sharply.

"Was it really hard?" he asks, half concerned, half curious.

I pause. Because was it? Was it the fact that I lived in a funeral home that made my life hard, or the fact that my brother was crazy and so we were ostracized?

173

I shrug. "I don't know. I think it was everything combined."

Dare nods, accepting that, because sometimes that's how life is. A puzzle made up of a million pieces, and when one piece doesn't exactly fit, it throws the rest of them off.

Like right now, for instance. I was lying naked in front him just a while ago, and now here we are, acting like nothing happened.

"Have you ever thought of moving away?" he asks after a few minutes. "I mean, especially now, I think maybe getting a break from...death might be healthy."

I swallow hard because obviously, over the years, that's been a recurring fantasy of mine. To live somewhere else, far from a funeral home. But there's Finn, and so of course I would never leave here before. And now there's college and my brother wants to go alone.

"I'm going away to college in the Fall," I remind him, not mentioning anything else.

"Ah, that's right," he says, leaning back in the sand, his back pressed against a splintered rib. "Do you feel up to it? After everything, I mean."

After your mom died, he means.

"I have to be up to it," I tell him. "Life doesn't stop because someone dies. That's something that living in a funeral home has taught me." And having my mother die and the world kept turning.

He nods again. "Yeah, I guess that's true. But sometimes, we wish it could. I mean, I know I did. It didn't seem fair that my mom was just gone, and everyone kept acting like nothing had changed. The stores kept their doors open and selling trivial things, airplanes kept flying, boats kept sailing... it was like I was the only one who cared that the world lost an amazing person." His vulnerability is showing, and it touches me deep down, in a place I didn't know I had.

I turn to him, willing to share something, too. It's only fair. *You show me yours, and I'll show you mine.*

"I was mad at old people for a while," I admit sheepishly. "I know it's stupid, but whenever I would see an elderly person out and about with their walker and oxygen tank, I was furious that Death didn't decide to take them instead of my mom."

Dare smiles, a grin that lights up the beach.

"I see the reasoning behind that," he tells me. "It's not stupid. Your mom was too young. And they say anger is one of the stages of grief."

"But not anger at random old people," I point out with a barky laugh.

Dare laughs with me and it feels really good, because he's not laughing *at* me, he's laughing *with* me, and there's a difference.

"This feels good," I admit finally, playing with the sand in front of me. Dare glances at me.

"I think you need to get off that mountain more," he decides. "For real. Being secluded in a funeral home? That's not healthy, Calla."

I suddenly feel defensive. "I'm not secluded," I point out. "I have Finn and my dad. And now you're there, too."

Dare blinks. "Yeah, I guess I am."

"And we're not in the funeral home right now," I also point out. We take a pause and gaze out at the vast, endless ocean because the huge grayness of it is inspiring at the same time that it makes me feel small.

175

"You're right," Dare concedes. "We're not." He pulls his finger through the sand, drawing a line, then intersecting it with another. "We should do this more often."

Those last words impale me and I freeze.

Is he saying what I think he's saying?

"You want to come to the beach more often?" I ask hesitantly. Dare smiles.

"No, I'm saying we should get out more often. Together."

That's what I thought he was saying.

My heart pounds and I nod. "Sure. That'd be fine. Do you care if Finn comes sometimes, too?" Because I feel too guilty to leave him behind all the time.

Dare nods. "Of course not. I want to spend time with you, however you want to give it to me."

Dare grins at me, that freaking *Dare Me* grin, and I know I'm a goner. I'm falling for him, more every day, and there's nothing I can do about it. In fact, there's nothing I *want* to do about it. Because it's amazing.

The Iredale is only a shell of a ship, so the wind whips at us and Dare shoves his hair out of his face. As he does, his ring shimmers with the muted light of the sun. A sudden feeling of déjà vu overwhelms me, as though I've watched his ring glint in the sun before, and we've been here in this ship, together.

We've been here before in this exact place and time.

That's all I can think as I stare at him, as I watch his ring shimmering in the light, as I watch him shake his hair in the wind.

Dare drops his hand and the feeling fades, but yet the remains of it linger like the wispy fingers of a memory or a dream.

I stare at him uncertainly, because the feeling was so overpowering.

Dare draws back and stares at me. "Are you ok?"

I nod, because *God, it's just déjà vu, Calla.* It happens.

But it felt so real. I shake my head, to shake the oddness away. I can't slip away from reality, I can't be like Finn. *God.*

Dare's hand covers my own, and we stare out at the ocean for several minutes more.

His hand is warm and strong, and I relish it. I relish the way he rests it against my back as we walk down the beach towards his bike. And I relish the way I fold against him as we ride back home. I relish it all because it's amazing. No matter what else is going on, *this* is amazing.

I feel like I'm floating as I slide off the bike and stand in front of him.

We pause, like neither of us wants to call an end to this day.

Finally, Dare smiles, a slow grin, a real grin that crinkles the corners of his dark *Dare Me* eyes. He reaches up and tucks an errant strand of hair behind my ear, and I swear to God I have to force myself to not lean into that hand.

"Wait here," he tells me and he disappears into his cottage, coming right back out with his picture. He presses it into my hand.

"I'll see you soon, Calla-Lily," he promises huskily. I nod, and watch him turn and walk away.

God, he looks good walking away.

And then I float upstairs to my room.

It's not until I'm staring out my bedroom window and see Finn that I come crashing down.

He's standing out on the edge of the trees.
And he's covered in blood.

23

VIGINTI TRES

In my head, all I can see is blood as I clatter down the stairs and rush to get to my brother.

What has he done?

I race outside, but when I reach where he was standing, he's no longer there. I spin in a circle, gazing about, but there's no sign of him.

Until I see a flash of green from the corner of my eye, the exact color of his shirt.

Viridem.

He's headed for the beach so I take off like a rocket, pummeling the ferns as I trip over them on my way to the shore. I skid over the rocks and the clay and the dirt, and when I hit the bottom, he's there.

Simply standing there on the edge of the water, waiting for me, like he's been there all along.

He stands limply, his hands at his sides, and blood runs from his elbows to his hands.

"What the hell?" I shout as I race to him, grabbing his arms and examining them. "What did you do?"

Long scratches stretch the length of his forearm, deep enough to bleed, perhaps even deep enough to scar. But not deep enough for stitches, or for permanent harm.

Thank you, God.

I look up frantically, and Finn stares down at me, his pale blue eyes so eerily calm.

"Why did you do this?" I ask, my voice shaking. "Are you upset because I went with Dare? Because you told me to do it."

"I didn't do it on purpose," he says limply. "I was out in the woods. The branches...." His voice trails off and he would really have me believe that the branches cut his arms.

I stare at him in disbelief.

"I'm stressed," he mumbles. "Maybe it was an accident."

I open my mouth, but he holds up a hand.

"Calla, I don't want to fight. And no, of course I'm not upset with you for going with Dare. I want you to go with Dare. I want you to be independent. Can't you see that? *I'm trying to show you.*"

His face is pained now, but he's still handsome and calm. He's still my Finn.

"I don't know what you want," I admit softly. "I don't want to feel guilty when I do something without you but when I do, I'm afraid you'll react like....*this*."

I purposely don't look at his arms, at the blood that drips on the sand, staining it crimson.

"What are we gonna do, Finn?" I ask quietly. "We've got to get a handle on this."

He smiles gracefully, his teeth perfectly white and straight. "You say *we* like it's your problem, Cal. I guess *that's* your problem. You've always assumed my issues like they're your own. They're not. We're different in that way. You're healthy, Cal. Act like it. It's time."

His voice is firm, an assertive tone that he rarely takes with me and I stand shocked, mesmerized by this new side of him.

"I don't understand," I tell him softly. "What do you want?"

He smiles again, and it's eerie now in the fading light. Eerie with it's calm, eerie with its knowingness.

"I want you to let go," he says simply. "Just a little. You have to."

I start to shake my head because a desperation wells up in my chest and threatens to overwhelm me. He holds up a hand.

"Let's not argue," he suggests. "I'm going to go clean up."

And so I trail behind him, back up the trail and into the house, where we clean him up and wrap his arms in bandages. He doesn't flinch when I spray him with first aid spray, even though I know it stings. He doesn't flinch when I tell him he has to be more careful. He just remains calm.

It's enough to terrify me.

Because one thing about my brother, he never remains calm. That's not his thing.

But today it is.

We curl up in my room and listen to music, to old albums that mom loved... the Beatles, the Cure, U2. It starts to rain and it runs down the glass like rivers and finally, Finn turns to me.

"I didn't do it on purpose."

"Okay."

"I'm tired, Cal."

And he looks so very tired. So pale, so skinny. I suck a breath in because it's like he's deteriorating in front of my eyes. Dad is so lost in his grief about mom that he doesn't even notice.

I'm the only one.

Like always.

"You've got to start eating better," I tell him.

"I know."

"Let's take a nap, Finn," I suggest. He nods and climbs into my bed. I cover him up with a quilt before I curl up beside him. He falls asleep quickly, and he doesn't stir.

Beneath him, between my mattresses, his journal rests. I know I have to force myself to read more of it, no matter how much it scares me, because I have to uncover the truth.

Something is bothering him, something is eating at him, and little by little, it will drive him completely mad... if I don't stop it first.

24

VIGINTI QUATUOR

Finn

I can't sleep. That's the problem. I seldom sleep now and the redness of my eyes is driving me to the brink. They burn and burn, and still sleep won't come.

Even now, I feel Calla watching me, waiting for me to be normal, waiting for me to sleep, so I feign it. I pretend to dream.

But I'm a faker.

Instead of dreaming, I lie here listening to the fucking voices.

SheDoesn'tDeserveYouSheDoesn'tDoesn'tDoesn't. Don'tYouSee? Can'tYOU? Can'tYOU? SheDoesn'tKnow Shedoesn'tknow. She doesn't.

They hiss and whisper and yell and scream and I fight the urge to flinch, to scratch, to shriek. But through it all, I lie as still as a corpse, as quiet as a ghost.

Serva me, serva bo te. Serva me. Serva me. Serva me.

Save me and I will save you.

I will save her. I will I will I will.

It's my voice now, rising above the others, ringing out loud and clear and most important. I can fend them off for a while, for long enough to do this. For long enough to save her.

My secret will come out. But before that, I will save her.

I will.

25

VIGINTI QUINQUE

Calla

I don't wake until morning, and when I do, Finn is gone. That's the first thing I notice.

I open my eyes and my hand runs along the cool smooth sheets of the empty side of my bed.

The second thing I notice is the piano music.

Since I know there isn't a funeral today, this is very odd. My mother was the only one who knew how to play in our family.

I crawl out of bed and pad down the stairs, inching into the Chapel, not sure what I expect to see. But nothing I expect prepares me for what it is.

Dare sits at the piano in the front, the sunshine pouring in from the windows above and reflecting off of his dark hair, like he's been chosen by God Himself. His eyes closed in concentration, he plays as if the music flows through him like blood or air, like he has to play to live.

I lean against the door, watching his hands span the keys, urging the music from them, with all the grace of an accomplished pianist. I don't recognize the song, but it's beautiful and haunting and sad.

It's just right for this place.

And even though Dare is wearing dark jeans and a snug black shirt and that trendy silver ring on his middle finger, he's right for this place too.

Because he's playing the piano as it should be played.

With reverence.

Here in this chapel, it's only right to revere our surroundings, the quiet peacefulness of a room used to honor the dead.

I close my eyes for a minute, unable to stop myself from imagining what it would be like if his hands worshipped my body in the same way as they worship the keys. My dreams have been like foreplay, because every night, he touches me. He claims my body as his own, and every night, I enjoy it. Right now, I recall those dreams, and my cheeks flush as I picture his fingers trailing over my hip, up my abdomen, pausing at my breasts. My lips tingle from wanting his kiss. My breath hitches, my tongue darts out, licking at my lips, my face slightly feverish.

It's only now that I realize the music has stopped.

I open my eyes and find Dare turned toward me, watching me. There is amusement in his eyes, like he knows exactly what I'd been daydreaming.

If ever there was a time to wish the floor would open up and swallow me, it is now.

"Hi," he offers. "I hope I didn't wake you. Your dad said I could come in and grab some orange juice. I saw the piano and…well, I intruded. I'm sorry."

His accent makes everything ok. And the fact that he plays the piano. More than ok, in fact, it might make him the sexiest man alive.

"You're not an intrusion," I tell him. Or if he is, he's a welcome one. "You play beautifully."

He shrugs. "It was one of my step-father's rules. Everyone in his family had to learn to play because that's what refined people do." He looks bored with the sentiment and closes the lid to the keys.

I raise an eyebrow. "Are you? Refined, I mean."

Because his LIVE FREE tattoo begs to differ.

He smiles. "I'm a bit of a rogue, I'm afraid."

I'm not. Afraid, that is.

"Your dad said to tell you that he had to run into town," he offers as he gets up and lithely moves toward me. I can't help but draw a parallel... between Dare and a graceful jungle cat. Long, lithe, slender, strong. He and I are connected by an invisible band, and he flexes that band as he strides down the aisle of the chapel before he stops in front of me like a panther.

Am I his prey?

God, I hope so.

In the light, his eyes are golden, and I find I can't look away.

"Thanks," I tell him. "I bet my brother went with him." I don't mention that my brother slept in my bed last night, because that would seem weird. Like always, I have to hide certain things for appearances sake.

"I don't know about that," Dare answers. "I haven't seen Finn today."

"He must've," I murmur. In fact, my father probably took Finn in to his group. I'm free to focus on what is standing in front of me.

Dare DuBray.

His smile gleams.

"I have another question to ask you," he tells me, with a certain smug look settling on his lips. I raise an eyebrow.

"What, already? You just asked one days ago."

He chuckles. "Yep. But not here. I want to ask it somewhere else."

I wait.

And wait.

"And that is…where?" I finally ask.

He smiles. "Out on the water."

I pause. "On the water? Like, on our boat?"

He nods. "Is that ok?"

Of course it is.

"It's just a little boat," I warn him. "Nothing fancy."

"That's perfect," he answers. "Because I'm nothing fancy, either."

Au contraire. But of course I don't say that. And it's a good thing I slept in my clothes because this way, we can go straight there without pause. But of course I don't say that either.

Instead, I simply lead the way outdoors and to the beach, not hesitating in the rain.

"We can still go," I tell him. "It's just a little rain, the waves aren't bad."

"I'm not worried," he grins. "I'm used to rain."

"That's right," I answer as I motion for him to climb aboard. "I forgot."

He steps across and I untie the boat from the dock, before I toss the rope to him. I leap before the boat can float away, and land unceremoniously beside him.

He lounges against the hull as I steer through the bay, and suddenly, the rain stops as suddenly as it started. The clouds part, the sun shines down upon us and I lift my face to the warmth.

I live for times like these, when my grief pauses long enough for me to enjoy something.

And I have to admit, I've been enjoying more and more moments since Dare came to my mountain.

"You make me feel guilty," I tell him quietly, opening my eyes. He's sprawled out, his legs propped up on a seat. He glances at me, his forehead furrowed.

"Why in the world is that, Calla-lily?"

The name makes me smile.

"Because you make me forget that I'm sad," I say simply.

Softness wavers in Dare's eyes for a minute before they turn back into obsidian. "That shouldn't make you feel guilty," he tells me. "In fact, that makes *me* happy. I don't like the idea of you being sad. Come sit by me."

He opens his arms and I sit on the seat next to him, leaning against his hard chest and into his beating heart. His arms close around me and for the first time in my life, I'm lounging in a guy's embrace. And not just any guy. Dare DuBray, who I'm guessing could have any girl he wants.

And right now, in this moment, he wants me.

It's unfathomable.

It's the perfect temperature as we drift in the sun, as the warmth saturates my shirt and soaks into my skin. I drag one hand over the side, letting it float on the surface of the water as I listen to Dare's heart.

It's strong and loud against my ear.

Thump. Thump. Thump.

The rhythmic sound reminds me of the day he was punching the shed.

I look up at him, reluctant to bring it up, but wanting to know the answer.

189

"That day outside," I begin. "When you were punching the shed. What exactly was making you so upset?"

He almost flinches, but he doesn't move. He keeps his arms wrapped tightly around my shoulders and his dark eyes closed.

"Why do we have to talk about that?" he asks, his voice husky with relaxation. "I thought you wanted to hear my question?"

"I do," I tell him quickly. "But I want to hear this first. You told me you were mad at yourself, that you were letting something get to you. What was it?"

Because I have to know.

He sighs, and then opens his gorgeous eyes.

"You," he says softly, the word grazing along the edge of my heart. "I'm letting you get to me."

I suck in my breath and draw back, trying to see more of his face, trying to figure his answer out.

"Why would that piss you off?" I ask him hesitantly. "I'm a girl, you're a guy, I think it's an entirely normal thing."

He closes his eyes again, but his arms are still wrapped around me. Thank God.

"It is. But you're not in a good place and I guess I was pissed at Serendipity for her bad timing."

I'm silent because I don't know what to say, and Dare opens one eye.

"Back home, girls often want to date me because of my step-father's family, because they have a lot of money. I hate all of it, but I especially hate the part where I never know when someone is sincere and wants to be close to me just because I'm me."

190

He pauses for a minute. "You have no idea who I am, but you like me just the same."

I'm desperately confused now. "And that's a bad thing?"

He shakes his head and opens his eyes and stares out at the water. "No, it's just a bad time. You're not ready for someone like me. You're not in a good place."

That sort of pisses me off and I shrug out of his arms. "Not in a good place? My mother just died. I'm hardly balancing on the edge or something. People die, and it sucks but it doesn't mean that I'm a fragile little flower."

He levels a gaze at me, a look as black as night. "Be that as it may," he concedes. "You're still grieving. And we can't begin something beautiful when there is still so much ugliness around us."

I'm stunned and sad and silent as I stare away from him, out toward the opposite side of the boat. So he likes me, but he can't be with me. What the hell kind of thing is this?

After a minute, he turns my chin with his thumb, making me look at him.

I don't want to, but then again, I do. Because even when he's infuriating, he's beautiful.

"Ask me what my question is," he instructs me.

I lift my chin.

No.

"Go on," he urges. "Ask me."

I want to know. I want to know why he wanted me out here in the middle of the water so he could ask it. I want to know what it is. I want to know what it could possibly be. So I ask.

"What is your question?"

He smiles and I swear it's brighter than the sun.

"Calla, I want you."

I suck in my breath at that. I wait and wait and wait for a question, all while his eyes penetrate my soul.

"I wake up in the night wanting you. I dream about you. But right now, you're tied up in a lot of painful, hard things. I need to make sure that you're not just drawn to me because you're confused. I want to make sure that you *really* want me. I'm willing to be patient and find out. So my question is, can you be patient and wait, too?"

He wants to be with me? That's all I can think of and never mind that he wants to wait until my mind is clear. Of course I'll wait.

I start to nod and to ask how long, but he continues.

"Can you wait, no matter what happens in the meantime?"

I pause because what a strange thing to say. I must look as puzzled as I feel because Dare reaches out a finger and touches my lips.

"Don't ask, because I can't tell you right now. Everyone has secrets, Calla, even me. But can you wait until we have a fair shot, despite the secrets?"

God, I'm tired of secrets.

But God, I want Dare even more.

"On one condition," I find myself saying. Dare lifts his head, surprised.

"And that is?"

"I don't have a lot of experience with guys like you," I tell him. *Or guys, period.* "But I want you. You're all I think about."

Dare's lips curve. "I feel the same way."

"So I don't know how you can ask me to wait. I only have the summer, Dare. And then I'm leaving for college." I pause and my heart flutters. "But if it's important to you, I'll wait for a little while. A *very* little while. But only if you do one thing for me."

He waits, his dark gaze pensive.

"Give me a reason."

The words are out before I can re-think them and take them back.

Realization clouds his eyes and before I can blink, I'm in his arms again, pulled to his chest and his mouth is ravaging my own. His lips, strong, yet soft, close over mine, pillaging them, bruising them, caressing them.

Kissing him is everything I thought it would be.

I sigh into his mouth and he inhales it as he inhales me. His hands trace the outline of my shoulder-blades, and then skim my back, down to my hips. They feel just as I'd imagined, strong, yet gentle.

He rocks me into him, and my hips meet a sudden rigidity, his very apparent desire for me. I'm taken aback by the hardness. But then it fuels the burning I feel, the burning that races along my veins, pumping through my heart. I burn because he's hard for me.

He wants me.

My tongue twirls around his, before I nip at his lips. He groans as I press tighter against him, wedging myself between his legs, stealing his breath. His hands come up, toward my breasts, grazing my hardened nipples with his thumbs. He lingers there, for a moment, turning my points into pebbles as he nuzzles the softness of my neck, his lips blazing a trail.

Finally, he yanks away, his breathing ragged, as though he's been burned. And I suppose he has. So have I. The chemistry between us is lightning hot.

He holds me at arm's length as he regains his composure.

Then he looks at me and grins the most devilish grin.

"Did that do the trick?"

His question is light and playful, but the meaning really isn't.

Because what he's really asking is... is that enough for now? Is it enough to hold me over? Enough to make me wait?

And the answer is...I don't know.

I don't know because if he's waiting until the worst of my grief is over, he could be waiting a while. Grief is an unpredictable thing, and honestly, I don't think it ever really goes away. I think we just learn to manage it.

And maybe that's really what he's waiting for. For me to manage it... my grief, my life, Finn. There's a lot there to manage. A lot of obstacles.

But as I stare at him, at the way the light turns his dark eyes to amber, at the way the sunshine bathes him in a golden glow and the connection between us sizzles hot and dangerous, I know one thing.

He's worth the wait.

Despite our secrets.

Or maybe even because of them.

26

VIGINTI SEX

Finn

I curl up in my room on the floor, where the dust has settled in the corners and the rain once again drenches the sill. I should get up and close the window, but I don't.

YouCan'tYouCan'tYouCan't.

The voice shrieks in my ear and I clasp my hands over them, holding tight, trying to drown them out, which of course doesn't work. Because the voices come from within.

I hear Calla come inside, I hear her singing in her shower, happy with things that I have no knowledge of, yet I do.

I know it's Dare making her happy.

He gives her hope, when all I give her is despair.

I drop my head into my hands.

Just a little longer.

Justalittlelittlelittlelittle.

She'sNotWorthThePainNotWorthItNotWorthIt.

The voices are insistent, but I know they lie. She *is* worth it. I can pull this off for her. I have to because she deserves it.

~~Act normal.~~

I sit up, brushing my damp hair away from my face.

For a little while longer.

I can do this. I can pretend.

For

A

Little

While

I watch the dust-motes twirl in the dying light, swatting at them before I curl up in a ball.

For Calla.

27

VIGINTI SEPTEM

Calla

I sit curled up in a chair on the side porch. From here, I have the perfect panoramic view of the ocean, the cliffs, and cascading mountainside.

I watch Finn chopping yet more wood, his pale skin glistening with sweat in the morning sun. He didn't sleep with me last night, so apparently he didn't have nightmares. But even still, he was out chopping wood when I got up, so he's clearly bothered by something. He told me once that it soothes his nerves, and lately, he's chopped piles and piles. So his nerves must be truly rattled.

Stirring my coffee, I take a sip, then take a deep breath of the clean mountain air. My father's crematorium isn't burning today, so there is no murky smoke to pollute the air.

"Would you like company?"

Dare's voice is quiet on the edge of the porch, as he lingers on the top step. My heart leaps a bit, just like it does every time I see him. I nod, with a smile.

"Of course." I shove the other chair away from the table with my foot. "It's a perfect morning."

He agrees as he sits down, a cup of coffee in his own hand.

As he looks out over the mountain, I shove Finn's journal further down into my pocket. I'd meant to read more of it this morning, since alone time is rare in my house. But I can do it later. I'll never turn away alone time with Dare, not now that he's decided we should *wait.*

Ugh.

I force a smile because that thought makes me grumpy.

"You're up early," I point out. He smiles back, his eyes sleepy.

"I didn't sleep well," he admits. "So I got up early for a jog. I still feel groggy, so I came up for coffee. Your dad gave me an open invitation to raid your kitchen."

I think about that for a second. My father is normally not all that social, despite the fact that he has to be for his job. He's gotten to be a pro at handling grieving people, at being appropriate and kind. But on his off time, he doesn't typically like to interact.

"He must like you," I decide.

"You sound surprised," Dare smiles. "People like me, you know."

"You said they like you for your step-father's money," I recall. "My dad doesn't know anything about that."

His lip twitches. "Well, people might actually like me, too. I don't know. But I think I'm fairly likable."

Fairly.

I remember the way his hips felt crushed against mine, and I flush.

"You're pretty when you blush," Dare says matter-of-factly, as he stares at me over the rim of his coffee mug. I flush more and he grins. "You're pretty all the time, though," he amends, which of course lights my cheeks on fire.

"You're trying to make me blush now," I accuse. He grins again, not the least bit sorry.

"Am I?" he asks without any chagrin whatsoever.

I nod absently, watching Finn over his shoulder. My brother is attacking the wood with a vengeance.

"Hey," Dare says, bringing my focus back to him. "I'd like to ask another question."

I wait.

He smiles.

"Tell me why you haven't had a real boyfriend." It's an instruction, not a question. It, of course, causes me to blush yet again, a wild crimson that spreads like fire to my chest. Dare shakes his head.

"Don't be embarrassed. I quite like it, really. I'm just curious as to how you've remained an undiscovered treasure."

God, I love the way he talks, so British and so refined.

I shrug. "I've always been Funeral Home Girl, remember? No one ever wanted to get close enough to know me. The mere fact that I live in a funeral home with my crazy brother is enough to creep them out."

"That can't be true," Dare argues. "You're beautiful. Teenage boys never think anything through logically. They think with the crotch of their pants, and their crotch would react to you. Trust me."

Oh, I do. Especially when I remember how his crotch had reacted to me yesterday. A flood of feminine power and lust spreads through me suddenly, like a wave, and I want to crest on it forever. But I don't. I turn my attention back to Dare and shrug again.

"I guess they hid it well, then, because I was pretty much ostracized. It's ok. Don't worry about me. I'm leaving here, remember? I'll never have to see them again, and neither will my brother."

My brother.

I glance toward the woodshed and I'm surprised to find him gone. I scan the trail and the beach, and I don't see him there, either. Maybe he went to shower.

I look at Dare. "What about you? Have you had any serious girlfriends?"

Surely so.

He shrugs, downplaying any role they might've played in his life. "Oh, there have been girls," he concedes.

I raise an eyebrow. "So you're a player?"

He laughs. "I plead the fifth."

I gaze at him. "You're not American. I'm not sure our constitution applies to you."

He laughs again.

"What's your favorite color?" he asks, instead of answering.

"Viridem," I answer immediately. "Green. It means life. I like that."

Dare nods. "I like that too. And I like that you know Latin."

I smile because of our thrust and parry game. "Finn knows Latin," I correct him. "I've just picked a few things up from him."

"Why does he love Latin so much?"

I shake my head, checking the trail for Finn again, but he's not there.

"He wants to be a doctor. A Psychologist, really. Latin is the base for medical terminology, so I guess he figures he'll get a jump start."

"Smart," Dare nods.

I have to agree. "Finn is brilliant," I tell him. "Truly."

"You're not just saying that because you're twins?" Dare teases. I shake my head.

"Nah. He's way smarter than me."

"I doubt that," Dare parries. "You seem rather brilliant yourself."

"Not smart enough to stay away from you," I answer without thinking about it. Dare almost rears his head back.

"Where did that come from?" he stares at me, his eyes wide.

I honestly don't know.

"I guess I'm just frustrated with your 'wait and see' mentality," I mumble. Dare cocks his head.

"Patience isn't a virtue of yours?"

I shake my head. "Unfortunately, no."

"But good things come to those who wait," Dare points out.

"I'm not ketchup," I thrust back. He looks at me in confusion.

"That was an old ketchup slogan a few years ago."

He shakes his head. "Americans. You do love your condiments."

I hear a car crunching in the gravel of the drive, and I glance around Dare to see my father pulling the hearse around.

"Ugh. There's a funeral today. You might want to vacate the place, if you don't want to be surrounded by tears."

Dare looks unconcerned as he takes a slug of coffee.

"Want to give me a tour of Astoria?" he asks casually, standing up and stretching. I'm distracted once again by the flat ribbon of his abdomen that shows as his shirt lifts up.

201

He catches me looking and grins. "My abs will be coming too," he adds arrogantly.

I roll my eyes.

"Are you trying to bribe me?"

His dark eyes meet mine. "I'll do whatever it takes. I'll go shirtless if you want."

My heart couldn't take that.

It's suddenly hard to swallow and I need a distraction. And I need to get away from the impending funeral.

"Okay," I agree. "Let's go. But only if you drive. With a shirt on."

"Done," he says triumphantly.

Only I'm the triumphant one a few minutes later as I wrap my arms around his waist and we glide down the mountain. The front of my body is pressed to his back, and we fit like perfectly placed puzzle pieces.

I take him to my favorite coffee shop first, where we sit outside and sip at espresso for a bit. We're sitting in the shade and the morning breeze is actually chilly, so when Dare notices my shiver, he lays his arm around the back of my chair and I snuggle into his arm.

I want to stay like this for the rest of the day, or perhaps even forever, but within twenty minutes, Dare stares down at me.

"What next, tour guide?"

I sigh.

"You're a punishing task-master."

But with my arms wrapped around him again on the back of his bike, I can hardly call it punishment.

"I want to see where you went to school," he calls back to me over the wind. So I direct him to Astoria High. He pulls up in front, and I only wish that my old classmates were here to witness Calla Price riding on the back of Dare DuBray's motorcycle. Victory would be mine, because he's leaps and bounds sexier than any of them could ever dream of being.

But it's summer, so no one is here to see.

Dare steps away from the bike and pulls his helmet off, the breeze ruffling his dark hair. He's absurdly handsome as he appraises the school, his hand shielding his eyes from the sun.

"So this is the fabled place of torment?"

I nod. "Unfortunately."

Dare glances at me. "It's just a building, Calla. It can't hurt you."

"The people inside can," I point out, the scars of their words imprinted in my memory. "Words can harm people every bit as much as a weapon."

He nods. "I know. But what happens as you get older, is that you realize that the people in high school were never very important to you in the first place. They're just stupid kids who don't know anything. You'll go on and do great things, and they'll stay here in this little town and do nothing. You'll win."

I stare at him. "And how exactly do you know that?"

He shrugs. "It's just math. I read a study once that said over half of the population will never move more than twenty miles from their hometown. There's not a lot of brilliant opportunity here, I'm guessing. So your classmates who stay will never save the world or anything."

"And I will?" my voice is sharp.

Dare doesn't flinch. "You'll change *someone's* world. I am positive of that."

My nether regions flood with warmth because I think he means himself. But then my blood turns ice cold with a realization. If I change anyone's world, it will be Finn's, so I doubt I'll have time to change Dare's too. I'm not talented enough to do both.

I'm feeling dejected about that as I turn around and gaze at the faded red bricks of my school, at the doors that I dreaded walking through every morning for four years.

I'm startled when the principal walks through them now.

He's startled to see me, too.

"Ms. Price," he says quickly, and crosses the walk toward me. I'm not used to seeing him in casual clothes, so his shorts and polo shirt throw me off.

"Hi Mr. Payne." The irony of his name is not lost on me.

"How are you doing?" he asks, his tone both warm and nervous. I get it. No one knows what to say to someone who has lost a loved one. It's a hard situation. "You've been in my thoughts a lot lately, Calla. My wife has asked me several times if I know how you're doing."

"I'm fine," I lie. "We're hanging in there."

"And your father?" he asks.

"He's doing as well as can be expected," I tell him. "I'll tell him you asked about him."

"Well, this is a small community, Calla. Everyone hated to hear of your loss. If you need anything, for college or for anything else, you just let me know."

I nod and he hurries away to his car as though he can't get away from me fast enough.

"Ugh," I shake my head. "He's all about helping now, but he never raised one finger when Finn kept getting shoved into lockers our freshman year by the football team. Or when they de-pants him our junior year. Or all of the times in between. And he can't even bring himself to directly ask about him now. They think he's crazy and not worth their time. It disgusts me. This whole town disgusts me."

I turn away for the bike and Dare grabs my arm, forcing me to pause.

"I understand your anger, Calla. But do me a favor, ok? One of the most beautiful things about you is your spirit. It's refreshing... to me, and to anyone else who sees it. So don't let anything make you ugly, ok?"

His words are so honest that they freeze me in my tracks, making me realize something. I can't let them make me as ugly as they are. I nod slowly.

"You're right, I guess. I can't fix their small minds. So I can't let it affect me."

Dare nods. "Exactly. Wanna get out of here?"

"Yes." My answer is immediate.

We get back on his bike and tear off down the road, and I try very hard to leave my bitterness back at the school where it belongs.

We drive all the way to Cannon Beach on a seaside road. We hike down to Haystack Rock and stare at the ocean as we lean against the rocks. We marvel at how big it is, while we're so small.

On the horizon, a sailboat glides across the water, it's white sails billowing into the sky like clouds.

We both stare at it for a while, until it disappears from sight. Finally, Dare turns to me.

"After my mom died, someone gave me a poem to read, and it actually helped."

I stare at him, unconvinced. "A poem?"

He smirks. "I know. But yeah, it did. It was about a ship and how the ship doesn't lose it's value or it's usefulness or its *being* simply because it sails away out of sight. It's still as large and valuable, and it still exists, even though we can't see it. So, in a way, dying is like a ship that sails away for another destination."

I stare at him, and there's something big between us, something unsaid, but big all the same.

"I've read that one," I tell him. Because I live in a funeral home, I've read all the poems about death. "That's a good one. That's probably better than the dragonfly story that Finn told me."

Dare smiles a small smile and he doesn't ask to hear the story, but on the way back up to his bike, he grabs my hand and holds it. I don't pull away, I just savor the feel of his long fingers woven between my own.

We drive forty minutes back to Astoria with the taste of the sea on our lips and the feel of Dare's chest beneath my fingertips. It's a good ride, and I hate to see it drawing to an end as we idle through the streets of Astoria.

I especially hate when we idle toward Ocean's View Cemetery.

I look away from its wrought iron gates and brick columns, from the trees that weep along the shadowy lanes inside. Because I know, that at the back of the neatly lined plots, there's a large white angel standing over a white marble stone. LAURA PRICE lies there beneath the surface, eternally sleeping, forever gone from me.

I squeeze my eyes shut, and I must squeeze Dare, too, because he turns slightly.

"Are you ok?"

I nod against his back. "Yeah."

Lie.

Dare notices the cemetery, and I feel him tense a bit.

"You're surrounded by it here," he tells me, his voice as soft and quiet as it can be on the back of this bike. "In order to move forward, you have to move away."

I nod, because I know.

As I move my head, I open my eyes, and as I do, I notice something.

Finn.

Standing in the gates of the cemetery, watching us ride away.

He doesn't call out, he doesn't chase me, he doesn't even seem angry. But the expression is still there on his face... the expression that tells me I let him down. I told him I'd go with him to visit our mother, and I didn't. And because I didn't, he went alone.

I close my eyes.

28

VIGINTI OCTO

Finn

It'sTime.

The voices are insistent, more so than usual, more so than ever.

It'sTimeIt'sTimeIt'sTime.

Time for what?

I buzz along the road from the cemetery, up the mountain to my home, where I linger in the trees and watch my sister as she says goodbye to Dare and waits for me. I know she's waiting for me, because she always does.

And unless I do something, that's what she'll always do.

DoItDoItDoIt.

I suddenly know what to do, and I head along the path for the pier. It doesn't matter that she wouldn't go to the cemetery with me, because I know she would've tried if I'd forced the issue. She would've tried and she would've been miserable because she's not ready. I can't force her to be ready. It has to happen in order.

It has to happen in order.

There's an order.

It

Has

To

Happen

In

Order.

Sail away and don't come back, a voice hisses.
MakeHerSeeTheOrder.

Don't, another one argues.
ThisIsHerFaultHerFaultHerFault.

The voices argue and I let them, as I continue walking in the sea breeze toward the boat. I climb inside and lift the anchor.

29

VIGINTI NOVEM

Calla

When we get back home, I walk Dare to his house.

"Thank you for today," I tell him softly. "I needed to get away."

"You did," he agrees with me. "And you still do."

I swallow hard, because he's right. I do need to get away, far from death and Astoria and here. But more and more, I feel that I can't. I'll never be able to truly get away, because I can't leave Finn. Even if I follow him to MIT, I'll still be surrounded by this forever.

But I don't say that of course, because it's depressing and he'd simply argue.

So instead, I simply lean up and kiss Dare's perfectly chiseled cheek, wishing with all of my might that I could fold into his arms and he could comfort me and kiss me and hold me forever.

But I can't because we're *waiting.*

Waiting for me to work through something that can't be worked through.

Dare disappears inside and I wait on my porch for my brother.

My butt is stiff from the hard boards and I've slapped at a hundred mosquitoes when my father finally comes out and hands me a glass of lemonade.

"Whatcha doing out here?" he asks as I sip the tart liquid.

"Waiting for Finn," I tell him. "I saw him at the cemetery. He went alone. He's going to need to talk about it."

My dad looks pained and I know it's because he hasn't been there yet, either.

"Don't feel bad, dad," I say quickly. "I haven't actually been there yet, either. I just drove past. I couldn't make myself go in."

He nods slowly. "One of these days," he starts to say, then trails off. And I know that's gone in the One Of These Days file in his head.

I smile and pretend that he'll actually do it.

He leaves me alone and I wish for a second that he hadn't, because I'm lonely and I could use some company while I wait. From time to time, I think I see Dare's curtains move, like he's keeping an eye on me, but I'm probably imagining it.

The lemonade finally runs through me, and I duck inside to use the restroom. As I'm washing my hands, a glint of silver catches my attention on the counter.

Finn's St. Michael's medallion.

It's a small silver disk honoring St. Michael that my mother bought Finn for Christmas last year. We're not Catholic, but she loved the idea that it's supposed to give courage and keep the wearer out of harm's way. She knew that Finn needed that protection, for sure. He never takes it off. He even sleeps in it.

211

But here it is, lying on the bathroom counter.

I pick it up with shaking fingers.

Where is he?

I rush back out of the house, intent on asking Dare to drive me back into town to look for him when I glance down at the beach and I see that our boat is gone from the slip.

Since dad's in the house and Dare is in the cottage, there's only one person that could've taken it.

Finn.

I jog down the trail to the beach, and sit with my legs dangling on the pier. Because there's only one thing to do.

Wait.

I wait until my body is stiff, until the sun sinks low in the sky, and still Finn hasn't come back in. I start to get pissed actually, because he had to know I'd be worried.

He's doing this on purpose, I decide. To teach me a lesson.

Anger boils my blood and I stomp back up to the house where I slam a few things together in the kitchen to make my dad a sandwich.

He looks up at me in surprise. "What's wrong with you?"

"Finn took the boat out alone," I snap. "He's obviously mad at me."

My dad pats my shoulder. "He's been sailing for as long as you have. He's fine," is all he says. I want to grab his hand and snap it off because he's so involved in his own sadness that he can't see anyone else's.

"You don't know that," I snap at him again.

"I do," he says confidently. "He'll be fine."

I can't even stand to stay and eat with him, so I slam back out the door, but on my way an idea occurs to me, something I've never considered doing before.

I pause at my dad's bar.

And then I grab a bottle of gin, my father's drink of choice.

He's certainly been drinking it a lot these past weeks, trying to forget his pain and his issues. I can do it too. If it works for him, it'll work for me. I clutch the cool bottle in my fingertips as I jog down the porch steps.

I think I see the curtains of the Carriage House moving, and I think I feel Dare staring at me through the glass, but I don't stop. And I don't put the bottle down. They can all judge me. I don't care.

I deserve a respite from reality.

I slide down the trail, pad through the damp sand and sit on the pier with my bottle of gin. After a few minutes, I open it, and take a swig.

I almost immediately spit the vile liquid out, coughing as the fiery stuff blazes a trail down my throat and into my belly. I can feel the heat of it, peeling off the tissue of my esophagus and I want to hurl the rest of the bottle out to sea.

It's disgusting. How can anyone willingly drink it?

But as I wait for minutes, then an hour, then two, I pick the bottle back up.

I stare at the empty horizon, and take a swig, forcing it down. I stare at the stars, at freaking Andromeda and her stupid love story, and take a swig. And before long, after fifteen swigs, my belly feels warm and my memory feels fuzzy.

A blissful sense of foggy detachment envelops me, and I no longer feel my raw throat or taste the disgusting liquid.

I drink more and more, until I fall back on the pier and stare at the sky, enjoying the way the stars swirl and twirl around me, like I'm on a carousel and they're in mirrors.

I close my eyes for a minute, and my eyelids spin too, round and round, until I actually start to feel dizzy.

I open my eyes, and Dare is standing over me, leaning over the edge of my horizontal periphery.

I smile. I think.

He smiles back.

"How much have you had?" he asks ruefully, picking up the bottle and examining it. There's only a couple of slogs left and I graciously wave my hand.

"You can have the rest," I tell him, as though I'm bestowing a gift.

My words are slurred through, my tongue thick and heavy, and even though that's what I meant to say, it comes out at gibberish. I try again.

Still gibberish.

I stare at him helplessly and he chuckles.

"That much, then?"

He bends down and offers me his hand. I shake my head.

"I've gotta wait for Finn."

Which sounds more like, "Lesh gofur a schim."

Dare shakes his head. "I don't want to swim, thanks. We need to get you to the house before you pass out."

I know I should stay right here on this pier and wait for Finn. I know I should be more worried about my brother because it's dark and he's alone and he never stays out this late by himself, but the gin has accomplished one thing aside from rendering my tongue muscles useless.

It's made me carefree.

I don't have a care in the world right now, which is a blissful, amazing gift. No wonder my dad likes this stuff.

I let Dare hoist me up, and then I promptly collapse against him when my legs give out.

"Hi," I say to his chest. His marvelously amazingly sexy chest.

"Hi," it says back. "Let's go, Cal."

Dare's hands pull me under my armpits, and then suddenly, I'm in his arms, cradled like a baby as he walks all the way up the trail.

"I'm too heavy," I mumble into his shirt.

"You're not," his shirt answers.

He doesn't stumble, he doesn't falter, he simply grips me tight and makes the climb. He's barely breathing heavily when we get to the top.

I open my eyes and see three blurry outlines of the funeral home above me, the jagged edges of the roof poking into the night. They blur together, then apart, then back together again. I close my eyes against the sight.

"I don't want to go in there," I manage to say clearly.

Dare stares down at me, and I swear I see sympathy in his eyes.

"Don't feel sorry for me," I snap.

He doesn't answer. He just carries me down the path to his Carriage House.

He deposits me carefully on his sofa and leaves me for a second, then returns with a big glass of water and some aspirin.

"Take those," he instructs firmly. "And then drink all the water. Trust me, you'll thank me in the morning."

I do as he says and then wipe my mouth with the back of my hand, before pulling him down next to me.

"Where do you think Finn went?" I ask worriedly, even though the gin has mostly paralyzed my worry muscle. Dare stares down at me.

"He'll be fine. You on the other hand, are going to have a big hangover tomorrow. Have you ever drank anything before?"

I shake my head and he sighs.

"Well, you certainly chose to start with a bang. Gin will put hair on your chest."

"I like my chest the way it is," I try to say. I must succeed because Dare's eyes gleam.

"I do too," he admits softly. I grab his hand and pull it to me, sliding it along my side, where he clamps down his fingers.

"Will you kiss me?" I ask. "I liked it when you kissed me."

He sighs again. "I did too. But you're drunk."

"I'm drunk," I snap. "Not dead."

It's a sentiment that makes very little sense, but I don't hesitate. I just grab Dare's face and pull him to my own, my lips crushing his. He tastes like spearmint and I taste like gin. It's somehow an intoxicating combination, and with numbed fingers, I stroke the side of his stubbly jaw.

He doesn't pull away for a minute, but then he finally does.

"You're drunk," he says again.

"Correct," I slide into him, my face against his shoulder.

I pick up his hand, and wrap it around my back. "I like being here, with you," I tell him. "I like how you smell. I like how you kiss. And I like how you're beautiful."

Dare stares down at me, amusement shimmering in his eyes. "I'm beautiful, then?"

"Don't fish for compliments," I mutter. "You don't need them."

He grins. "Don't I?"

"I'd like for you to kiss me again," I announce, sitting up straight. I think.

"I can't," he says firmly. "You're drunk."

"I am," I agree. "Didn't we already establish that?"

The room spins a bit, but then rights itself, and I decide to take matters into my own hands. I collide against him, my chest smashed to his, as I kiss him.

I consume him, basically.

I kiss him hard, my need for him overwhelming everything else. His mouth is hot and at first he hesitates, then he kisses me back, his tongue plunging into my mouth. Clumsily, I run my hands down his chest, across his hips, and coming to a stop where his hardness bulges against me. My fingers brush against him and he sucks in his breath, absorbing my gasp. And then he yanks away.

"Jesus, Calla," he bites out, his voice harsh, his breathing ragged. He holds me away as I try to wiggle closer. "Seriously. I'm going to pour ice water on you."

I freeze, suddenly terrified of something.

"You don't want me, do you?"

Dare looks at the ceiling, apparently trying very hard to be patient.

Lifting my hand, he places it squarely onto his lap, where he strains against the crotch of his jeans, throbbing and hard.

"Does that seem like I don't want you?" he asks mildly, removing my hand, even though I desperately want to keep it there. "I'm looking out for you, even if you don't want me to."

"I don't want you to," I agree. "I just want you."

Dare looks at the ceiling again, but I see the tiniest hint of a flush along the curve of his cheekbone. He's struggling for self-control, I realize. The thought makes me smile, but then the room spins again, faster this time.

I slump into Dare, he pulls me up, and I immediately slump again.

"I like being drunk," I tell him, mumbling into his shirt. "I can't feel anything."

"You're gonna feel it in the morning," he assures me.

I somehow know he's right, because the room spins and spins, and my mouth suddenly fills up with spit.

"I'm gonna throw up," I realize. Dare grabs me up and rushes me to the bathroom. I kneel in front of the toilet and retch and retch and retch.

The gin, if possible, tastes worse coming up than going down.

That's saying something.

Cool hands pull my hair away from my face as I vomit, holding it back and I wave my hand.

"Go away," I mumble in between heaves.

"You're fine," Dare says comfortingly, patting my back with one hand as he holds my hair with the other. "You're fine."

I'm not fine. I'm dying. I'm vomiting up every last vestige of food that I've consumed in the past four years. Of that, I am sure. And still I heave. Until there's nothing left and then I heave some more.

Finally, I curl up on the floor, my face pressed against the cool tiles.

Nothing has ever felt better than this, I decide, loving each and every one of the cool porcelain tiles with a blinding and personal passion.

I close my eyes and keep them closed, even though I feel myself being moved. My pants are tugged off, though my shirt is left on and I'm floundering around like a rag doll. And better yet, I don't care.

Cool sheets are pulled up around me, and I don't bother opening my eyes. The only thing I know is that the sheets smell like Dare...woodsy and male. In this moment, that's all that matters.

When I open my eyes again, it takes a minute to focus, but then I see the moonlight shining against the wall. It's the middle of the night.

My mouth is dry, like wood or sawdust, and I swallow hard.

I'm in Dare's bed.

Dare. DuBray's. Bed.

It's a thought that takes a minute to register, and then I register too, that unfortunately, Dare DuBray isn't in his bed.

I scan the room, and he's not in here at all.

So I get up, wrapping the sheet around me, and pad into his living room. He's sprawled out on his couch, completely clothed and dead asleep.

In sleep, his face is vulnerable and bathed in moonlight. I stare at him for a long time, because when he's awake, I don't get this luxury. I only turn away when I start to feel dizzy again, when my head begins to pound and pound and I finally grasp what he meant when he said that I'd feel it tomorrow.

It's not tomorrow yet, but I certainly feel it now.

I cross the room as something jackhammers the back of my head, and I dig through the cabinet over the stove to find more aspirin. I find them, take several, and wobble back to the living room.

I'm standing above Dare watching him again when he opens his eyes.

His beautiful onyx eyes.

"I don't want to be alone," I murmur.

He doesn't say anything, he simply opens his arms.

I lay down in front of him and he closes his arms around me, shielding me from the night. This is how I fall asleep, cradled against his chest and listening to his heartbeat.

In the morning, the sunlight wakes me up while Dare still sleeps.

It takes me a second to remember where I am, how I'd gotten drunk last night, how I'd thrown myself at Dare and then thrown up in front of him.

I'm dying of humiliation as I glance up at the windows, at the door, and then I freeze.

Finn is staring inside, a look of horror on his tired face. He's still dressed in the clothes he was wearing from yesterday, which make me believe he's only just now getting in.

I'm sprawled in Dare's arms, wrapped in a sheet, and I realize how it must look.

Finn has the entirely wrong idea.

I scramble up to tell him, I throw open the door, but he's already gone.

30

TRIGENTA

I chase Finn up to my room where he's waiting for me, sitting calmly on my bed, his shoes muddy from the beach.

"It's not what it looked like," I tell him quickly, although I still have Dare's sheet wrapped around my waist because my shorts are in his bedroom.

Finn shakes his head and looks out the window. "I don't care what you were doing with him, Cal. It's not my business. I'm your brother, not your keeper."

"But I'm *your* keeper," I snap back. "And you went out alone yesterday. What the hell were you dong?"

"I needed some alone time," he says quietly, still looking out the window. "After the cemetery, I mean."

That causes me to pause, which was his intention. "I'm sorry," I say simply, my hands still clutching the sheet. "I should've been there with you. I let you go alone. I'm so sorry, Finn."

He shrugs with his skinny shoulders, his arms pale in the morning light. "It's fine, Calla. You aren't ready yet. I get it."

"But I should still have gone for you," I argue. "I'm sorry. Do you want to go back today? Because I will. If you need to go again, I will."

Finn looks at me sadly. "You need to go for *you,* Cal. But you're not ready. It'll happen in layers... in order. I promise."

He's talking nonsense, which worries me. "You're taking your meds, right?" I ask him worriedly. He nods.

"Please stop worrying about me, Cal. I'm fine."

"You're not." I can't help but take in his wrinkled clothes, pale skin, dark circles around his eyes. "You're not sleeping again. Your hands are shaking. We've got to get you some help. I'm going to talk to dad."

Finn's arm snakes out faster than I can blink and grabs mine. "Don't," he says quickly. "Please. We'll handle this on our own, Calla. You and me, just like always."

And I want to tell him that it's not fair to me, that this weight is too heavy, that it's too much responsibility, but of course I don't. Because we're Calla-and-Finn and that's how it's always been, and that's how it will always be.

I finally just nod. "Ok. I won't tell him."

I glance at him again and remember that he's not wearing his St. Michael's medallion.

"You took your necklace off," I tell him, trying not to sound accusatory. He looks away and shrugs.

"I decided I don't need it anymore. You can have it, if you want."

I stare at him, my mouth open. "You haven't taken that thing off since you got it, because mom liked the idea that you're protected when you wear it."

His icy blue gaze impales me. "Mom's not here anymore, Calla."

I swallow and it hurts. "I know that," I answer, the words raspy. He nods.

"Good. So you can have it if you want it." He gets to his feet wearily and my heart explodes into a puff of dust.

"I've gotta shower," he says quietly and leaves without another word.

I'm quiet as I stare out the window, staring at the ocean. Boats glide on the horizon and I can't help but wish I was on one, floating far, far away from here.

But if that were the case, I'd be sailing away from Dare. And I can't do that. Not now.

I shower and brush my teeth, then lock my bedroom door before pulling out Finn's journal. Curled up in my window, I force myself to read the words because I've been putting it off and now is the time. Turning the mysterious tarot card over and over in my fingers, I stare at the weird symbol and Finn's words.

DEATH IS THE BEGINNING.
MORS SOLUM INITIUM EST.
THE BEGINNING BEGINNING BEGINNING
BEGINNING
I NEED TO START

I startle as I read the scratched words, the ink ground into the paper like Finn had used all of his strength. He needs to start what?

A new beginning?

Or death?

My heart pounds hard against my ribcage as I mark my place with the tarot card, cram the journal back between the mattresses and clatter down the steps.

"Have you seen Finn?" I ask my father when I meet him on the stairs.

"No," he answers. "Are you ok?"

"Yes," I sigh because I'm so sick of him asking. "I just need to find Finn."

I find him where I always find him lately, down by the woodshed, chopping wood. More wood, although we have fifteen piles already.

"Why do you keep doing this?" I ask him hesitantly. I approach him slowly so I don't startle him because he's holding an ax, after all.

He looks up at me, the light shining in his pale blue eyes.

"The exercise burns stress."

"Ok," I answer. "Finn, you'd tell me if you were feeling really bad, right? Like, you wouldn't do anything stupid?"

His forehead wrinkles and he leans against the ax handle. "Stupid like what, Cal? What are you talking about?"

I sigh because he knows what I'm saying, he's just trying to make me say the words.

"You wouldn't try to hurt yourself, would you?"

The words taste hateful and awful, but I ask them anyway.

Finn stares at me seriously.

"Calla, if I wanted to hurt myself, I wouldn't try. I'd just *do*." But when I start to cry out, he hurriedly continues. "But no. I don't want to hurt myself."

I stare at him, desperately wanting to believe him, but so sure he's lying.

"I think you should go to Group today," I tell him slowly, gauging his reaction.

He shrugs. "Ok. I was planning on it anyway."

"Yeah?" I raise an eyebrow.

"Yeah," he answers firmly. "Let me finish here and then take a shower."

He splits another piece of wood and tosses it into a new pile. I shake my head as I walk to the house. Dad will have enough wood to last five winters.

I hesitate at the porch, playing with the idea of going to talk to Dare, but as I stand there trying to decide, I see him pacing back and forth behind the cottage, talking animatedly on his cell phone. He paces up, waves his hands, his face set in stone, then he paces back, doing the same thing.

He glances up and sees me, and his dark eyes hold mine for just a moment, black, black, black as night, then he turns his back and paces away.

Who is he talking to so intently?

Questions swirl around me as return to my room to fold up Dare's sheet so that I can take it back to him later. Who is he talking to? For that matter, as long as I'm asking questions, who is Dare here to visit? He'd said he was visiting someone in the hospital. He never said who, and he never said why he wanted to rent an apartment here when he lives in England. I've been so wrapped up in my own stuff and in my own fascination with Dare himself, that I've never asked.

That's going to end today.

I wait patiently for thirty minutes because that's got to be enough time to wrap up a conversation.

I take the sheet and knock on Dare's door.

He opens it immediately and looks devastatingly handsome in a snug dark shirt that complements his dark eyes.

"Hey," he greets me. "You look like you feel better."

"Thank you for taking care of me last night," I tell him, flushing a bit. It's embarrassing that he saw me puke my guts up. "I'm a bit humiliated."

"Don't be," he says politely, oddly formal considering I slept all night in his arms. He doesn't make any kind of move to invite me in, but instead stands planted in the middle of the doorway.

"Well, I am," I answer back in confusion. "Is something wrong? I can't help but notice that we're still standing on the porch."

He shakes his head. "Of course not. I'm just a bit busy at the moment."

He's so cool and detached, sort of aloof. I stare at him, not sure what to say.

"Did you need something?" he prompts me, his eyes glinting in the light.

"I...yeah," I stammer. I thrust the sheet at him. "I just came to give this back to you. And to get my shorts."

"Sure. Hang on."

And I swear to God, he closes the door in my face. I'm still stunned when he re-emerges a few minutes later with my shorts.

"Here you go," he hands them to me.

I stare at him, never more confused in my life.

"Are you sure nothing's wrong?"

His face seems to soften for a minute, then it smooths back into an unreadable mask. "Yeah, I'm sure. I'm just busy. I'm sorry."

"It's ok," I say slowly. "I'll just catch up with you later." I turn to leave, but pause, turning half-way on the sidewalk.

"Hey, you never said who you were here in Astoria to visit," I tell him slowly, watching his face for a reaction. "You said you were visiting someone in the hospital, but you never said who."

He doesn't miss a beat. He simply nods. "I didn't, did I?"

And he doesn't offer it now.

I wait, but there's nothing. He just steps back inside his house.

"I'll talk to you later, Calla."

And then he closes the door.

I'm absolutely stunned as I stare at the wood, frozen on the path.

Everyone has secrets, Calla. That's what he told me and I guess it's truer than I realized. The question is, are his secrets important? Should I care about them? Because I've got so much to worry about already.

But his contradictions confuse me. His want and his detachment confuse me. His hot blood and cold attitude confuse me. Over the past week, he's anchored me amid all of this crazy. Is it possible that he just doesn't want to be that anchor anymore?

My chest feels numb with the thought, because somehow, I've come to depend on him already. I depend on him to make me smile, to lift me out of this mire into a world where hope survives.

But he just closed a door in my face and I can't help but wonder if it was a metaphor for something bigger.

I try and put it out of my mind as I wait for Finn, then drive him into Group. All I can do right now is keep going through the motions, keep my head above water.

Dare doesn't define me.

That's going to have to become my new mantra.

I fall sleep with that thought in my head, with the very best of intensions. But I'm awakened at three a.m.

Piano music plays softly, filtering through the house.

Startled, I sit up in bed and look at the clock again.

Yes, it's the middle of the night.

No, the piano shouldn't be playing.

I pad down the stairs toward the chapel and with each step, the soft music gets a little louder. When I hit the bottom step, the music stops. Silence seems to echo loudly in my ears as I rush down the hall and round the corner into the room.

The piano seat is empty.

Stunned, I walk numbly to the front, trailing my finger along the empty piano bench.

I know it was playing. I know it's what woke me. The lid to the keys is open, which is unusual. It's usually closed when it's not in use.

And then I smell it.

The barest hint of Dare's cologne.

My heart in my throat, I look out the window, to see a lamp turned on in his cottage.

He's still up. He'd been here.

Somehow I know, without anyone having to tell me, that he still wants me as much as I want him, regardless of how cool he'd acted earlier. I don't know his reasons, and I don't know his secrets.

But I know one thing as I collapse onto the seat of the piano.

Even though he tried, he couldn't stay away.

31

TRIGENTA UNUS

Calla

In the morning, I want to go see Dare. But at the same time, I don't want to be desperate. I don't want to play games.

The memory of his piano music drifting through my house last night buoys me, though, keeps me from panicking.

He's trying to do an honorable thing. I feel it in my bones. And just as much, I feel the connection to him, loud and strong, tugging and tugging me toward him. I know he feels it too. And because of that, I can't let myself worry.

It'll work out. It has to.

So with a last glance over my shoulder, I walk away from his door, certain that I'll see him sooner rather than later.

With the sun shining on my shoulders, I decide to take a walk.

I wind through the trails, working my way up toward the cliffs rather than down toward the sea.

When I get to the top, I'm surprised to find Finn sitting too close to the edge.

Startled, I stop, my pink chucks freezing in place.

Finn's black ones dangle over the side and he kicks his feet casually, not looking one bit concerned that the edge could break away at any moment.

"Finn," I say slowly, trying not to startle him, "Move away from the edge."

He looks over his shoulder at me, unconcerned. "Hey, Cal. Did you know that nutmeg is incredibly deadly if it's injected?"

This freezes me, too.

"You don't know that firsthand, right?" I stare at him, examining his arms for injection marks.

He rolls his eyes. "You know I hate nutmeg."

I can't breathe. "I also know you're sitting too close to the edge. Move back. Carefully."

He doesn't move, and I see tiny balls of clay rolling around him, dropping off the edge. My heart pounds in my ears.

"Want to go to the lighthouse today?" he asks, like he didn't even hear me. He stares out over the water toward the beacon, watching the gulls fly around it.

"Yeah," I tell him quickly. "Let's go right now."

With another shrug, Finn clumsily gets to his feet, one of his shoes breaking off a piece of the edge. It plunges over the side, but Finn doesn't even notice. He just walks to me like sitting on a cliff is the most natural thing in the world, like he is completely oblivious to the danger.

I throw my arms around him and hug him tight.

"What is wrong with you?" I whisper into his neck, inhaling his sweaty skin. "Why would you do that?"

"Do what?" he asks innocently. "I just wanted a good view."

"You know it's dangerous." I pull away and stare into his eyes. "You know that."

"And you know that I was far enough back to be safe."

He tells me the same thing I told him the other day, only it's not true in his case.

"You were on the edge," I tell him shakily. To that, he shrugs.

"I still am."

He walks away down the trail, whistling a tune that sends goose-bumps down my spine. The song that Dare played on the piano last night.

He heard it. He knew Dare was in the house and it upset him. That's what this has to be about.

I skid down the trail to catch up.

"Are you upset because I'm close with Dare now? Because you have to know that you're the most important thing to me, Finn. You'll always be the most important thing. No matter what."

He pauses and looks back at me.

"Calla, you're overthinking this. Nothing is wrong with me. I'm not mad at you."

And then he continues on his way.

I trip along side of him, trying to stay calm, and I do a very good job of it, too, until we walk halfway up the beach, and I see something silver glinting in the sand. Jogging ahead, I bend down and pick up Finn's St. Michael's medallion.

Speechless, I let it dangle in my fingers while Finn catches up.

"Why did you throw this out?" I demand. "I get that you don't want to wear it right now, but this was a gift from mom. She gave it to you, Finn. You can't just throw it out."

He shrugs and I'm getting tired of all his shrugs.

"If you want it, you can have it," he tells me nonchalantly and I want to scream.

"I don't want it. I want *you* to want it. It's yours. *Our dead mother gave it to you.* You should want it."

I'm practically yelling now, and Finn doesn't flinch, and doesn't react at all. He just stares at me, with his pale blue eyes the same color as the sky.

"But I don't," he says lightly. I stay frozen in place, the necklace clutched in my hand while Finn walks out onto a rock walkway and sits staring out at the water. He's quiet, he's pensive, and something is most certainly wrong.

I feel it in my bones, in my heart, in the hidden and dark place where a twin knows.

So I do the only thing I can.

I've got to get help from a professional, from someone who Finn tells the things he won't tell me.

I rush back home and climb in my car. I drive down the mountain, through town and to the hospital. When I get there, I shove the medallion in my pocket. God knows I can't give it back to Finn. He's likely to throw it out and I'll never find it again.

I walk numbly through the halls, past the abstract bird painting and into the Group room. I'm interrupting a session and everyone turns to stare at me curiously. Jason, the therapist, gets up and crosses the room. He's short and blond, and his steps are long. He reaches me quickly.

"Calla," he says, assessing my face. "Is everything all right?"

With his arm on my elbow, he leads me into the hallway, so I don't instill panic into his precious patients.

"There's something wrong with Finn," I tell him abruptly. "I can't figure it out, and he won't tell me. Do you know?"

Jason stares at me, his hand patting my back, as he tries to figure out how to calm down a frantic woman. I'm annoyed, because like my father and his grieving clients, Jason is supposed to know how to handle upset people. He's a therapist, for God's sake.

Finally, he shakes his head. "I don't know, Calla. He hasn't said anything to me. But even if he had, you know I can't share that with you. It's confidential."

"Even if he's a danger to himself?" I demand. "He was on the edge of the cliffs this morning. And then he told me that *he* was on the edge and it wasn't a metaphor, Jason. He's in serious trouble. His hands have been shaking and I'm afraid he's stopped taking his meds. Has he said anything to you?"

Jason hesitates, then stares seriously into my eyes.

"I can't say. But what I *can* say is that Finn hasn't been to group in weeks."

Those words slam into me with the weight of a freight train and I stand limply in front of the therapist.

"Weeks?" The word scrapes my lungs. "That's impossible. I've been driving him myself."

Jason shakes his head regretfully. "You might be driving him here, but he's not coming in. I'm sorry, Calla."

He's sorry. My brother is losing it, and his therapist is sorry.

My blood boils and I whirl around.

"Why didn't you tell someone?" I demand before I walk away. "You're supposed to be helping him, for God's sake.

It's no wonder Finn always calls out for me. I'm the only one he can count on.

I storm through the hospital and slam my car door hard enough to shatter the half-open driver's side window.

I'm covered in pellets of safety glass as I sit hunched over the steering wheel.

Perfectus.

To make matters worse, because it's Oregon, it starts to rain as I drive. I lean away from the door as the rain blows the precipitation in. By the time I get home, I'm drenched.

I slam the car door again, as hard as I can.

It echoes through the yard, or so I imagine.

I take the stairs three at a time, and before long, I'm standing in front of my father again. He's startled by my drowned rat appearance.

"I just came from the hospital," I tell him harshly. "Finn hasn't been going to Group. So if you weren't worried before, you should be now."

My father stares at me blankly, something that infuriates me.

"Dad, you've got to live in the present right now. I know you're sad. I know you have gin in that coffee cup." He looks at his glass and then looks up me guiltily. "Did you wonder why your open bottle was gone the other night? It's because I drank it and you didn't even notice. Dare cleaned me up and took care of me, not you."

My father looks horrified and appalled but I don't pause.

"Finn needs you. He needs you right now."

My father's head drops and he stares at his hands, at the mug in his hands. "I'm sorry, Calla. I'm sorry that you think I've checked out. I haven't. I love you, and I love Finn."

My heart softens at the sight of his broken expression. "I know," I tell him softly. "I'm sorry I'm so angry. I'm just... Finn. I'm worried about Finn."

"I know," he tells me. "We'll figure it out. I promise."

"Do you know where he is?" I ask as I head toward the stairs.

"No."

I don't turn back around, I just leap up the stairs. Finn's not there. Not in his bedroom or mine or on the top floor at all. I go back downstairs and search every room, even the Visitation rooms. He's simply not here.

As I stand in the kitchen, trying to figure out where he might've gone, my attention is drawn to a pad of paper lying on the counter.

One word is scrawled over and over.

NOCTE.

And with that, I know where I have to go.

32

TRIGENTA DUO

I clatter down the porch steps, just in time to see Dare emerging from his cottage.

Like always, he's dressed in slim dark jeans and a snug t-shirt. He's heading for his bike and he looks like he's going to continue on his way, until he notices my face. His eyes narrow as he sees my state of distress. He immediately changes course and heads for me.

"What's wrong?" he asks in concern, his hand reaching for mine.

I pull away. "Oh, now you're worried about that?" I can't help but ask. The emotions of the day are threatening to overwhelm me.

He shakes his head. "Don't do that. I've already explained. Everything is just complicated."

I swallow hard. "Finn's gone. I can't find him. I think he went to Nocte."

Dare nods toward his bike without hesitation. "Then let's go."

We pull on helmets and are on the road within a minute. My arms wrap around his waist like they belong there, and I suddenly realize that they do. My arms belong wrapped around this man, no matter what. No matter what secrets he might have, or what might be going on with me.

237

When I'm upset, he calms me. When I'm breathless, he gives me air. When I'm sad, he buoys me. That's all that matters, right?

I decide that soon, I'll sit down and tell him all of these things.

But not right now. Because right now, I have to find Finn.

We pull right up outside the hole in the fence and then we duck through it.

I take off at a run through the park, headed straight for the old house of horrors. Dare runs with me, easily keeping pace.

"There isn't a car here," he points out to me as we jog. Our wet shoes squeak on the midway.

I know his point is logical, but I know in my heart that Finn is here.

I know like a sister knows, like a twin.

I don't deviate from my path, and within a couple of minutes, I'm standing on the porch of Nocte, bent over to catch my breath.

Dare runs his hand up and down my back, relaxing my muscles as my lungs fill with air. He's my air. I give him a grateful look, then push forward, through the door and into the abandoned house.

I hadn't thought to bring a flashlight this time, but luckily, enough light shines through the dirty windows that we can see where we're going.

"Finn!" I call out as I race along, over the electric cords and through the rooms. "Where are you?"

There's no answer. But I still feel him here.

"He's here," I tell Dare over my shoulder. "I know it. We have to find him before he hurts himself."

Dare nods and we race along the darkened pathways, into the part of the house that I hadn't shown Dare before.

I stop in the middle of a dusty parlor. An empty noose swings from the chandelier above, while gargoyle's faces leer from the sides of the fireplace. I feel an instant air of relief that Finn isn't hanging from the rope. Shivering, I scan the place. Once upon a time, a "rotting" butler walked through this room, scaring visitors as they passed through. The room is empty now.

"He's not here," Dare tells me needlessly.

My shoulders drop and my breath exhales and I sink into a dusty velvet sofa.

"Where is he?" my voice is frail and threatens to break.

Dare sits next to me, his arm around my shoulders and I turn into his chest because all of a sudden, I can't keep it together. The weight of it is too heavy.

All of the emotions I've been feeling lately come crashing down. The desperation of wanting to help my brother, the rejection I've felt from Dare, the anger I've felt toward my father. It spirals around me, too much to bear, and I sob into Dare's shirt.

His hands are large as he comforts me, as he pats my back and strokes my shoulder.

I feel comfort here in his arms, unlike any comfort I've ever felt before.

He's mine. No matter what happens, I can't lose him.

The fear of that loss, even though it's imagined, floods me and I grab him.

"I can't lose you, too," I tell him, my voice still strained. "I'm sorry that I can't seem to hold things together. I promise I'll get a handle on things. If you promise to stay." I pause and there's silence and I stare at him. "Promise me, Dare."

He looks at me oddly, and presses a kiss to my forehead. "Promise."

His voice is so husky, and it strokes my skin. And it's not enough. With shaking hands, I reach for him, pulling him to me and his mouth, hot and minty, closes over my own.

He kisses me with abandon, like he's not afraid of the consequences, like it's only him and me, and there's nothing else around us. There is no Finn, there is no funeral home, there is no grief.

There is only Dare and Calla.

I inhale it, breathing it in my throat, and holding it deep inside by my heart.

He starts to pull away, but I stop him with a whisper.

"Please don't. I need you. Make it all right. Please. Make it all right."

My whisper is broken and desperate, but I don't care. Because it gets me what I want. Dare clutches me to him, his hands stroking me everywhere, lingering over my hips, my arms, my ribs, my breasts.

My hips lift to meet him, my pelvis crushing his. But it's an exquisite pressure, something that builds and builds within me, begging for an eruption, screaming for a release.

"Please."

I whisper one more time.

Dare groans, and touches me again, his fingers finding me in the dark, long and smooth and cool. I clutch his shoulders, trying to get closer and closer, but I know I'll never be close enough. Even when he's finally inside of my body, it won't be enough. Because I want all of him.

Now.

I pull at the button on his jeans, at his shirt, at his arms.

And he almost lets me.

Almost.

But then, with a ragged breath, he pulls away.

I reach for him, but he shakes off my arm.

"Give me a minute, Cal."

I sit trying to breathe, as he does the same.

All I can hear is our raspy breath as we breathe and breathe, until finally, Dare looks at me again.

"I'm sorry for that."

I'm incredulous. "For what? For doing what I want?"

He shakes his head. "Don't you understand? You're completely beside yourself over your brother. Do you really want to have sex in in a house of horrors while you're crying over Finn?"

"Isn't that up to me?" I ask shakily, trying to reach for him again, because *I need him.* He won't let me, though.

"No," he finally answers. "Not today. You're not thinking clearly."

"I'm thinking clearly enough," I answer firmly, but I don't move toward him again. His face is set and determined.

"Why do you have to be such a gentleman?" I demand. "Is this a British thing?"

He chuckles, able to laugh now. "I guess it's just a Dare thing."

I roll my eyes and rub the chill away.

He stares at me hard. "Calla, when we... when this happens, it's not going to be in a house of horrors. It's going to be something you remember."

I look away, annoyed. "Shouldn't that be my choice to make?"

He smiles, humoring me. "I'm trying to help you make a good choice here, Cal. Work with me."

I can't help but chuckle too because he's trying to help me, in spite of myself.

"Most guys would've jumped at that, no matter what," I tell him snarkily as we climb to our feet.

Dare pauses, his eyes oh-so-dark. "But those guys don't love you. I do."

I'm completely frozen, completely still as that sinks in.

"You do?" I breathe.

He nods. "More every day. You're like no one I've ever met. We're not going to rush this, Cal. Good things come to those who wait, remember?"

And with those simple words, every single problem I have floats away, off of my neck, off of my chest. I don't even roll my eyes over the ketchup reference.

Dare loves Calla.

It's impossible. But it's real.

My feet and heart are light as we walk back to the door, and just when we're stepping out into the light, I see something, something fluttering against the porch railing.

A red ticket.

I bend down and grab it, curious.

Quid Quo Pro.

"This is Finn's favorite band," I tell Dare. "He was at their concert the night mom died."

I turn around and stare at him, confusion rippling through me. Confusion, then realization.

"He was here, after all."

Dare guides my elbow toward the steps.

"Well, he's not here now."

I can't argue with that.

I stuff the ticket in my pocket and we make our way home.

33

TRIGENTA TRES

Finn

The rain pelting me by the ocean is cold, and the wind blows it into my eyes.

IgnoreItIgnoreIt.

I do. But I try and ignore the voices too. It's the story of my life.

They woke me up from my nap and I know what I have to do.

It'sAlmostTimeAlmostTimeAlmostAlmostAlmost.

Yeah, I have to agree. It's almost time.

I've hidden the secret for so long, it's eating at me, clawing to get out and I almost can't keep it inside anymore.

I grip the St. Michael's medallion firmly in my hand and walk into the water, straight out without pause.

DoItDoItDOITDoItDo.

~~Do it.~~

I dive under the waves and swim straight down. It's at least twenty feet down and the water grows murky before I see the faded red paint of the car. I swim to it, my oxygen already starting to run out, and stick my head through the open passenger door.

Reaching my hand in, I hang the necklace on the rearview mirror. It dangles in the water, twisting and turning in the murk.

St. Michael's face seems to mock me.

Protect me? I think not.

My lungs feel hot and swollen, so I push off, away from the car toward the surface. I burst through with a cough, the sun on my face as though I'd never left.

~~Breathe.~~

I do. I take deep hacking breaths and then pull myself out of the water onto the damp sand of the beach. I look back out at the choppy surface.

No one would ever know what lies beneath that water.

You can't see it.

But I know.

I know.

I know.

I know.

But Calla doesn't.

34

TRIGENTA QUATUOR

Calla

When we get home, Finn is in bed. I stand at his doorway and watch him sleep for a minute, watching the restless way he tosses and turns and moans, and the way he's got mud smeared on his cheek.

What's he been up to?

With utter trepidation, I know how to find out.

I curl up in my room and stare at the pages of his journal. For some reason, I can't bring myself to read much at a time. The words press down on me, suffocating me, because it's such a glaring piece of evidence of what Finn's mind has come to be.

The writing has become erratic, as his thought processes spiral to and fro. Scrawled, scratched words line the pages and they no longer make any kind of sense.

PROTECT HER PROTECT ME ST. MICHAEL.
PROTECT US HER ME ME ME.
SERVA ME, SERVA BO TE. SAVE ME, SAVE HER
AND ME.
CALLA CALLA CALLA.

IT'S KILLING ME. KILLING ME KILLING KILLING
KILLING MEMEMEMEMEMEME.
PUT ME OUT OF MY MISERY.
DO IT DO IT DO IT.

I swallow hard, biting back helpless tears as I flip through several pages of the nonsense. But then I see one phrase. One phrase that dries my tears and freezes the breath on my lips.

SECRETS. EVERYBODY'S GOT EM.

I can practically hear those words coming out Dare's mouth. But why did he say such a thing to Finn?

If it weren't so late, I'd barge into his home right now and ask. But as it is, I wait.

I wait until I've slept through the night, showered and have thought about it some more. I still haven't calmed down though. Because something isn't right here.

As soon as it's a decent hour, I head for Dare's cottage. He answers his door shirtless, and it takes great effort to ignore that.

"Have you talked to Finn lately?" I ask him without greeting, my eyes frozen on his, never traveling south of his chin.

He looks at me oddly. "No, why?"

"Because I was reading his journal last night and he wrote something that you said. Verbatim, Dare."

He lifts an eyebrow. "And what piece of wisdom was this?"

"I'm not kidding," I snap. "He said, *'Secrets. Everybody's got 'em.'* That's exactly what you said to me. Why would you be talking about secrets with Finn? Has he told you what's going on with him?"

Dare seems utterly confused now, and he gestures for me to come in. I hesitate.

"Please," he urges. "I should get a shirt on."

I follow him in and wait on the sofa as he pulls a shirt on. When he comes back out, he sits next to me, picking up my hand.

"To answer your question, no. I haven't spoken to Finn about any secrets. Is it possible that he overheard us talking? I think we were discussing secrets here on the property one time."

Maybe.

That actually makes sense. Finn does have a way of quietly slipping around.

I relax, my shoulders slumping. Dare stares at me.

"Did you really think Finn would get into a deep conversation with me?" He eyes me doubtfully. I shrug.

"No. I guess not. I'm just... frustrated. He's hiding something. It's making him worse and he won't talk to me about it. He'll never be able to go to college alone at this rate."

Which means that I won't be able to, either.

It's something that makes me feel panicky, guilty and dejected about at once.

"I thought that's what you wanted," Dare presses me. "I thought you wanted to go with him."

"I do," I say quickly, too quickly. "I mean. Yes. I do. But at the same time, I guess I was warming up to the idea that he wants some separation. I thought it would give me an opportunity to maybe have a love life. With you, for instance."

I feel sheepish now, ashamed, embarrassed. What kind of sister am I?

Dare lifts my chin with his finger. "Don't feel guilty about that," he tells me. "You have the right to a life of your own, too, you know. That doesn't make you a bad person."

I nod, not believing him.

He grins at me, and for a second, just one, I feel like everything is fine. "Let's get out of here today."

I nod immediately. "Ok. Where?"

Dare stares out his window, toward the ocean. "Out there. Where we're boundless."

LIVE FREE.

"Ok," I agree.

We're in my boat within five minutes. Me in a short sundress and sunscreen, and Dare in his dark jeans and none.

"You're going to get skin cancer," I stare at him.

"I'm not," he answers. I don't argue because I like his bare chest, and the way the muscles ripple across his shoulders as he moves. I pause on my way to the helm, long enough to run my fingers over the letters of his tattoo. His skin is hot beneath my fingertips, and the friction makes me grit my teeth.

"I'm going to show you someplace new," I tell him, guiding the boat out of the bay and toward a small rock pier down the beach. It only takes ten minutes to get there, and I urge the boat aground so that we can step out onto land.

I hold my hand out to Dare and he takes it, climbing down next to me. We walk all the way out to the tip of the land finger, where the fingernail would be.

Dare sits, and I sit next to him, our feet splayed out in front of us on the rocks.

We're surrounded by nothing but the air and water, we're utterly alone out here, with no one to overhear or watch us like we're fish in a bowl.

The salty breeze blows Dare's hair around his face and I turn to him.

"I'm ready to use another question," I tell him. He grins.

"So soon? It's only been days since the last one."

I ignore that. "Why are you such a gentleman?"

Meaning, *why are you so resolute to keep your distance until I figure my shit out?*

He shifts his weight and crosses his feet at the ankles. "So you've noticed."

His tone is wry. I roll my eyes.

"Seriously. Why are you trying to force me into doing something for my own good that I don't want to do? All for the sake of being a gentleman? Maybe being a gentleman is overrated and archaic."

He scoffs at that, shielding his eyes from the sun with long fingers of one hand. I stare at his silver ring glinting in the light.

"It's not, trust me." The way he said that is so knowing, so strange.

I raise an eyebrow and he sighs.

"My step-father, while refined and rich, was not a gentleman behind closed doors. From the time I was very small, I decided that I would always be the opposite of him. My mother always gave me lessons on what a gentleman should do. She spoke of those traits with such...reverence that I knew that's what I wanted to be." He pauses. "Are you going to make fun of me now?"

He stares at me, his jaw so sculpted, his eyes so guarded. I find all I want to do is reach out and stroke the coarseness of his stubble with my hand. "No," I tell him. "Not at all."

Because he made that hidden part of me ache, the maternal place, the place that wants to protect him from everything, even if that means from me.

"What did your step-father do?"

My question is quiet in its simplicity and Dare sighs again.

"You're really burning through your questions today."

I nod, but I don't back down.

"My stepfather was unfortunately, very much like his mother. A very calculating, controlling person. He had to have everything his way exactly and those people who didn't comply were punished severely."

I swallow hard at the closed look on Dare's beautiful face.

"How severely?"

He turns to look at me, his black eyes staring into my soul.

"Severely."

My heart twinges at the vulnerable pain in Dare's eyes. He thinks he's concealing it, but he's not. "And being the rogue that you are, I'm guessing you were punished a lot."

He nods and looks out at the sea and I pick up his hand, spinning his ring round and round.

"And no one interfered? Not your mother or your grandmother?"

He looks at me now, stricken. "She's my step-grandmother. And of course she wouldn't interfere. She never approved of me. She thinks I deserved everything I got and then some. My mother... she couldn't stop it. She couldn't stand against the two of them. They were an unstoppable force."

"Why didn't your mom leave him? If he was so bad, I mean?" I ask hesitantly.

"It's not always that easy," he answers tiredly. "Where would she have gone? She didn't have anywhere to go."

The feel of this conversation is dark and ominous and scary. I examine his face, the planes and angles, and grip his hand harder. "Well, now that your mom is gone, you're done with your step-father's family. Thank goodness. You're here in America and they can't hurt you anymore."

He sighs, a ragged sound, his slender fingers weaving around my own. "Can't they?"

I start to answer and he interrupts. "You've burned through most of your questions, Cal. It seems to me like you've only got a couple left."

I nod, because he's right. "I've only got one more to ask today, and then I'll save my last one for later."

Nerves cause my heart to pound, adrenaline to rush, rush, rush through my veins as I look at him, the Adonis sitting next to me. *Do it. Do it.* Everything about him touches me... his voice, his story, his vulnerability that he tries so hard to hide. All of it. I want him. All of him.

"You've been such a gentleman," I start, before I lose my nerve. "And it's sexy as hell, I'll admit. You're sexy. And beautiful. And I want to be close to you, Dare. I want it more than I've ever wanted anything."

Dare swallows. I see his throat move, I see him grip his leg with long fingers.

"And?" he asks hesitantly. "What is your question?"

He swallows again.

"Be with me," I urge him. "Today. Right now. Out here where it's only the two of us. Please."

Dare closes his eyes, and his face is bathed by the sun.

"That's not a question," he states softly. But his hands are gripping his legs so tightly his knuckles are turning white.

I move over, close, close, closer. Until my thigh is pressed against his, and I unclasp his fingers from his thighs. Leaning over our intertwined hands, I kiss his neck, beginning at the base, slowly and softly working my way up to his ear.

"Will you be with me? *Today?*" I whisper in his ear. With my last raspy word, I release his hand and slide mine along his inner thigh. I feel him harden beneath my fingers, pulsing through his jeans.

He closes his eyes and I tighten my fingers, increasing my grip.

"Don't," he whispers. His voice husky and so sexy.

"That's not an answer," I tell him, stroking him through the denim. A surge of feminine power shoots through me, lifting me up, propelling me onward, until my own hormones explode and cloud my thoughts.

NOCTE

"I want you, Dare," I tell him hotly, all logic and reason abandoning me. And then I kiss him, pressing my body into his, plunging my tongue into his hot mouth. His hands come up and lift me until I'm straddling him and I feel his hardness, his rigidity, pressing between my legs.

He's hard for me.

I swallow hard, absorbing his moan, sucking it down.

"You don't know what you want," he rasps into my neck.

"I do," I insist quietly, rocking in his lap, grinding my hips into his, creating an exquisite, amazing friction. "I've wanted you all along."

Dare pulls away, his dark eyes heavy-lidded with want for me. Warmth floods me, wetting my panties and I cling to him.

"Are you sure?"

"Yes." My answer is simple.

With a growl, Dare scoops me up, and carries me down the peninsula, to a place where the ground is soft. He lays me down, on his knees above me, gloriously back-lit.

"I shouldn't," he wavers.

"You have to," I tell him, grabbing him and pulling him down on top of me.

His weight is delicious and perfect and he molds into me, making it seem like we're one person as we writhe together, trying desperately to get closer.

His tongue finds mine, as his fingers explore my body, every inch, every hidden place. I arch against him, palmed in his hand, as he finds where I want him the most.

"Please," I say softly, my breath escaping me. Dare smiles against my lips, knowing the effect on me, knowing and loving it.

He leans forward and rests his forehead against mine, and we're so very close that I can feel his breath mingling with mine as his hands work absolute magic. Pleasure laps against me, like the water against the shore and I lose all cognizant thought, and instinct takes over.

I tug at his jeans, unbuttoning them and pushing them away, and suddenly, he's naked and in my hand, long and thick and bare.

I can't breathe.

I can't think.

I can only move.

I slide my hand along him, softly, gently, then harder, harder.

He bucks into me, his eyes shuttering closed.

"I've waited for this," he murmurs into my neck, as he wedges his rigidity into my thighs, closer, closer. "For so long."

"Please," I say again, my hand cupped around his neck, pulling his mouth to mine, so I can taste him, inhale him. He pulls off my sundress, and stares at me in the sunlight, as the light exposes every plane of my body to his searching eyes.

"You're beautiful," he whispers, his eyes glittering in the sun. "You're so much better than I deserve."

Wordlessly, he pulls back for a moment, and I protest, but then I hear the crinkle of a wrapper and he's back, and he's sliding into me and I can't think anymore.

Motions become blurs, blurs become colors, and all I can do is feel.

His hands, his mouth, his skin. The way he slides in and out of me, the friction causing me to crest in waves, his fingers bringing me to it faster.

"I…you… *God*," I manage to say, because the words I want won't come.

Dare smiles slightly and slides back into me, moaning my name.

"I want you to know me," he says, his voice a husky chant. "I want you know me."

I'm *knowing* him now like I've wanted to for weeks. Intimate and close and I can't believe this is finally happening, I can't believe it's so amazing, I can't focus, I can't focus, I can't focus.

The lights, the sun, the sea, Dare's scent, his fingers, his hands.

I grip his back, where his words say LIVE FREE and I've never felt freer in my entire life.

And then my world explodes in a kaleidoscope of colors and lights.

I'm limp as I cling to him, as he finally arches against me and groans and says my name in a ragged whisper before collapsing against me, his head against my chest, his beautiful hands holding me close.

I can't even answer. My legs are shaky, my mind is spinning. But as I come back to myself, as my thoughts form logically together again, as the sun hangs heavy in the sky, with the oranges and reds on the water, something comes to me. Something Dare said in the heat of the moment, exact words that I've heard before in my dreams.

You're better than I deserve.

35

TRIGENTA QUINQUE

My swollen lips part and I stare at him, at the face I love, at the lips that just spoke words from my dream.

It's impossible.

Yet it's not.

"You... there's something...." my voice trails off and he looks at me questioningly, a smile lingering on his lips, the after effects of something beautiful.

Something that's now tarnished by ugliness.

By confusion.

"You said I'm better than you deserve," I say shakily, not wanting to speak the truth, because the truth sounds crazy. "Why would you say that?"

He shrugs. "Because you're soft and honest and beautiful. You're better than I deserve."

"But why?" I demand persistently, refusing his answer. "You must have a reason."

He shakes his head, still staring, still questioning.

"It doesn't make sense," I tell him.

"Life doesn't make sense sometimes, Cal," is his only reply. He takes his hand away now, the warmth gone from me, and my fingers turn instantly cool with the breeze.

It's his turn to examine me, to study me in the breeze.

"Do you feel ok?" he asks hesitantly. "Are you... do you... you seem different."

I shake my head. "I'm just the same. I just... those words stood out to me somehow, like I've heard them before, *like you've said them before*."

If I didn't know better, I'd say he turned pale. He shakes his head slowly, with such a strange expression on his face.

"Do you know why?" he asks strangely, an odd glint in his eye, his beautiful lips pulled tight.

"No. Do you?"

He gives me a droll look. "Why would I know your mind?" he asks vaguely, but his face tells a different story as an expression that puts my nerves on edge floods his face.

"How cryptic," I murmur.

He shakes his head. "I'm not trying to be. It's just... I thought... never mind. You've got enough to worry about right now without adding more to it."

"Everyone has secrets," I say blankly, my heart numb. He nods.

"Yeah. I guess."

My blood is ice, my heart is heavy, my very being filled with terror and foreboding, when just a scant moment ago, I was filled with exquisite belonging. It's been shattered now, by the sheer expression on Dare's face.

"What are yours?" I ask calmly. "Your secrets, I mean. What are they, Dare? You're hiding something and I know it. Just tell me."

He looks sad as he looks away from me, and that terrifies me even more. My heart picks up a little as I wait, pounding in my chest, echoing in my temples.

He's hiding something.

"I can't tell you. Not right now. It's not a good time." His voice is expressionless, solemn.

"Will there ever be a good time?" I ask. He shrugs.

"I don't know. I hope so."

I don't like that answer.

"We just... I... I trusted you," I tell him limply. "And I know you're keeping a secret and I know it affects me. I can't...I can't."

I crawl off the slippery rocks and walk quietly back to the boat without another word. Lately, I feel more and more like I'm the crazy one, like I'm losing my mind, like the whole world is composed of secrets and I don't have the slightest clue how to figure them out.

Dare follows me and lifts my hand to help me into the boat.

The quiet between us is loaded and charged and I don't know why. I don't know why I feel like I'm standing on a precipice and if I make one move, I'll fall.

When we're halfway across the bay, Dare sits straight up.

"Let's go to your little cove," he suggests softly.

He sits on the hull, his shirtless chest gleaming in the dying light, his eyes vulnerable and hopeful and I can't say no.

Instead, I just wordlessly steer toward the cove and wedge the boat on the sand. I don't know why, I just don't want to stay here. I have to move. I have to think. I have to try and stay sane, because it feels like I'm fraying.

I don't know why.

All I know is... I suddenly feel lost.

Dare holds my hand as we walk through the water, to the enclosed little inlet that I so love. Without a word, I dig out the little bag holding the lighter and I make a little driftwood bonfire.

With the violet light surrounding us , we sit facing each other over a tide pool. The moon rises over the edge of the water and this place seems ethereal and peaceful and infinite.

"Do you trust me?" Dare asks seriously, his eyes ever-so-dark. He brushes a tendril of my hair behind my ear. "I mean, really trust me?"

I'm puzzled by that, by his uncertainty.

I'm scared by the hidden meaning of his words.

I reach up and trace the lines of his face, the cleft in his chin, the strong jaw, his forehead.

"Why wouldn't I?" I ask finally. "Is there some reason I shouldn't?"

"That's not an answer," he replies.

"Then yes," I tell him quickly. "I trust you."

Don't I?

He stares into my eyes, his hands on my knees. "Would you still trust me if I told you that I want to tell you everything. That I want to spill all of my secrets, everything that you've been wondering about... but I can't?"

There is genuine angst in his voice, and his face is pained and I can't figure it out.

"Are you a mass murderer?" I ask, trying to lighten the mood, but it doesn't work. His face doesn't change.

"No. But there are things... that I wish I could say, but can't."

I drop my hand, stricken by the look in his eye.

"Like what?" I ask bluntly. "Just tell me right now. Tell me *all the things,* Dare."

He ignores that.

"Do you believe me when I say I love you?" he asks instead, his fingers running along my cheek.

"I'm not sure why, but yeah. I believe you."

He looks startled. "Why *wouldn't* I love you?"

I shrug. Because no one else ever has.

Aside from my parents and Finn.

But I don't say that.

Instead, I face him squarely. "You're scaring me. If you love me, then you shouldn't be afraid to tell me the truth... about anything. Tell me, Dare."

He stares at me, pausing.

"I can't. It's about me... who I am. You wouldn't understand."

I stare back, my spine straightened like steel. "Try me."

He shakes his head, firm. "I can't."

Despair like I've never felt it before settles around me like a cloud. I thought he was my anchor, but if he can't trust me enough to tell me who he even is, then I can't trust him with my heart.

Even I know that my heart is too fragile for that right now.

"That's not good enough," I tell him slowly, each word fighting my lips. I don't want to say them, but I have to. I have to.

I have to do what is good for me. What is smart for me.

"I've got enough secrets around me at the moment... whatever Finn is hiding. And his drama. I can't take it from you too, Dare. I just can't. If you can't tell me what is

261

going on with you... then...." The pain breaks my voice off and tears well up in my eyes.

Dare doesn't fold. He just stares at me, daring me to say it. *Dare me.*

"If I can't tell you what's going on with, then *what*?" he pushes.

"Then I can't be with you. Not if you don't trust me enough to let me in."

Dare sighs and takes my hand, his thumb stroking mine, but I pull it away.

"I mean it."

"You don't understand," Dare tells me, his voice harsh. "I'm doing this for you. To protect you. There are things you don't know. You can't know, not right now. I love you, Calla. I do. But you've got to trust me."

"I only trust people who are honest with me," I reply evenly. "You're not being honest."

For the life of me, I don't know how we went from having an amazing day to this, in the blink of an eye. Dare looks confused too, and shell-shocked and unsure of what to do.

"God, I want to be," he tell me, his voice razor sharp. "I'm in a bad position, Calla. You don't understand."

"I only understand one thing," I tell him and my heart threatens to break. "And it's that I can't do this right now. If you ever decide that you're ready for something else with me, that you want to grow up and be honest, come get me. Until then, leave me alone."

I get up and walk down the beach, fighting the urge to collapse at every step. What did I just do? Am I insane? I feel Dare watching me, I feel his gaze, and against my will, I glance over my shoulder.

He's staring at me and the look in his eyes tears my insides apart. There's pain there, raw, honest pain, and that's all I can see. It swirls around and around, and then the stars whirl and suddenly, the world spins.

It's too much to handle.

Anyone would crack.

So I do.

36
TRIGENTA SEX

I'm in my bed.

The sunshine is bursting through my windows, flooding the room with light. I open my eyes, to find Finn sitting next to my bed.

"Dramatic, much?" he asks, his eyebrow raised.

I gaze around the room, only to find it empty, but for my brother and me.

"Where's Dare?" I ask quickly. Finn looks away, shielding his thoughts from me.

"Gone," he simply says.

Gone? Without another word? Or explanation? Or anything? I know I told him to go, but still. *God.*

My stomach balls up, like it's being constricted in a vise.

"Dad's downstairs getting you some breakfast."

"I don't want breakfast," I say petulantly, staring out my windows. The sky is still blue, the sun still shines... even though Dare is gone.

"Are you ok?" Finn asks finally. "You passed out on the beach. Dare carried you here, but once dad found out that you'd gotten upset while you were fighting, dad made him leave. What happened?"

"Nothing," I mutter. "I'm just surrounded by secrets and craziness and I can't let Dare keep secrets too. I want him here, I want to be with him, but I'm going to lose my mind if the people in my life don't start being straight with me."

Finn stares at me, startled. "What do you mean by that?"

I don't blink. "I think you know."

But before he can reply, we're interrupted by my father.

He breezes through the door with toast and juice, like it's an ordinary day.

"Good morning!" he calls out, setting the tray on my stand. "I'm glad you're awake."

I stare at him icily.

"You sent Dare away."

My father stares back, standing his ground.

"You literally passed out on the beach," Dad tells me concisely. "While you were having a fight with him."

"My love life is my business," I remind him. "I decide who to send away. Not you."

My father shakes his head. "I decide who can stay on my property," he tells me. "And you're under enough pressure without adding more to it. Dare understood. He agreed, actually."

"Dare agreed that he shouldn't be with me?" I ask doubtfully. Dad's expression slips a bit.

"Not exactly. He just agreed that he shouldn't be here last night. I'll let you decide when you want to talk to him next. But when you do, you need to make sure you're ready. Being emotionally involved with someone is a big

265

NOCTE

deal, honey. Especially when your emotions are fragile already."

I ignore that. "Where did he go?"

"I don't know," my father answers firmly, walking back to the doorway. He walks out and I stare at the wall, fighting the red hot tears that well up in my eyes.

"I sent him away and he was the only one outside of you and dad who has ever loved me," I tell Finn without looking at him. He looks flustered and scared and sad.

"There was mom," he offers hesitantly.

"She's dead," I say icily.

He can't argue with that.

"I want to be alone," I tell him finally. *Alone with my thoughts, alone with my pain. Because I gave myself to him and he left me. I sent him away and he accepted that and he's gone.*

Finn startles, staring at me in surprise. Because I've never wanted to be alone before.

"Are you sure?"

I nod.

"Ok," he finally agrees. "But if you need me, I'm right down the hall."

He slips out after looking over his shoulder reluctantly, but I don't call him back. Instead, I pull the blankets up and stare at the oceans, at the boats on the horizon. I wish one of them could take me, and sail me to wherever Dare is.

He might be hiding things from me, but the pain on his face was real.

He loves me.

No matter what, I have to believe that.

It's what anchors me.

I close my eyes and sleep.

266

When I wake, I find Finn's St. Michael's medallion on my night stand. He left it with me because apparently, I *am* the one who needs it. Also, it's evening. I slept all day.

Hesitantly, I swing my legs out of bed and sit at my desk instead, opening my laptop.

I punch Adair DuBray into a search engine.

I'm half-surprised that 1. A ton of results are returned. And 2. I'm only just now doing this.

I scroll through the results hesitantly.

Apparently, his family, or his step-family, rather, are very affluent in England. They're old money, and every Savage (that's their last name) goes to Cambridge University. Dare went there himself, and graduated a year early.

There are tons of pictures of him posted ... pictures of him at various parties, with various women on his arms. The articles mention how he's a disappointment to the Savage matriarch, because of his wild ways, his inability to settle down, his refusal to conform. His partying ways are compared to that of Prince Harry.

You've got to be kidding me.

What kind of family is he from that gossip sites are so interested?

He lives on some huge estate called Whitley, with his grandmother.

Eleanor Savage.

A widow, she had two children, Laura Savage and Richard Savage II, both deceased.

She has three grandchildren, but only one is named. A step-grandson, Adair DuBray.

I stare at the picture of Eleanor. Even in the picture, her mouth is drawn tightly into a frown, like she's perpetually displeased, like she's unable to be satisfied. No wonder Dare doesn't like her. No wonder he's a self-proclaimed rogue.

I read an article interviewing him after he graduated Cambridge early and with honors. He told them that he was off to America for a while. That was earlier this year, back in the Fall.

So he's been here since the Fall, and he was only just hunting for an apartment when he met me?

How strange.

I look again at the pictures of him. He's surrounded by drunk women, beautiful women. All long golden legs and blond hair. In one photo, he's got his arms wrapped around one girl, with a drink in his hand as he flippantly toasts the camera. His eyes stare into the lens... black, black, black as night.

Black as anything I've ever seen.

Blacker than my sadness.

I gulp back tears because I already miss him. Because I gave my body to him. Because I don't want him to ever take a picture with another blond girl because *he's mine*. Because he's hiding something from me and because I want him anyway. Does that mean I'm weak?

I choke back a cry and pick up my phone.

I text him quickly, although I've never texted him before. I didn't have to before... he lived a hundred feet from my house. But now he's gone.

I miss you. Even though you have your secrets.

I slide the phone across my desk and climb back into bed.

I don't know how long I sleep, I only know that it's daylight once again when I open my eyes. Finn is sitting in my desk chair, watching me, concerned. He's pale, his skinny hands clasped in his lap.

"You've got to eat something," he tells me.

I turn my face away. "I don't feel like it."

"You've been sleeping for two days," he points out. That surprises me, but I don't show it. "At least take a drink."

He pushes a glass of water at me. I lean up, take two sips, then lie back down.

"Go away, Finn."

He studies me, his blue eyes appraising me, searching me. "You know, if you're trying to show dad that he was right, this is the way to do it," he points out. "You're acting crazy... clinically depressed. Is that what you're trying to do?"

"It takes crazy to know crazy," I mutter and then I feel guilty when Finn flinches. Pain gushes through me, remorse. "I'm sorry," I say quickly. "I didn't mean that."

He shrugs, pretending it didn't hurt. "That's all right. It's just the truth. You're acting crazy right now. If dad's wrong and you're really in a place where you should be dating someone, get out of bed and act like it. Show them, Calla."

He stares at me plaintively with that challenge and I hate him right now for being so logical.

For being so right.

"I'm still tired," I tell him miserably. I want to stay in here where it doesn't matter that I'm alone. I want to stay here where nothing to get to me. Not mom's death, not Finn's crazy, and most of all, not Dare's absence.

Finn shakes his head. "I'll check on you later."

I watch him leave, then grab my phone.

269

No new messages.

Dare didn't answer.

I close my eyes.

"Get up."

I open my eyes, and it is dark once again.

I have no idea how long I've been in bed, but I'm assuming it's been another day. Or twelve hours. Or twelve years. Who knows and who cares?

I stare up at Finn.

"Enough, Calla. You're stronger than this. Maybe you don't care, but I do. I need you. I need you up, I need you to be strong. Sleep through the night if you want to, but in the morning, I need you to get your ass out of bed and quit feeling sorry for yourself."

He's firm and stern and brotherly.

My eyes fill up with tears, so I close them.

I hear him sigh as he walks away and closes my door.

****
Finn

I sit in my sister's desk chair and watch her sleep. I stare at the tears streaked down her face, the way her hair is matted and wet.

This is pathetic.

Her pain causes me to hurt.

FixItFixItFixIt, the voices chant.

I can't. That's the bitch of it. I can't fix it.

She's fragile and scared and alone, and now she's broken.

He broke her.

Scowling, I pick up her phone, making sure that he didn't text again. I deleted his answer before, the pitiful *I miss you too.*

Fuck him.

Fuck anyone who wants to hurt her.

I can't save her if she keeps getting hurt.

But the world is like that. The world is ugly and painful and that's how I'll fix it. The answer comes to me as clear as a bell. The world is too painful. There's only one way to stop it, to fix it.

Fix it.

I will.

I will.

Fix it.

Consider it done.

I tell that to the voices and it seems to appease them because they're silent for a minute as I bend and kiss my sister's forehead, then crawl in bed behind her.

There's a way. Only one Only one Only one.

~~Fix it.~~

37

TRIGENTA SEPTEM

Calla

Sunlight floods my room and I wake up feeling... alive again.

I don't know why.

Maybe it was Finn's indignation last night, his plea, his demand to get my ass out of bed in the morning.

I'm not sure what it was that worked, what broke through my self-pity, but here I am, sitting on the edge of my bed.

It's lunchtime and I'm up.

I smell food drifting through the house, so I pad down the hall and find my father and Finn in the kitchen.

I sit down without saying a word. I haven't combed my hair, I haven't put clothes on. But they both pretend not to notice.

Finn makes a plate for me, sliding it across the table.

"Are you feeling better?" he asks carefully.

I nod, staring at my food, taking a bite.

"You've been in bed for four days," he adds, his eyes trained on my face.

"Four?" My gaze shoots up and meets his, then my father's. My father nods, his face carefully expressionless.

I look back down.

"I was tired." I pause, noting how white my hands look holding the fork. Pale, skinny, listless. I do need to get up. I need some fresh air. I need to stop being pathetic. But first… "Did Dare call?" I can't help but ask.

There's a pause, then my dad nods.

"And?" I hear the hope in my voice and hate it.

"And nothing," he says firmly. "He was just checking on you. You're not ready for this, Calla. You've been through too much these past couple of months. You've got to focus on yourself, not Dare."

Pain shoots through me and I look away from him, out the window, out at Dare's empty Carriage House.

They don't understand. He's what has kept my head afloat these past few weeks. I don't know why I'm depending on him so much, I just am. And then I sent him away, because apparently, I'm a lunatic.

I take a second bite. "Thanks for the plate," I tell Finn. He nods.

I chew and swallow, careful not to look at my father. I'm still pissed at him.

I'm so pissed that my lungs feel hot and my throat feels tight.

I take a third bite. As I chew, it begins to feel like sawdust in my mouth, like I'll never be able to swallow it because my throat is too hot, because I can't breathe.

What the hell?

Confused, I look at my plate. Polish sausage, sauerkraut, apples… and pecans.

Pecans.

My hands immediately fly to my throat because after three bites, it's already swelling shut.

I wheeze, trying to breathe. Warmth spreads through my chest as all the vessels in my lungs start to enlarge. I can feel each individual one, pulsing in my ribcage, stretching, swelling.

"Dad," I manage to say, getting up from the chair. He rushes to grab me, and I fall into his arms, trying to breathe with stiff lungs.

I suck in a breath, but it won't come. The air can't get into the swollen tissue of my throat. It's like a vise, constricting and squeezing.

I'm a fish out of water, and everything turns to noises, but I can't understand the words. The light blurs into one large color, and I think of one last thing before there's nothing more.

Someone just poisoned me.

***

Before I open my eyes, I know where I am. I also know why.

Someone fed me nuts.

Someone.

Finn.

That knowledge is dizzying, and so I focus instead on where I am.

I recognize the sterile medicinal smell of the hospital. I listen with my eyes closed, hearing the rubbery squeak of the nurses' shoes, the beeps of the machines, the low murmurings out in the hallway.

I have a tube in my nose. Oxygen. The room spins, and I shift it back into focus.

Concentrate, Calla.

I open my eyes and the room spins. I shift it back into focus.

"Calla?"

My dad's voice is calm and low. Shifting my gaze without moving my head, I find him in the corner chair, watching me in concern.

"I'm not dead?"

He smiles. "No. Thank God."

My memory is blurry. "There were nuts," I recall. "In my food."

My father cringes. "Yes. I'm sorry, Calla. I didn't see...."

"How long have I been here?" I ask. My voice is scratchy, my throat raw. I know from experience that they probably shoved a breathing tube down it.

"About four hours. We called an ambulance. You were out the whole time. You'll be fine now. By tomorrow, you'll be good as new, but they want to keep you overnight for observation."

I nod.

I feel heavy, groggy, slow.

"What's wrong with me?" I ask slowly.

"They gave you something to calm you down," my father says hesitantly. His eyes are on my face, like he's worried I'm going to fly off the handle. Did I before?

"Where's Finn?"

My father looks away. "He can't be in here, honey."

"Why?"

My father sighs, and looks back to me. "You know why, Calla."

I close my eyes. Because Finn knows I'm allergic to nuts. He knew and he gave them to me anyway.

Is that his version of saving me? Saving me from what? Sadness? Was his plan to kill me, then himself?

Pain ripples through me, slow, then hard, then unbearably, like a wave.

"I need to see him," I say, the words cutting my lungs.

"No." My father's voice is firm.

I curl up on my side, looking away, out at the clouds having over the parking lot.

"Where is he?" I ask without looking at my father. He doesn't answer, which sends chills down my spine.

"It's my fault," I tell him, turning over so that I'm looking him in the eye now. "It's not Finn's fault. It's mine. I read his journal, I knew he was slipping and I should've told you, but I didn't. He wants to save me from pain, dad. He wasn't trying to hurt me. It's not his fault, it's mine."

My voice takes on a jagged, desperate edge and my dad rubs my arm. "Calm down, sweetie. Everything's going to be ok."

"It's not," I insist, my voice shrill. "Don't punish Finn. Don't put him in the hospital, dad. It's my fault. Not his. *Not his.*"

I'm practically screaming now, writhing in the bed trying to get up, but my dad holds me down, pleading with me. Before I know it, nurses have come in, two of them, one for each side. One injects something into my IV and then all of my agitation slips away. My anger is gone, my frustration non-existent.

"Please call Dare," I whisper. "Please."

And then everything is black.

38

TRIGENTA OCTO

Finn

"Let me go!" I shout, squirming to get away from the nurses. "I didn't hurt her. I didn't! I just had to help her. Don't you see?"

No one can see and no one cares. They just wrap my wrists with elastic bands and fasten them to the bedframe.

I whimper into the pillow before I bite it. I'd never hurt Calla.

Never.

I'm doing all of this *for her.*

"Let me go," I plead them. "I can't leave her by herself. Please. I'll be good. I'll be good!"

But they ignore me and when I look up, I see my father's face pressed against the glass.

I call out to him, but he doesn't answer. In fact, his face slips away and doesn't come back.

"Come back," I whisper.

But he doesn't.

My tears are hot, as I think about my sister, huddled somewhere in this hospital, alone and scared and thinking that I tried to kill her.

I would never. *Would I?*

YouDidYouDidYouDid. Don'tYouRemember? The voices are laughing at me, hissing and shrieking. *YouDidYouDid.*

I didn't.

I couldn't.

But my hands are handcuffed to this bed and there is no arguing that.

I fed her the nuts. There's no denying that, either.

I close my eyes against the chanting in my head, trying to block them out. *SisterKillerSisterKillerSisterKiller. You'reaMonster. Monster. WeControlYou WeControlYou.*

Monster.

39

TRIGENTA NOVEM

Calla

When I open my eyes, I immediately focus on Dare sitting next to me.

He's sprawled in the recliner, his eyes closed, his hands gripping the armrests. He's long and slender and lithe. He's beautiful and dark and *here.*

He's here.

I take a deep breath and blink to make sure I wasn't imagining it.

He's still there.

"Dare," my whisper is throaty and raw. I figure he won't hear me, but he does. His eyes fly open and meet mine.

And then he's out of his chair and on his knees next my bed, his forehead pressed to mine.

"Cal," he says, his lips brushing my skin. "Thank God."

"How are you here?" I ask in confusion. "Did my dad…"

Dare nods. "You asked him to call me, and he did."

Bless him. A surge of gratitude rushes through me. "Where is he? Is he with Finn?"

"I don't know," Dare answers. "I told him I would sit with you until he came back, though."

I close my eyes and inhale him, his musky outdoorsy smell. "Don't leave me," I tell him. "Please. You promised once, remember?"

He nods. "I do. And I won't. Don't tell me to again."

I nod. *I won't.*

He strokes my hand, his fingers smooth. "What do you remember, Cal?"

"Finn made me a plate," I tell him. "I took three bites and then realized that there were nuts. Pecans."

Dare closes his eyes. "You're lucky to be here," he tells me without opening them. "Your dad said even one nut could kill you. You barely made it to the ER."

"But I did," I remind him. "I'm here now. Please don't let them keep Finn. He didn't mean to hurt me. I know he didn't. He would never...."

But Dare sits up and rocks back on his heels. "I don't know what they're going to do," he says vaguely. "It's not up to me."

I close my eyes, pain ripping through my chest. "Maybe you were right. Maybe I do need to leave here. Maybe I'm a crutch for him... or maybe I'm even a worry for him. He hates that I'm sad about mom. Maybe he just wanted to end my grief. If I left, he could focus on himself... not on me."

"And you could focus on *yourself,*" Dare adds. I open my eyes and his face is so tired, so drawn. I reach out and touch it, my blue hospital bracelet sliding down my forearm. When did I lose weight? My arms are so skinny.

"I trust you," I blurt suddenly. "I trust you to tell me about yourself whenever you're ready."

Dare flinches now. "It's not about me being ready. It's just... I can't add to your burden, Cal. After *this*, can't you see that?"

This. My burden. My brother trying to kill me.

Will it never end?

"I'm sorry for all of this," I tell him quietly as I stare at his tired face. "I'm sorry that my life is crazy."

He looks around and shudders. "You almost died, Calla."

"I was handling it," I defend myself and Finn. "Finn needs me. I was handling it."

"Were you?" Dare raises an eyebrow. I look away.

"His journal is in my bedroom. As soon as I get out of here, I've got to finish it. I just feel, somehow, that it's the key. I've got to read it all."

Dare stares at me, his gaze as dark as night.

"Are you sure?"

I nod. "I'm positive. I've been reading it bits at a time, but it's time that I finish it. Do you know when they're letting me out?"

Dare shakes his head. "I don't know. I think they said maybe in the morning, depending on how you're doing. You were really upset last night."

"Of course I was!" I snap. "They're going to lock my brother away."

Dare stares at me, sympathetic.

"Do what they say today, and I'm sure they'll let you out in the morning."

I nod and he holds my hand.

"What if I decide that I want to move to Berkeley early?" I ask him before I go to sleep.

He squeezes my fingers. "Then I'll go with you."

"And if I want to stay here?"

"Then I'll stay with you."

"No matter what?"

"No matter what."

That's all I need to hear. Peace fills me up and I fall asleep. And in the morning, they let me go.

"I want to ride with Dare," I tell my father.

Dad stares at me, his eyes at once sad and resigned.

"Ok."

"And if Dare wants to rent the Carriage House again, I want you to let him."

He nods.

"Anything else?" His voice is brittle.

"Yes. I love you." I throw my arms around his neck because even if he interfered where he shouldn't have, he did it because he loves me. When he pulls away, his eyes are misty.

"Go on, then. I'll be home after while."

"Can I see Finn before I go?"

He stares at me regretfully. "I'm afraid not."

I nod, a lump forming in my throat.

"Will you bring him home with you?"

"I'll try," he promises.

That'll have to be enough.

Dare walks me out of the hospital and to his bike, handing me my helmet. I wrap myself around his waist and we ride with the wind in our faces.

Freedom has never felt so good.

LIVE FREE. I understand that phrase now more than I thought I ever could.

When we get home, Dare pauses.

"I want to stay with you when you read the journal. Is that ok?"

He's hesitant and sweet as he lingers on the bottom step of my porch. I'm self-conscious that he thinks I'm so fragile, but I nod anyway.

"Ok."

He follows me to my room and sits at my desk while I curl up on my bed.

"Just pretend I'm not here," he advises.

I shake my head, but that's exactly what I do.

I ignore the sexy British heartthrob sitting two feet from me, and instead, focus on saving my brother.

To do that, I dive into his journal. I've only got a quarter of it left to read. I begin skimming through it, and it weaves its way back and forth between being lucid and crazy.

IGNORE HER.
IGNORE IT ALL.

DEUS ADIUVA ME. GOD HELP ME. ME. ME.
GOD HELP ME.
NOCTE LIBER SUM.
BY NIGHT I AM FREE.
I HAVE TO PROTECT MY SECRET. HAVE TO HAVE TO
HAVE TO.

This gibberish continues for pages, with pictures and phrases and words, until I come to one particular page.

There's a drawing of me and Finn, sitting on top of the cliffs. Finn is throwing his medallion over the side.

SHE NEEDS IT NOW. NOT ME NOT ME NOT ME.
PROTECT HER FROM ME. PROTECT HER FROM ME.
PROTECT HER FROM ME.
LOVE IS STRONGER THAN DEATH THAN DEATH THAN
DEATH.

LOVE IS STRONGER THAN DEATH.
END THIS END THIS END THIS.
END THIS ALL.
PLEASE GOD.
PLEASE.

"Protect her from me," I whisper, ice water pumping through my veins. "Finn knew he was going to do something to me. He was afraid of it. He kept trying to give me his St. Michael's medallion to protect me. But I kept giving it back."

I feel limp and shell-shocked as I stare at Dare.

"He knew he was going to hurt me. He couldn't help it."

Dare's eyes are stormy. "So he gave you the nuts to protect you?"

I nod, the knowledge cutting through me to my heart. "He'd never hurt me. He only wanted to help me. It's the only way he knew how in the state he's in."

"Have you figured out his secret?" Dare's question is solemn. I shake my head.

"No. He keeps referencing it. He says *I have to protect my secret.* But he doesn't say what it is."

Dare opens his mouth to speak, but Finn's voice is louder, thunderous, coming from the door.

"What are you doing with my journal?" he demands, his skin pale and his blue eyes paler. His expression is stormy though, furious. "You said you couldn't find my journal, Calla. Did you have it all along? Did you hide it from me?"

I stammer, trying to form a reply, but he won't let me.

"This is bullshit, Calla," he snaps. "I've been killing myself with guilt and trying to figure out a way to help you, and you've been going behind my back all along."

He stands still, so furious that he's shaking. "You want to know my secret?" he asks, icily calm now. I nod, terrified. "Then come find out."

He whirls around and storms out, down the stairs and out the door. I'm stunned for a minute, then I leap to my feet. I can hear Dare on my heels as I rush to follow my brother.

40

QUADRAGINTA

Finn

I fly over the trails, skidding up the path, with my sister right behind me. I don't stop until I reach the cliffs, because God, I have to end it. I can't do this anymore. I can't hide it. She has to know She has to know She has to know.

I can't take it anymore.

She has to know.

"Finn!" Calla calls out. I turn around slowly, and I can hardly stomach the look on Calla's face. She's in so much pain, and I'm causing it.

It's me.

It's me.

It's me.

"I didn't mean to hurt you, Cal," I tell her quietly, every word hurting my heart. "I just can't take it anymore. The voices... they're louder than my own. They tell me to do things, and I can't tune them out. I don't want you to hurt anymore. And I don't want me to hurt. You're a part of me and I'm a part of you and we shouldn't have to hurt."

Calla freezes, her hand in the air, because she hears the desperation in my voice.

"The secret is killing me, Cal," I tell her. I sound desperate and weak and pathetic. "I can't take it. It's not fair to you, and it's not fair to me."

"What is your secret, Finn?" she asks slowly, careful not to approach me. "Can you back away from the edge and tell me?"

I laugh, a hysterical sound, like a deranged hyena.

I'm unhinged unhinged unhinged.

I've come unhinged.

"Aren't you tired of talking me off the edge?" I demand. "Aren't you? Aren't you tired of balancing on these cliffs and being afraid that we'll tumble over the edge? I know I am. This isn't life, Calla. This isn't living. Love is stronger than death, Cal and this isn't living."

Her breath is loud, and I hear Dare coming up behind her, but he takes her cue and doesn't say a word.

"It *is* living," she says. "It's living because I love you. I'll do anything for you. You're part of me, and I'm part of you and that's the way it works. Please, God, please... don't do this, Finn. Don't do this."

She's crying now, shivering in the wind with her tears, but I feel lighter than I've felt in ages. In weeks. In months.

"It'll all be ok, Calla," I tell her. "It'll be over soon."

I smile and tilt my face toward the sky.

The sun feels good on my face.

Warmth = Life.

"No," Calla cries out, lunging toward me, but I step backward.

"Don't move," I tell her. "Or I'll do it right now."

"Why are you doing this?" she sobs, her blazing red hair whipping around her from the wind. "Why, Finn?"

"Because things have to happen in order," I tell her, as calmly as I can, only it sounds like I'm shouting. "You weren't moving in order, Calla. I had to make you. This is how I'm making you. My secret. I'm helping you, you just don't see it."

"*What is your secret?*" she shrieks, tears falling onto her nose, her mouth, her shirt. "Tell me and I'll help you, Finn. Save me and I'll save you, remember? Let me save you!"

She's sobbing and I am too and I can't tell the difference between us anymore.

DoItDoItDoIt! The voices chant. *JumpJumpJumpJump. Show her show her show her.*

"Shut up!" I shout, covering my ears. "I tried, Calla. I tried. But I can't do this anymore. Not even for you."

I picture my list in my head, because it's the only thing that drowns out the voices. It's a clean page without mar or smudge. In my head, I carefully write the words, then cross them off because I'm about to complete my task. Finally.

~~End it now.~~

"I love you," I tell my sister. I step back.

"Nooooo!"

The harsh shout breaks through my concentration and I pause on the edge, with the wind blowing through me, because the voice wasn't Calla's. It was Dare's.

Confused, I look up to find Dare standing exactly where Calla had just been.

Red hair blows around my shoulders while my shoes balance on the edge.

Pink converses.

They should be black.

"Calla, step away from the edge," Dare pleads. "Please."

Calla, step away from the edge.

What the hell?

I stare at Dare, balanced precariously, as I try and sort through what is happening with jagged, phrenetic thoughts. The pieces fly apart and whirl and come back together, partially cohesive. Through all of it, though, one thing is clear.

Finn isn't here.

I'm standing on the edge where Finn had just been. Panic and confusion seize me, as I whirl about, hunting for my brother, but already knowing something deep down.

I finally know Finn's secret.

He's not here.

He never was.

41

QUADRAGINTA UNUS

Calla

I'm panicked as I stare at Dare, disoriented and terrified, as the wind whips my hair around my face.

No. This isn't right. This can't be.

Images and memories and pictures flood my mind with lightning speed, fitting together, pulling apart, forming a collage, then another and another.

Memories.

My life.

All of it.

I fight to find words, but I can't and so I start to sob instead, stepping away from the edge and sinking to the ground. Dare wraps his arms around my shoulders, pulling me to safety.

"I'm crazy," I hear myself cry, clinging to Dare. His voice is husky and calm.

"You're not," he insists. "You're not."

"Where's Finn?" my voice is broken because deep down, I know where Finn is. I know it in my heart, I know it in my soul. I've been hiding it from myself all along.

Dare remains quiet, his large hands stroking my back, urging me to calm.

I have to know. I have to see.

Wrenching away from Dare, I leap to my feet and take off for my house. I throw open the doors and bound through the dark house, taking the stairs two at a time until I'm standing in front of Finn's bedroom door.

I stare at the wood, at the grain, at the indention, at the handle. I don't want to open it because I know what I'll find.

But I have to. I have to see it.

Reaching down, I turn the knob.

The door creaks open, revealing what my heart knew I'd find.

An empty room.

The bed is still there, neatly made. Finn's posters are still on the wall, of Quid Quo Pro and the Cure. His black converses sit next to the door, like he's going to wear them again, but he's not. His dirty laundry is still in his hamper. His books line the shelves. His favorite pillow waits for him, his CDs, his phone. All of it.

But he's not coming back.

Dare's hand is on my back, comforting me. I can't feel anything.

I step inside and sit on the bed, listening for my brother.

There's not a sound.

I hug my knees, as wave after wave of memory comes back.

My reality hasn't been real.

"Finn died with my mom," I say aloud, the pain wracking my heart, my bones, my soul. I see the images in my head, flitting together to form scenes.

I watch him getting into his red car. The car we never shared because we each had our own.

"He was going to a concert, Quid Pro Quo. He started down the mountain and was on his way when I called mom. Mom crossed the centerline on her way up the mountain. She was hurrying because she was late and she hit him head-on as she came around a curve."

I can't take the pain.

It blinds me, deafens me, turns everything into a roar.

I can't hear. I can't see.

"She was going too fast," I continue lifelessly, my memories unrolling like a movie in my head. "She was distracted because she was talking to me on the phone. I killed my mom and my brother. *Finn.* God."

My head drops into my hands.

The pain is more than I ever thought it would be, more than I ever thought I could bear. Flashes of Finn rip through my mind... of when we were small. Of when we played in the ocean. Of Finn calling to me when we played hide and seek, of Finn calling to me when he was scared. And of that night, when he poked his head into the salon before he left...the last time I'd seen him alive.

See you later, Cal. Are you sure you don't want to go?

"I didn't go with him," I whisper, the words cutting a path along my throat. "He was going with a friend from his Group and I didn't go with him. Because I wanted... I wanted...you."

I knew Dare back then.

I've known him for months and months. *This can't be happening. What is happening? Am I crazy? Have I lost it?*

Dare holds me tight, letting me cry, trying desperately to shield me from my pain.

He can't.

He can't shield me from the pain anymore.

"I wanted to stay at the funeral home so that you could come meet me so we could be alone."

My heart pounds, as I see glimpses of Dare in my head. His smile, his face, his hands. I stare at his hands now, the silver ring.

"I gave that to you for Valentine's Day," I remember.

He nods.

"You...me...we've been together for a while. We were... that night... I let my brother go to the concert alone because I wanted to be alone with you."

God, I'm a monster.

God, I'm crazy.

I look at him. "What's been happening to me?"

I feel dazed, confused, lost.

Dare swallows. "Your mind has been trying to protect itself. You've experienced an overwhelming loss. You felt like you were at fault when you weren't. It was more than you could bear. The day after they died, you woke up and thought Finn was still here, in fact, there were times that you thought *you were Finn*. The doctors said you needed to come out of it on your own, that to try and bring you into reality would hurt you."

"So everyone went along with it," I realize in horror. "I'm crazy. I'm crazy and never even knew it."

Dare's dark eyes connect with mine. "No, you're not," he says firmly, resolutely. "You had a mental break because your reality was too hard to bear. They called it PTSD and Disassociative Memory Loss. You're not crazy."

"That's why you couldn't be with me," I realize slowly, putting the pieces together. "Because I'm a lunatic and I didn't remember you. How in the world could I forget such a big piece of my life? I don't know why you stayed with me. I'm so crazy."

I'm crying again, or still, because maybe I never stopped, and Dare holds me tight against his chest.

"I love you, Calla. You forgot me because you felt too guilty to remember. Because you thought it was your fault. Because you thought you didn't deserve to have something good."

"Maybe I don't," I cry hotly, squeezing my eyes closed, but when I do, all I see is my brother's face.

"You do," Dare says firmly. I open my eyes and look at him. "You love me, Calla. And I love you."

I remember the first time he said those words to me, months ago, but the memories are hard to see. They're foggy and distant, like I'm trying to pull them to me through murky water.

"I can't remember everything," I say in frustration. "My memories around you are... there aren't many."

Dare nods. "The doctors said they'll come back in stages. At first, I... tried to stay away, but it was too hard, and you weren't making any progress. We decided that I'd re-enter your life as a stranger to see if it'd jog your memory at all."

I feel so foolish....so crazy.

"You staged meeting me again for the first time? At the hospital?"

Dare stares at me, his eyes carefully expressionless. "Yeah."

"That's why it felt like I knew you," I realize slowly. "That's why you felt familiar, why I felt pulled to you from the very beginning." *The déjà vu, the dreams.*

"You have no idea how hard it's been," he tells me. "To pretend that I didn't know you."

I gulp, because I can only imagine, and because all of it, the whole elaborate thing, was my fault. Then something else occurs to me, something horrifying.

"The pecans," I breathe, my eyes wide and appalled. "Finn didn't feed them to me. I fed them to myself. The hospital... I wasn't there to visit Finn... I was there for *me.* They were watching me... to see if I'd try and hurt myself again."

Dare doesn't anything, but his silence is everything.

I stare around the room, at the empty, empty room.

"My brother is dead." The words taste bitter.

Dare doesn't say anything but he squeezes me tighter.

"You knew all along." My words are hard. Dare looks down at me.

"I couldn't tell you. The doctors said you had to remember on your own."

"I'm so stupid." Tears run down my cheeks and I wipe them away, ignoring my pounding heart because it hurts too much. "I'm insane."

"You're not."

"Are you trying to convince you or me?" I ask painfully.

"You," he says firmly.

I look out the windows, at the rain, at the cliffs. The wind, the rain, the clay... all of it blurs together with my tears and it all turns red, because red = dangerous.

My loss is overwhelming.

My brother.
The pain.
It's all red.

"Ever since we were born, we were Calla and Finn," I tell Dare blankly. "Who am I now?"

Dare holds me close, oblivious to the weather, oblivious to everything else but me. "I'm one half of a whole. Finn's my other half. What am I supposed to do without him?"

My sobs scrape my ribs, cutting them, making them bleed because I'm red now. I'll never be green again.

"I don't know," Dare admits helplessly. "I want to tell you it'll be ok. I'll tell you that I'll do anything I can to make it that way. But I think... only time..."

"Don't say time heals all wounds," I interrupt sharply. "That's a lie."

"I know," he says simply. "But with time, you can manage it. That's all. The pain will become less and your memories will keep you afloat. That's what I know."

"He wanted saving... from his own mind, I mean," I try and make my heart numb, but I know that's dangerous now. I can't hide from it anymore. I have to feel this for all of the miserable pain that it is. "In his journal... he asked over and over to be saved. He asked me to save him." I look into Dare's eyes. "I couldn't save him, Dare."

Dare doesn't break our gaze. "He wasn't yours to save, Calla. He didn't die from his mental illness. He died from a car accident. There was absolutely nothing you could've done to save him."

"Except I shouldn't have called my mom during the storm. That would've saved them both."

Dare grips my arms, forcing me to look at him.

"That's simply not true and you know it. When's it's time, it's time. We don't get to decide. God does."

I'm empty inside. I hear Dare's words, but I can't feel them.

"I need to rest," I decide, curling onto my side in my brother's bed. I close my eyes against reality, seeking comfort from the blackness. Dare doesn't argue. He just lays down behind me, his arms holding me tight.

"You don't have to stay."

"I do." His words are firm. "Your dad's not here and I'm not leaving you alone. I'm not leaving you again, period."

Tears streak my face and I keep my eyes pressed closed.

I turn into Dare, inhaling his smell, listening to his heart while it beats strong and loud and true. He's alive, and I am too.

But Finn's not.

"I don't know how I'm going to survive this," I whisper.

Dare kisses the top of my head, his breath a mere whisper.

"One day at a time."

I look up at him, my eyes hot and red. "With you?"

He nods. "With me."

The pain floods me and so I do the only thing I know to do.

I sleep.

And I dream.

Because all along, my dreams have been memories.

42

QUADRAGINTA DUO

"He's gone, honey."

I stare at the wall, my phone in my hand. I'd been waiting and waiting for Finn to call, waiting for his voice, waiting for him to be okay. Dare's arms are wrapped around my shoulder, holding me up.

My dad stares at me, his eyes pale blue like Finn's, and shocked.

"Calla?"

I turn my face to look at him, but looking at him makes it feel too real, so I close my eyes instead.

I can't do this.

"Calla, they found his car. It's in the bay. He drove off the edge... your mom was in the ravine, but Finn's car plunged the opposite way. Down the rocks, into the water."

No, it didn't.

He couldn't have.

"No," I say clearly, staring at my father dazed. "He was wearing his medallion. He was protected."

My father, the strongest man I know, turns away and his shoulders shake. After minutes, he turns back.

"I want to see," I tell him emptily. "If it's true, I need to see."

My father is already shaking his head, his hand on my arm. "No."

"Yes."

I don't wait for him to agree, I just bolt from the house, down the steps, down the paths, to the beach. I hear Dare behind me, but I don't stop. There are fireman and police and police tape and EMTs congregated about, and one of them tries to stop me.

"Miss, no," he says, his voice serious, his face aghast. "You can't go over there."

But I yank away because I see Finn.

I see his red smashed car that they've already pulled from the water.

I see someone laid out on the sand, someone covered by a sheet.

I walk toward that someone calmly, because even though it's Finn's car, it can't be Finn. It can't be because he's my twin, and because I didn't feel it happen. I would've known, wouldn't I?

Dare calls to me, through thick fog, but I don't answer.

I take a step.

Then another.

Then another.

Then I'm kneeling in the sand, next to a sheet.

My fingers shake.

My heart trembles.

And I pull the white fabric away.

He's dressed in jeans and a button-up, clothing for a concert. He's pale, he's skinny, he's long. He's frail, he's cold, he's dead.

He's Finn.

I can't breathe as I hold his wet hand, as I hunch over him and cry and try to breathe and try to speak.

He doesn't look like he was in a crash. There's a bruise on his forehead and that's it. He's just so white, so very very white.

"Please," I beg him. "No. Not today. No."

I'm rocking and I feel hands on me, but I shake them away, because this is Finn. And we're Calla and Finn. And this can't be happening.

I cry so hard that my chest hurts with it, my throat grows raw and I gulp to breathe.

"I love you," I tell him when I can breathe again. "I'm sorry I wasn't with you. I'm sorry I couldn't save you. I'm sorry. I'm sorry."

I'm still crying when large hands cup my shoulders and lift me from the ground, and I'm pulled into strong arms.

"Shhh, Calla," my dad murmurs. "It'll be okay. He knew you loved him."

"Did he?" I ask harshly, pulling away to look at my father. "Because he wanted me to go with him, and I made him go alone. And now he's dead. I called mom and they're both dead."

Dad pulls me back into his arms and pats my back, showing a tenderness that I didn't know he possessed. "It's not your fault," he tells me between wracking sobs. "He knew you loved him, honey. Everyone knew. Your mother, too."

My mother. I choke back another gasping sob.

This can't be happening.

This can't be happening.

This isn't my life.

I shake off my father's arms and walk woodenly back up the trails, past the paramedics, past the police, past everyone who is staring at me. I walk straight up to Finn's room and collapse onto his bed.

Out of the corner of my eye, I see his journal.

I pick it up, reading the familiar handwriting written by the hands that I love so much.

Serva me, serva bo te.

Save me, and I will save you.

Ok.

Ok, Finn.

I close my eyes because when I wake up tomorrow, I'll find that this was all a dream. This is a nightmare. It has to be.

Sleep comes quickly.

I wake up with a start, the memories from that night so vivid, so awful.

Sunlight floods my room, exposing every corner, every empty corner.

I shudder and climb from bed, looking out the window. Dare and my father sit on the porch below, talking earnestly.

I throw some clothes on and slip out the back door and toward the road. When it starts to rain, I pull my hood up, but I keep going.

I have someplace to be.

I pick up the pace, jogging, until I get to the cross and ribbons.

Gulping, I stand at the side, looking down at the ravine, at the broken trees, at the black marks and bent limbs.

My mother died here.

But I always knew that.

Turning, I cross to the other side, to the side facing the ocean.

Living things are broken on this side too. The bracken and bushes and trees. They're bent and broken but still living. They thrive on the side of the mountain, coming back from the brink.

The viridem.

The green.

It's still here, but Finn isn't.

His car flipped down the side of this mountain and plunged into the water.

Staring out over the glass-like surface, you'd never know that Finn died there. But I do. I know it now.

And it's too much to bear.

It's too much.

I sink to my feet and pull my knees to my chest, closing my eyes, feeling the hot tears form beneath my eyelids. Focusing hard, I picture Finn's face. I picture him sitting right next to me, right now.

"Hey Cal," he would say. "Do you know that the sloppy handwriting of physicians kill more than 2,000 people each year—from getting the wrong medications?"

I shake my head sadly at him. "No."

He nods, smug in his superior knowledge of strange death facts. "It's true."

"But that's not what killed you."

My voice is stark, and I realize that I'm speaking out loud. And I don't care.

Imaginary Finn shrugs. "No. But everyone is just as dead, regardless of the cause."

"I'm not ready, Finn," I tell him weakly. "You can't go."

My body is like ice, my nerves are wood. He smiles at me, the old smile that I love, the one that lights up his pale blue eyes.

"I couldn't help it, Cal," he tells me seriously. "But you've got to deal with it. You've got to move on."

"To where?" I ask him simply. "I can't go anywhere without you."

The pain in my voice is scalpel sharp, cutting through me with precision.

"You have to," Finn replies. "You've got no choice, Calla. You have to."

"Calla?"

The voice comes from behind me, from beside the road. Within a minute, Dare is sitting next to me, staring out to sea with me.

"Who were you talking to?" he asks, trying hard to hide his concern.

"Finn," I tell him honestly. "But don't worry. I know he's not real. It's just... you don't understand what it's like. He's part of me, Dare. And he's just gone. And I don't know how I'm supposed to live with that."

My voice breaks and I cry and I feel weak. But I can't help it. The tears just come and come and come.

Dare pulls me to him, against his chest and cradles me there, protecting me from the world, from my own sadness.

"Let's go back to the house," he suggests. "You don't need to be here."

Here where my brother died.

I nod, agreeing, complying, because the truth of it is that I don't know where I should be. Not anymore.

I let Dare lead me to the house, and I let him prepare lunch for me, and sit with me on the porch until it's time to eat again for dinner. And this is how my life is for the next several days.

I go through the motions and I feel like wood, and Dare and my father wait for me to rejoin the living.

43

QUADRAGINTA TRES

I'm dreaming again on the fourth day.

I dream that Finn and I are walking on the trails, doing yoga on the cliffs, swimming in the ocean, crab fishing. It's always Finn and me, because he's not in my reality anymore. He's gone. But in my dreams, he lives.

In my dreams, he's everywhere, surrounding me.

And then when I wake up, when I look at all of those places he should be, he's not there.

He's gone.

Today, when I wake, Dare's waiting for me in Finn's desk chair. It's morning and he looks impossibly casual and elegant in his slim, fitted clothing as he sprawls out in the sun.

"I don't think I can stay here," I tell him, my voice husky with sleep and harsh with memories. "Everywhere I go... reminds me."

Dare nods. "I know."

"What should I do?" I whisper.

He shakes his head. "I can't decide for you."

"I don't want to leave Finn," I say shakily. But Dare shakes his head again.

"Finn's not here, Calla-Lily."

I gulp, because he's not.

"It's so strange," I muse woodenly. "I kept thinking that Finn was trying to convince me to go to the cemetery to say goodbye to my mom. But it was really my own mind, trying to make me see reality, wasn't it?"

Dare stares at me, sympathy in his eyes. "I don't know. Maybe so."

"I need to say goodbye to them both," I tell him. "But I can't today. I just need a minute to wrap my mind around it."

"Take as much time as you need," Dare says wisely. "You can't rush it. We'll go as slow as you want."

He pulls me to him and I stand there, my forehead against his chest, his hands rubbing my back.

My hands burn and I pull away, examining them.

I've got blisters across my palms, reddish and peeling, because they're in the process of healing. I hadn't even noticed them until now, although it's clear they've been there for a while.

"You've been chopping wood," Dare offers, and I cringe. I cringe because I know *why*.

"That was Finn's job," I say aloud. "I must've... I must've thought I was Finn. And that my dad would need wood when we went away to college."

Dare nods solemnly in agreement and I still can't figure out why he would stay with me. I'm such a mess.

"It's like my mind was a rope, splintering and unraveling until it was hanging by a thread."

Dare shakes his head and pulls me close again.

"You needed time to process what happened. That's all."

"I'm still not ready." My voice breaks at the thought of moving on without Finn.

"I know."

Four more days pass before I bring it up again. Four days of my father and Dare watching me for signs that I'm cracking, four days of rain and sleep and silence.

Four days of mourning.

Four days of having it hang over my head until one morning, I've had it.

"I've got to do it today," I decide at breakfast. Dare immediately stands up.

"Ok."

I ride on the back of his back on the way to the cemetery, my face pressed against his strong back. I close my eyes and inhale the fresh air, absorbing the sunshine, feeling the warmth.

Warmth = Life.

We pull to a stop outside the gates and Dare kills the motor, careful to respect the sacred grounds of the burial place.

"It's so odd," I tell him as we walk through the manicured grounds, stepping around stones. "I remembered my mother's funeral, but I didn't remember a thing about Finn's. We had a joint funeral, but my mind blocked out anything that had to do with Finn. But I remember it now. You were there. I saw your face. You were in the back."

Because at that point, I didn't even remember him. God.

Dare squeezes my hand and we walk straight to the back, straight to the white marble headstones that mark the ground.

I look at my mother's first, because even though it's gut-wrenching, it's easier.

LAURA PRICE. I trace the name with my finger, sinking to my knees.

"I'm sorry, mom," I whisper to her. "I'm so sorry I called. I'm so sorry you answered. Please forgive me. I love you. I love you."

I kiss my fingers and press them to the stone, and then I do the hardest thing I'll ever have to do.

I turn and say goodbye to my brother.

My Finn.

Finn's memorial stone is white and glows in the late afternoon sun. The writing on it brings tears to my eyes, because I recognize it immediately....it's very similar to one Mark Twain had inscribed on his daughter's stone.

The words on Finn's blur as tears fill my eyes once again, or still.

Good night, sweet Finn. Good night, good night.

I tear up for a thousand reasons, and one of them is my dad. He must've paid attention to me over the years after all, because I'd told him once how heart-wrenching and beautiful I thought this particular epitaph was. And when it was time to pick Finn's stone, I wasn't in a position to help.

But my dad had remembered, and this is perfect.

It's exactly what I would've chosen for my brother.

I sink to the ground in front, not caring that the earth is muddy and wet, and trace the words with my fingers.

Good night, sweet Finn.

He *was* sweet. And kind and good and funny. He was brilliant and witty and sharp. He was my brother, my best friend, half of my soul. He was all of those things and more. He was *more than* anyone else ever knew or ever would know. Because I was the only one lucky enough to really know him.

"I miss you," I whisper. "God, I miss you."

I slump against the cool marble, and I talk to my brother. I talk to him like he's sitting right here with me. I tell him about dad, Dare and my mental break.

"So I'm crazy, too," I tell him. "And I always thought I needed to worry about *you.*"

I feel Dare sigh behind me, because I know he wants to tell me that I'm not crazy, but he doesn't interrupt. He just stands aside and lets me do what I need to do.

"I think I have to leave," I tell Finn. "I don't want to leave you, but you're not really here, and I can't stay. Not right now. It's too hard. Do you understand?"

His cold marble stone doesn't reply and I lean my cheek against it, desperately wishing that Finn were here.

But he's not.

I'm wiping away a tear when I see it.

I stiffen and startle and stare.

A dragonfly hovers nearby.

Large and shiny, it's greenish-blue wings shimmer in the late afternoon sun. It watches me, unafraid, as it hangs in the air, it's gorgeous wings fluttering fast. It seems to be here for me, because it doesn't move away. It simply waits with me, watching me.

My heart pounds and I'm frozen in shock.

"Finn," I breathe.

I'm not crazy enough to believe the insect is Finn. However, I *am* crazy enough to think that Finn is here, somewhere, and that he sent the dragonfly as a sign.

He's ok.

I'm suddenly surrounded by a strange peace, by something ethereal and other-worldly and I think it must be real.

Finn is bringing me comfort, like he always has.

"I love you," I whisper. "I will *always* love you."

The sunlight hits the dragonfly just so, and it makes it look like it winks at me. I smile, and it flies away. I watch it go, and the peace that has wrapped around me spreads inside, to my heart.

I'm still in pain, but for the first time in over a week, I feel calm, quiet, hopeful.

The air around me feels reverent and sacred somehow, and I hesitate to move, to get up, to take a step. But I have to, because I know that's the most important thing. That's the point, that's what Finn was here for.

To move me forward.

To show me that he's okay, that I'm okay, and that I need to move forward without him.

It's scary because I've never been without him before. But at the same time, I know that I'm not alone.

I look up at Dare.

"That was real, right?"

He looks at me, confused.

"The dragonfly. Did you see it?"

He nods. "Yeah, why?"

"Because... the story." I tell him the story that I thought Finn had told me, the one that I'd actually read in his journal. The one about the dragonflies. And Heaven. And peace.

When I'm finished, Dare's eyes are wide.

"Do you think it was Finn?" I ask seriously.

Dare shakes his head. "I don't know. But it was a sign. Whether it was from God or from Finn or your mom. It was a sign. I believe that, Calla."

I'm not crazy.

I smile and close my eyes, soaking in the warmth.

It is here, in the sun and against my will, that I feel peaceful for the first time since Finn died. It's an amazing feeling, and I'm afraid to move, out of fear that when I do, the feeling will be gone.

But when I open my eyes again, it's still here.

I'm still warm.

I'm still alive.

And Dare is with me. He smiles down at me, holding out a hand to help me up. I get to my feet, then stare at my brother's name again.

Good night, sweet Finn.

"I love you, Finn," I tell him, as I lean forward and kiss the top of his stone. "I'll see you later."

We walk through the cemetery arches but before we climb back onto the bike, I pause, staring up at the most handsome face in the world.

"It was you," I tell him softly. "You're the thing that brought me back. You gave me reality. You tethered me, anchored me, loved me. I thought you were going to break me, but that's just because I didn't understand. You were trying to help me all along."

He pulls me to him and kisses me softly. "I love you, Calla."

"I know." And I do. For the first time in months. I can see it. And I believe it.

I climb on the bike behind Dare, pressing my cheek to his back.

Beneath my hands, his heart beats, vibrant and strong and alive.

I have to live, too.

I have a reason, and that reason is warm and alive and sitting in front of me.

The sun warms my back as we ride up the mountain.

44

QUADRAGINTA QUATTUOR

I sit with my brother's journal on my lap, curled up on his bed. This is where I feel him the most, here among his things. It brings me comfort.

I open the tattered book, and flip through the pages until I find what I'm looking for... the last several entries. My blood runs cold as I stare at the words... the insane, crazy gibberish lining the page.

The handwriting is mine.

"I thought I was him," I murmur. "But there at the end, his journal was mine."

Dare sits next to me, careful of my brother's space. He knows it's sacred to me, especially now. "The human body is an amazing thing," he says by way of explanation. "Your mind knows how to shield itself from too much pain."

I trace the tarot card in my hand, following the ragged edges with my finger.

"I wonder what this means," I whisper. "I didn't know Finn ever had his cards read."

Dare stays silent, because of course we'll never know the answer.

I drop the journal and watch the pages flutter as it falls to the floor.

I drop the journal and watch the pages flutter as it falls to the floor.

When it hits, the cover closes… a metaphor for Finn's life.

The story is over.

I gulp.

"He did love a good metaphor," I say aloud.

"What's that?" Dare leans closer. I shake my head.

"Nothing."

"Let's take a walk on the beach," Dare says with a small smile. "We should get some fresh air."

We make our way down the trails and I cringe as we pass the Chapel because I remember the funerals now. I cringe when we pass the woodshed because I remember Finn chopping wood. And I cringe when we pass the pier, because Finn and I went out on the boat so often.

"That night… when I got drunk. I was waiting and waiting for Finn to come back with the boat. But it was me all along. I was out on the boat."

Dare stares out at the water. "I watched for you, and when you stepped onto the pier, I knew right away you were drunk."

I grip his hand tighter, but look away. Because God, how embarrassing. All of this.

"And Nocte," I murmur. "Those initials were ours. We've been there several times before."

"Yep. You and me. And also, you, me and Finn."

I look at him, sharply now, because I've been focusing so much on my own pain, that I haven't considered his. He and Finn had been friends for most of the year.

"I remember you helped Finn with his senior science project," I recall, a memory suddenly re-surfacing of Finn and Dare hovering over the kitchen table with test tubes.

Dare smiles. "Yes. He probably would've blown the house up on his own."

I giggle in spite of myself. "Probably."

I glance at him. "I haven't asked you how *you're* doing."

Dare looks down at me. "I'm doing better now. For a while, I thought I'd lost you both."

I swallow hard, remembering the day I'd found him punching the woodshed.

"It must've been so frustrating."

"You have no idea."

But I do. "At least you still have your memories. My mind is like swiss cheese."

I chew on my lip for a second. "The drawing of me that you did. I was naked and in high heels…"

Dare levels a gaze at me. "Do you remember the day I based that drawing off of?"

Oh, I do. I definitely do now. It was right before school ended and it had been amazing.

"I do. But… I found that drawing in Finn's journal. He'd written MINE all over it. But it wasn't Finn. I think it was me."

Dare sighs. "You asked me for the drawing the night you caught me drawing it."

I stare at him, shocked. "I did? I don't remember that part."

I don't remember it at all. Why would I write all over my own drawing?

Because I thought I was Finn. Because subconsciously I couldn't let go of Finn.

I shake my head and look away. "This is maddening. I remember some things, but other things…especially when it comes to you, things are still fuzzy."

He gives me a dark look. "Maybe your mind is still trying to protect you."

That gives me pause and I freeze in place, my feet sinking in the damp sand. "What would it have to protect me against?"

Dare shrugs, his face a perfect expressionless mask.

"You know I can't say."

Frustration makes me want to scream. "The doctors said I need to remember on my own," I tell him sharply. "They didn't say you can't give me hints."

He shakes his head. "It'll come to you. Just know that I'll never hurt you. Not on purpose."

"It's your past," I tell him confidently. "Where you came from. I'm sure of it. Because that's the part that's fuzzy. How we met. But I did an internet search on you. Nothing was unusual."

Except for the part where he's richer than God, and has had a million blond girlfriends. I absentmindedly twirl a piece of my long red hair around my finger, because I'm the farthest thing from blond there is.

We sit on the beach finally, staring out at the water, listening to it crash against the rocks.

I lay my head against Dare's shoulder.

"It can't be too bad. Whatever it is, I was fine with it before. I know that because we were still together when… it happened."

When I lost everything.

Dare grabs my hand, his thumb playing with mine. The only sound is the water, crashing into the shore then sucking back into the ocean. To and fro. It's a lulling, soothing sound.

"I'll figure it out," I say softly, no longer worried.

"Yes, you will." There seems to be slight trepidation in Dare's voice.

For days, I think about it.

For days, nothing comes.

Dare stays with me like a champion. He comes to my house every day. He sits with me, goes through pictures with me, plays the piano for me.

Every day, I remember why I love him.

Every day I love him more.

Then one night, I'm curled up on Dare's couch, my head on his lap as he reads.

"I love you," I say simply, out of the blue, my words cutting through silence.

Dare looks up from his book, his dark eyes smoldering. "Are you sure?"

I smile. "Of course. What's not to love?"

He pulls me up, his book dropping to the floor as I'm crushed to his chest, his hands pressing, pulling, feeling.

Warmth from his hands soaks into me, thawing me, and for the first time in days and days, it ignites in me, making me want more.

"Thank you for staying with me," I murmur. "You didn't have to. Thank you."

I pause, then kiss him.

His lips are warm and firm and they light a fire in my belly, a fire that I forgot existed. It extinguishes my sadness for the moment, and I arch into him, pulling him closer.

There's so much familiarity here... so much want.

His hands trace my collarbone, running down my arms, setting my nerve endings on fire. They burst into flame, burning away anything else but the desire to be with him, right here and right now.

"You think you don't deserve me," I whisper against his neck. "But that's not true. I'm the one... I don't deserve *you.*"

I kiss him again, and he groans in my mouth, the sound of it driving me to the brink because I know he wants me too.

"You want me," I tell him urgently, pulling at him. "I know you do."

"I've always wanted you," he tells me roughly.

"It's just you and me now," I tell him. "You and me. That's all that matters."

Make me feel something besides pain.

I kiss him again and his hands splay around my hips, positioning me so that I'm lodged against his hardness. I suck in a breath and look up into his eyes, eyes that hold a thousand secrets, but eyes that I love.

I love him.

"No matter what," I whisper. He pauses from kissing my neck and looks at me questioningly as he lifts his hand to brush my hair back. The light glints from his ring, and I'm frozen.

Because fragments come flying into my mind. Memory fragments. Images of that same exact expression, of his ring glinting in the moonlight as he tells me something. It's a confession and he's alarmed, upset, anxious.

It's the night of the accident. *Before* the accident. I see his lips moving, but I can't hear the words. It's like he's in a wind tunnel, the words are static, and I've seen this exact scene before in a dream.

I strain to hear the words from my memory.

"What's wrong?" Dare asks me now, lowering his head once more, sliding his warm lips across my neck as he leans me back.

At this exact inopportune moment, as Dare's touch lights my skin ablaze, the fragments finally fit into place. Puzzle pieces fitting together. *At last.*

The memory forms and I suck in an appalled breath as I yank away from him.

"I remember," I whisper. Dare pauses in apprehension, his onyx eyes glittering, his hands frozen on my arms. "You... you were here for me all along. *You came here for me.*"

His eyes close like a curtain and I know that I'm right.

His breath is shaky and his hands tremble as he touches me, as he refuses to pull away even now.

"You have one question left, Calla," he reminds me, his voice somber. "Ask it."

So with fear in my heart and ice in my veins…I do.

TO BE CONTINUED…

To read more of Calla and Dare's story, please read
VERUM, book two in the Nocte Trilogy.

About the Author

Courtney Cole is the author of several bestselling titles, including the New York Times and USA Today bestselling *Beautifully Broken* series. She was born and raised in Kansas, but has since relocated to Florida, where she writes beneath palm trees. To find out more about her and to sign up for her newsletter which will give you new release announcements, a FREE book and fans-only perks, please visit www.courtneycolewrites.com.